This Book Belongs To

_____

Jack Archer

A Tale of the Crimea

G. A. Henty

Copyright©2004 by Quiet Vision Publishing
All rights reserved.

No part of this book may be reproduced or transmitted in any form or by any means, electronic or mechanical, including photocopying, recording, or by any information storage or retrieval system, without permission of the publisher in writing.

ISBN: 1-57646-857-7

Quiet Vision Publishing
World Wide Web: http://www.quietvision.com

Printed and bound in the United States of America
Published - November 2004

Publisher's Note

Quiet Vision editions of classic works are taken from as close to original editions as practical. All works are presented without comment or commentary by our editors.

The Publisher

Chapter I
THE MIDSHIPMAN

THE first day of term cannot be considered a cheerful occasion. As the boys arrive on the previous evening, they have so much to tell each other, are so full of what they have been doing, that the chatter and laughter are as great as upon the night preceding the breaking-up. In the morning, however, all this is changed. As they take their places at their desks and open their books, a dull, heavy feeling takes possession of the boys, and the full consciousness that they are at the beginning of another half year's work weighs heavily on their minds.

It is true enough that the half year will have its play, too, its matches, with their rivalry and excitement. But at present it is the long routine of lessons which is most prominent in the minds of the lads who are sitting on the long benches of the King's School, Canterbury.

As a whole, however, these have not great reason for sadness. Not more than a third of them are boarders, and the rest, who have in truth, for the last week, begun to be tired of their holidays, will, when they once get out of school, and begin to choose sides for football, be really glad that the term has again commenced.

"So your brother is not coming back again, Archer?" one of the boys said to a lad of some fifteen years old, a merry, curly-haired fellow, somewhat short for his age, but square-shouldered and sturdy.

"No. He is expecting in another six months to get his commission, and is going up to town to study with a coach. My father has lodged the money for him, and hopes to get him gazetted to his old regiment, the 33d."

"What is he going to a coach for? There is no examination, is there? And if there was, I should think he could pass it. He has been in the sixth for the last year."

"Oh, he is all right enough," Archer said. "But my father is sending him to an army man to get up military drawing and fortification. Dad says it is of no use his going on grinding here at Greek and Latin, and that he had much better spend the time, till he gets his commission, in learning something that may be of use to him. I wish I had done with Latin and Greek too, I'm sure they'll never be of any use to me, and I hate them."

At this moment the conversation between the boys was abruptly broken off by Archer being called up by the class master.

"Archer," he said, looking up from the papers on the desk before him, "these verses are disgraceful. Of all in the holiday tasks sent in, yours appears to me to be the worst."

"I'm very sorry, sir," Jack Archer said, "I really tried hard to do them, but somehow or other the quantities never will come right."

"I don't know what you call trying hard, Archer, but it's utterly impossible, if you had taken the trouble to look the words out in the Gradus, that you could have made such mistakes as those here."

"I don't know, sir," Jack answered. "I can do exercises and translations and all that sort of thing well enough, but I always break down with verses,

Jack Archer

and I don't see what good they are, except for fellows who want to write Latin verses for tombstones."

"That has nothing to do with it," the master said; "and I am not going to discuss the utility of verses with you. I shall report you to Dr. Wallace, and if you will not work in your holidays, you will have to do so in your play-hours."

Jack retired to his seat, and for the next ten minutes indulged in a diatribe against classical learning in general, and hexameters and pentameters in particular.

Presently one of the sixth form came down to where Jack was sitting,—

"Archer, Dr. Wallace wants you."

"Oh, lord," Jack groaned, "now I'm in for it! I haven't seen Marshall get out of his seat. I suppose he has written a report about those beastly verses."

The greeting of Dr. Wallace was, however, of a different nature from that which he had anticipated.

"Archer," he said, "I have just received a note from your father. You are to go home at once."

Jack Archer opened his eyes in astonishment. It was but an hour and a half since he had started from Harbledown, a mile or so distant from the school. His father had said nothing at breakfast, and what on earth could he want him home again for?

With a mechanical "Yes, sir," he returned to his place, gathered up his books hastily together, fastening them with a strap, and was soon on his way home at a rapid trot. He overtook ere long the servant who had brought the note—an old soldier, who had been Major Archer's servant in the army.

"What is the matter, Jones? Is any one ill at home?"

"No, sir; no one is ill as I knows of. The major called me into his study, and told me to take a note to Dr. Wallace, and, of course, I asked the master no questions."

"No," Jack said, "I don't suppose you did, Jones. I don't suppose you'd ask any questions if you were told to take a letter straight to the man in the moon. I wonder what it can mean."

And continuing his run, he soon left the steady-going old soldier far behind. Up High Street, under the great gate, along through the wide, straggling street beyond, into the open country, and then across through the fields to Harbledown. Jack never paused till, hot and panting, he entered the gate.

His father and his elder brother, who had seen him coming across the fields, were standing in the porch.

"Hurrah! Jack," the latter shouted; "you're going to be first out after all."

"Going to be first out?" Jack gasped. "What on earth do you mean, Harry?"

"Come into the parlor, Jack," his father said, "and you shall hear all about it."

Here his mother and two sisters were sitting.

"My dear boy," the former said, rising and throwing her arms round his neck, "this is sudden indeed."

"What is sudden, mother? What is sudden?" Jack asked. "What is it all about?" and noticing a tear on his mother's cheek, he went on, "It can't be those beastly verses, is it?" the subject most upon his mind being prominent. "But no, it couldn't be that. Even if Wallace took it into his head to make a row about them, there would not be time. But what is it, mother?"

"Sit down, Jack," his father said. "You know, my boy, you have always said that you would like to go to sea. I had no interest that way, but six months ago I wrote to my nephew Charles, who is, as you know, a first lieutenant in the navy, and asked him if he thought he could get you a midshipman's berth. He wrote back to say that he was at present on half pay, and feared it would be a long time before he was afloat again, as there were but few ships in commission, and he had not much interest. But if he were appointed he might be able to get you a berth on board the ship. As that didn't seem very hopeful, I thought it better to say nothing to you about it. However, this morning, just after you had started for school, the postman brought a letter from him, saying that, owing to the threatening state of affairs in the East, a number of ships were being rapidly put in commission, and that he had been appointed to the 'Falcon,' and had seen the captain, and as the latter, who happened to be an old friend of his, had no one in particular whom he wished to oblige, he had kindly asked the Admiralty for a midshipman's appointment for you. This he had, of course, obtained. The 'Falcon' is being fitted out with all haste, and you are to join at once. So I shall take you to Portsmouth to-morrow."

Jack was too much delighted and surprised to be able to speak at first. But after a minute or two he recovered his breath, uttered a loud hurrah of delight, and then gave vent to his feelings by exuberantly kissing his mother and sisters.

"This is glorious," he said. "Only to think that I, who have just been blown up for my verses, am a midshipman in her Majesty's service. I can hardly believe that it is true. Oh, father, I have so wished to go to sea, but I have never said much about it because I thought you did not like it, and now to think of my getting it when I had quite given up all hope, and just at a time, too, when there seems to be a chance of a row. What is it all about, father? I have heard you say something about a dispute with Russia, but I never gave much attention to it."

"The cause of the dispute is trumpery enough, and in itself wholly insufficient to cause a war between two great nations. It began by a squabble about the holy places at Jerusalem, as to the rights of the Greek and Latin pilgrims respectively."

"But what have we got to do with either the Latin or the Greek pilgrims?" Jack asked. "I should have thought that we were quite bothered enough with Latin and Greek verses, without having anything to do with pilgrims. Besides, I didn't know there were any Latins now, and the Greeks ain't much."

Major Archer smiled.

"The Latin pilgrims are the members of the countries which profess the Roman Catholic religion, while the Greeks are those who profess the religion of the Greek Church. That is to say, in the present case, principally Russians. There have for years been squabbles, swelling sometimes into serious tumults, between the pilgrims of these creeds, the matter being generally complicated by the interference of the Turkish authorities with them. The Russian government has been endeavoring to obtain from Turkey the protectorate of all Christians in her dominions, which France, as the leading Catholic country, naturally objects to. All this, however, is only a pretext. The real fact is that Russia, who has for centuries been casting a longing eye upon Turkey, thinks that the time has arrived when she can carry out her ambitious designs. It has always been our policy, upon the other hand, to sustain Turkey. We have large interests in the Mediterranean, and a considerable trade with the Levant, and were Russia to extend her dominion to Constantinople, our position would be seriously menaced. Moreover, and this perhaps is the principal point, it is absolutely necessary for us in the future to be dominant in the east of the Mediterranean. Egypt is rapidly becoming our highway to India, and many men think that in the future our trade with that great dependency will flow down the valley of the Euphrates. Consequently, it is necessary to prevent Russia, at any cost, obtaining a footing south of the Black Sea."

"And do you think, father, that there will really be a war?"

"I'm inclined to think that there will be, Jack, although this is not the popular opinion. We have so long, in England, been talking about the iniquity of war that I believe that the Emperor Nicholas has persuaded himself that we will not fight at any price. In this I am sure that he is wholly mistaken. So long as there was no probability of war, the people of England have quietly permitted the cheese-paring politicians who govern us to cut down the army and navy to a point when we can hardly be said to have an army at all. But I am convinced that the people of England are at heart as warlike as of old. Few nations have done more fighting than we, and, roughly speaking, the wars have always been popular. If the people at large once become convinced that the honor and interest of England are at stake, they will go to war, and the politicians in power will have to follow the popular current, or give way to men who will do so. At present, however, the general idea is that a demonstration upon the part of England and France, will be sufficient to prevent Russia from taking any further steps. I think myself that Russia has gone too far to draw back. Russia is a country where the czars are nominally all-powerful, but where, in point of fact, they are as much bound as other sovereigns to follow the wishes of the country. The conquest of Constantinople has long been the dream of every Russian, and now that the Czar has held out hopes that this dream is about to be realized, he will scarcely like to draw back."

"But surely, father," Harry Archer said, "Russia cannot think herself a match for England and France united."

"I don't know that, my boy. Russia has an enormous population, far larger than that of England and France united. Every man, from the highest to the lowest, is at the disposal of the Czar, and there is scarcely any limit to the force which he is capable of putting into the field. Russia has not fought since the days of Napoleon, and in those days the Russian troops showed themselves to be as good as any in Europe. At Borodino and Smolensko they were barely defeated after inflicting enormous losses on the emperor's army, and, as in the end, they annihilated the largest army even Napoleon had ever got together, they may well think that, fighting close to their own borders, while England and France have to take their troops across Europe, they will be more than a match for us. And now, Jack, we must go down to the town.

G. A. Henty

There is much to do and to think about. The principal part of your outfit I shall, of course, get at Portsmouth, where the tailors are accustomed to work at high pressure. But your underclothes we can get here. Now, my dear, if you will go upstairs and look through Jack's things, and let me know exactly how he stands, I will go down with him to the town, and get anything he requires."

"And will you be able to spare me for a quarter-of-an-hour, father? I should like to be outside the school when they come out at one o'clock, to say good-bye to them. Won't they be surprised, and jolly envious? Oh no, I should think not! They would give their ears, some of them, I know, to be in my place. I should like to say good-bye, too, to old Marshall. His face will be a picture when he finds that he is not going to drop on me for those verses, after all."

It was a day of bustle and business, and Jack, until the very moment when he was embracing his weeping mother and sisters, while his father stood at the door, in front of which was the pony-chaise, which was waiting to take him down to the station, could hardly realize that it was all true, that his school-days were over, and that he was really a midshipman in her Majesty's service.

Harry had already gone to the station on foot, as the back seat in the pony-chaise was occupied by Jack's luggage, and the last words that he said, as he shook hands with his brother, were,—

"I shouldn't be surprised, old boy, if we were to meet in the East before long. If anything comes of it, they will have to increase the strength of the army as well as of the navy, and it will be bad luck indeed if the 33d is left behind."

On arriving at Portsmouth, Major Archer took up his quarters at the famous George Inn, and, leaving their luggage there, was soon on his way down to the Hard. Half a century had gone by since Portsmouth had exhibited such a scene of life and bustle. Large numbers of extra hands had been taken on at the dockyards, and the fitters and riggers labored night and day, hastening on the vessels just put into commission. The bakeries were at work turning out biscuits as fast as they could be made, and the stores were crammed to repletion with commissariat and other stores. In addition to the ships of war, several large merchant steamers, taken up as transports, lay alongside the wharves, and an unusual force of military were concentrated in the town, ready for departure. By the Hard were a number of boats from the various men-of-war lying in the harbor or off Spithead, whose officers were ashore upon various duties. Huge dockyard barges, piled with casks and stores, were being towed alongside the ships of war, and the bustle and life of the scene were delightful indeed to Jack, accustomed only to the quiet sleepiness of a cathedral town like Canterbury. Inquiring which was the "Falcon," a paddle steamer moored in the stream was pointed out to them by a boatman.

"Oh dear," Jack said, "she looks small in comparison with those big men-of-war."

"She is none the worse, Jack, for that," his father said. "If there should be fighting, it will scarcely be at sea. The Russian fleet will not venture to engage the fleets of England and France united, and you are likely to see much more active work in a vessel like the 'Falcon' than in one of those

Jack Archer

floating castles. Hullo, Charles, is that you?" he broke off, lying his hand upon the shoulder of a naval officer, who was pushing his way though the crowd of boatmen and sailors to a man-of-war gig, which, with many others, was lying by the Hard.

"Hullo, uncle, is that you?" he replied. "I am glad to see you. I was expecting you here in a day or so. I thought you would run down with the youngster. Well, Jack, how are you? Why, it must be eight years since I saw you. You were quite a little chap then. Well, are you thinking of thrashing the Russians?"

"The boy is half out of his mind with pleasure, Charles," Major Archer said, "and he and all of us are greatly obliged to you for your kindness in getting him his berth. I think you will find him active and intelligent, though I fear he has not shone greatly at school, especially," he said smiling, "in his Latin verses."

"He will make none the worse sailor for that," Charles Hethcote said with a laugh. "But I must be going on board. I have a message from the admiral to the captain and every moment is precious, for things are terribly behindhand. The dockyard people are wellnigh out of their wits with the pressure put upon them, and we are ordered to be ready to sail in a week. How it's all to be done, goodness only knows. You need not come on board, Jack. I will tell the captain that you have arrived, and he would not thank me for bringing any live lumber on board just at present. You had better get him his outfit, uncle, at once, and then he can report himself in full trim to-morrow."

Giving the major the address of the tailor who could be trusted to supply Jack's uniform without loss of time, and accepting an invitation to dine at the "George" that evening, if he could possibly get away from the ship, Lieutenant Hethcote stepped into the gig, and made his way to the "Falcon."

Major Archer and Jack first paid a visit to the tailor, where all the articles necessary for the outfit were ordered and promised for next day. They then visited the dockyard, and Jack was immensely impressed at the magnitude of the preparations which were being made for the war. Then they strolled down the ramparts, and stood for some time watching the batches of recruits being drilled, and then, as the short winter day was drawing to a close, they returned to the "George."

Chapter II
AN ADVENTURE AT GIB

IT was on the 1st of February, 1854, that the "Falcon" sailed from Portsmouth for the East, and ten days later she dropped her anchor at Gibraltar harbor. Jack Archer was by this time thoroughly at home. In the week's hard work during the preparation for sea at Portsmouth, he had learned as much of the names of the ropes, and the various parts of the ship, as he would have done in a couple of months at sea, and had become acquainted with his new ship-mates. So great had been the pressure of work, that he had escaped much of the practical joking to which a new-comer on board ship, as at school, is generally subject.

He had for comrades four midshipmen; one of these, Simmons, had already nearly served his time, and was looking forward to the war as giving him a sure promotion; two others, Delafield and Hawtry, had already served for two or three years at sea, although only a year or so older than Jack, while the fourth, Herbert Coveney, was a year younger, and was, like Jack, a new hand. There were also in the berth two master's mates, young men of from twenty to two-and-twenty. With all of these Jack, with his high spirits, good-tempered face, merry laugh, soon became a favorite.

During the first two days at sea he had suffered the usual agonies from sea-sickness. But before reaching Gibraltar he had got his sea-legs and was regularly doing duty, being on the watch of the second lieutenant, Mr. Pierson.

The wind, which had blown strongly across the Bay of Biscay and down the coast of Portugal, moderated as the "Falcon" steamed past Cape St. Vincent with its picturesque monastery, and the straits were calm as a mill-pond as she slowly made her way along the Spanish coast and passed Tarifa. Up to the time when she dropped her anchor in the Bay of Gibraltar, the only incident which had happened on the way was that, as they steamed up the straits, they passed close by a homeward-bound P. and O. steamer, whose passengers crowded the sides, and cheered and waved their handkerchiefs to the eastward-bound ship.

The "Falcon" was not a fast vessel, seldom making, under favorable circumstances, more than eight knots an hour. She carried sixteen guns, twelve of which were eighteen-pounders. It had been intended that the "Falcon" should only stay a few hours at Gibraltar, proceeding immediately she had taken in a fresh supply of coal. The engineers, however, reported several defects in her machinery, which would take three or four days to put in order.

Jack was pleased at the delay, as he was anxious to set his foot for the first time ashore in a foreign country, and to visit the famous fortifications of the Rock. The first day he did not ask for leave, as he did not wish to presume upon his being the first lieutenant's relation.

Charles Hethcote differed widely from the typical first lieutenant of fiction, a being as stiff as a ramrod, and as dangerous to approach as a polar bear. He was, indeed, a bright, cheery fellow, and although he was obliged

Jack Archer

to surround himself with a certain amount of official stiffness, he was a great favorite among officers and crew.

It was not till the third day of his stay that Jack, his seniors having all been ashore, asked for leave, which was at once granted. Young Coveney, too, had landed on the previous day, and Hawtry, whom Jack was inclined to like most of his shipmates, now accompanied him. They had leave for the whole day, and, as soon as breakfast was over, they went ashore.

"What a rum old place!" Hawtry said, as they wandered along the principal street. "It looks as Spanish as ever. Who would have thought that it had been an English town for goodness knows how long?"

"I wish I had paid a little more attention to history," Jack said. "It makes one feel like a fool not to know such things as that when one comes to a famous place like this. Look at that tall fellow with the two little donkeys. Poor little brutes, they can scarcely stagger under their loads. There is a pretty girl with that black thing over her head, a mantilla don't they call it? There is a woman with oranges, let's get some. Now, I suppose, the first thing is to climb up to the top of the Rock."

With their pockets full of oranges, the boys started on their climb, which was accomplished in capital time. From the flagstaff they enjoyed the magnificent view of the African coast across the straits, of Spain stretching away to their right, of the broad expanse of the blue Mediterranean, and of the bay with its ships, and the "Falcon" dwarfed to the dimensions of a toy vessel, at their feet. Then they came down, paid a flying visit to the various fortifications and to the galleries, whence the guns peer out threateningly across the low, sandy spit, known as the neutral ground.

When all this was finished, it was only natural that they should go to the principal hotel and eat a prodigious luncheon, and then Hawtry proposed that they should sally out for a ramble into Spain.

They had been disappointed in the oranges, which they found in no way better than those which they had bought in England. But they thought that if they could pick them off the trees, they must somehow have a superior flavor. Accordingly they sallied out by the land gate, passed unquestioned through the line of British sentries, and were soon in the little village inside the Spanish lines.

"It's awfully hot," Hawtry said, mopping his forehead. "Who would have thought that it would have been so hot as this in any place in Europe in the middle of February? Just fancy what it must be here in July! Look, there is a fellow with two mules. I expect he would let them. I vote we go for a ride. It's too hot for walking altogether.

"I say, old boy," he said, approaching a tall and powerfully-built man, who was smoking a cigar, and leaning lazily against one of his mules; "you let mules, we hire them, eh?"

The Spaniard opened his eyes somewhat, but made no reply, and continued to smoke tranquilly.

"Oh, nonsense," Hawtry said. "Look here."

And he put his hand into his pocket and pulled out some silver. Then he made signs of mounting one of the mules, and waved his hand over the surrounding country to signify that he wanted a general ride.

The Spaniard nodded, held up five fingers, and touched one of the mules, and did the same with the other.

G. A. Henty

"He wants five shillings a head," Hawtry said.

"I don't know," Jack said doubtfully. "I don't suppose he knows much about shillings. It may be five dollars or five anything else. We'd better show him five shillings, and come to an understanding that that is what he means before we get on."

The Spaniard, on being shown the five shillings, shook his head, and pointing to a dollar which they had obtained in change on shore, signified that these were the coins he desired.

"Oh, nonsense!" Hawtry said indignantly. "You don't suppose we're such fools as to give you a pound apiece for two or three hours' ride on those mules of yours. Come on, Jack. We won't put up with being swindled like that."

So saying the two lads turned away, and started on their walk.

While they were speaking to the Spaniard, he had been joined by one of his countrymen, and when they turned away, these entered into a rapid conversation together. The result was, that before the boys had gone thirty yards, the Spaniard with the mules called them back again, and intimated that he accepted their terms.

They were about to jump up at once, but the man signed to them to stop, and his companion in a minute or two had brought out two rough rugs which were secured with some cords over the wooden saddles.

"That's an improvement," Jack said. "I was just wondering how we were going to sit on those things, which are not saddles at all, but only things for boxes and barrels to be fastened to."

"I wonder which way we'd better go," Hawtry said, as he climbed up with some difficulty, aided by the Spaniard, on to one of the mules. "My goodness, Jack, this is horribly uncomfortable. I never can stand this. Hi, there! help me down. It would be better a hundred times to ride barebacked."

Accordingly the saddles were taken off, the rugs folded and secured on the animals' backs by a rope passed round them, and then the boys again took their seats.

"I hope the brutes are quiet," Jack said, "for I am nothing of a rider at the best of times, and one feels an awful height at the top of these great mules, with one's legs dangling without stirrups."

"If you find yourself going, Jack," Hawtry said, "the best thing is to catch hold of his ears. Come on, let's get out of this. All the village is staring at us."

The mules, upon the reins being jerked, and boys' heels briskly applied to their ribs, moved on at a fast walk.

"We shall have to stop under a tree and cut a stick presently," Hawtry said. "It will not do to get down, for I should never be able to climb up again. Mind, we must take our bearings carefully, else we shall never get back again. We have neither chart nor compass. Hallo! here comes the mules' master."

They had by this time gone two or three hundred yards from the village, and, behind them, at a brisk trot, seated on a diminutive donkey, was the Spaniard.

"Perhaps it's best he should come," Jack said. "There will be no fear of being lost then, and if one of us gets capsized, he can help him up again."

Jack Archer

Upon the Spaniard coming up to them, he gave a sharp shout to the mules, at the same time striking the donkey on which he rode with a stick. Instantly the mules, recognizing the signal, started into a sharp trot, the first effect of which was to tumble Hawtry from his seat into the road, Jack with difficulty saving himself by clutching wildly at the mane.

"Confound it!" Hawtry exclaimed furiously, as he regained his feet, to the Spaniard. "Why didn't you say what you were going to be up to? Starting the ship ahead at full speed without notice! I believe I've broken some of my ribs. Don't you laugh too soon, Jack. It will be your turn next."

The Spaniard helped Hawtry to regain his seat, and they were soon clattering along the dusty road at a brisk rate, the boys quickly getting accustomed to the pace, which, indeed, was smooth and easy. For hours they rode on, sometimes trotting, sometimes walking, taking no heed whither they were going, and enjoying the novelty of the ride, the high cactus hedges, the strange vegetation, little villages here and there, sometimes embowered in orange trees, and paying no heed to time.

Presently Jack exclaimed,—

"I say, Hawtry, it must be getting late. We have been winding and turning about, and I have not an idea how far we are now from Gib. We must be through the gates by gun-fire, you know."

They stopped, and by pantomime explained to the Spaniard that they wanted to get back again as soon as possible.

He nodded, made a circle with his arm, and, as they understood, explained that they were making a circuit, and would arrive ere long at their starting-place.

For another hour and a half they rode along, chatting gayly.

"I say, Jack," Hawtry exclaimed suddenly, "why, there's the sun pretty nearly down, and here we are among the hills, in a lonelier looking place than we have come to yet. I don't believe we're anywhere near Gib. I say, old fellow, it strikes me we're getting into a beastly mess. What on earth's to be done?"

They checked their mules, and looked at each other.

"What can the Spaniard's game be, Hawtry? We've had a good five shillings' worth."

"Let us take our own bearings," Hawtry said. "The sun now is nearly on our left. Well, of course, that is somewhere about west-sou-west, so we must be going northward. I don't think that can be right. I'm sure it can't. Look here, you fellow, there is the sun setting there"—and he pointed to it—"Gibraltar must lie somewhere over there, and that's the way we mean to go."

The Spaniard looked surly, then he pointed to the road ahead, and indicated that it bent round the next spur of the hill, and made a detour in the direction in which Hawtry indicated that Gibraltar must lie.

"What on earth shall we do, Jack? If this fellow means mischief, we are in an awkward fix. I don't suppose he intends to attack us, because we with our dirks would be a match for him with that long knife of his. But if he means anything, he has probably got some other fellows with him."

"Then hadn't we better go in for him at once," Jack said, "before he gets any one to help him?"

Hawtry laughed.

G. A. Henty

"We can hardly jump off our mules and attack him without any specific reason. We might get the worst of it, and even if we didn't how should we get back again, and how should we account for having killed our mule-driver? No. Whatever we are in for, we must go through with it now, Jack. Let us look as though we trusted him."

So saying, they continued on the road by which they had previously travelled.

"I don't believe," Hawtry said, after a short silence, "that they can have any idea of cutting our throats. Midshipmen are not in the habit of carrying much money about with them, but I have heard of Guerillas carrying people off to the mountains and getting ransoms. There, we are at the place where that fellow said the road turned. It doesn't turn. Now, I vote we both get off our mules and decline to go a step farther."

"All right," Jack said. "I shall know a good deal better what I am doing on my feet than I shall perched up here!"

The two boys at once slid off their mules to the ground.

"There is no turning there," Hawtry said, turning to the hill. "You have deceived us, and we won't go a foot farther," and turning, the lads started to walk back along the road they had come.

The Spaniard leapt from his donkey, and with angry gesticulation endeavored to arrest them. Finding that they heeded not his orders, he put his hand on his knife, but in a moment the boys' dirks flashed in the air.

"Now, my lad," Hawtry said. "Two can play at that game, and if you draw that knife, we'll let daylight into you."

The Spaniard hesitated, then drew back and gave a loud, shrill whistle which was, the boys fancied, answered in the distance.

"Come on, Jack. We must run for it. We can leave this lumbering Spaniard behind, I have no doubt," and sheathing their dirks, the boys set off at full speed.

The Spaniard appeared inclined to follow them, but distrusting his powers, he paused, gave a long, shrill whistle, twice repeated, and then mounted his donkey and driving the mules before him, he followed the boys at a hand gallop.

They had, however, a good start, and maintained their advantage.

"I don't think," Jack said, "we have passed a village for the last hour. When we get to one, we'd better rush into a house, and ask for shelter. These fellows will hardly dare to touch us there."

Had the race been simply between the boys and their immediate pursuer, it is probable that they would have won it, for they were light, active, and in good condition, while the animals behind them had already been travelling for five hours, at a rate considerably above the speed to which they were accustomed. The road, however, was an exceedingly winding one, which gave time to the confederates of the mule-driver to make a short cut, and, as the boys turned a sharp corner, they saw three men barring the road in front.

"It's all up, Jack," Hawtry said, pausing in his run. "It's no use making any resistance. We should only get our throats cut straight off."

Jack agreed, and they walked up to the men in front just as the muleteer came galloping up with his troupe.

"What do you want with us?" Hawtry said, advancing to the men.

11

Jack Archer

There was a volley of maledictions at the run they had given them. The boys were seized by the collar, their dirks, watches, and money roughly taken from them, their arms tied to their sides by the ropes taken from the mules, and they were motioned to accompany their captors. These at once left the road and struck up the hill, the muleteer proceeding along the road with the animals.

With their arms tied, the boys found it hard work to keep up with their captors, who strode along with long steps. The sun had by this time sunk, and presently they heard the distant boom of the sunset gun from Gibraltar.

"That gun must be fifteen miles away," Hawtry said. "What fools we have been, Jack, to be sure!"

In one of the three men who accompanied them they recognized the peasant who had spoken to the muleteer when he refused to accept their first offer, and they had no doubt that he had arranged with the man to lead them to a certain spot, to which he had proceeded direct, while their guide had conducted them by a circuitous route.

They walked for four hours without a pause, ever ascending among the hills, until they at last reached a sort of plateau, upon which some six or eight men were gathered round a fire. Upon three sides the hill rose abruptly, on the fourth the ground sloped away, and in front, seemingly almost at their feet, some 2000 feet below them stretched away the waters of the Mediterranean, sparkling in the moonlight.

"They have got something to eat that smells nice," Jack said, as they approached the fire. "I hope to goodness they are going to give us some. I feel awfully peckish."

The men gathered round the fire rose at the approach of the new-comers, and an animated conversation took place. Then the boys were motioned to sit down, and the rest threw themselves round the fire. Some meat which was roasting on a rough spit over it was taken off, and one of the men undid the cords which tied their arms, and a share of the meat was given them.

"This is stunning," Jack said. "What on earth is it? It does not taste to me like mutton, or beef, or pork, or veal."

"I fancy it's kid," Hawtry said. "Well, it is evident they have no idea of cutting our throats. If they had been going to do that, they would have done it a quarter of a mile after we left the road. I suppose they are going to try to get a ransom for us. Where it's coming from as far as I'm concerned, I don't know, for my father is a clergyman, and has as much as he can do to make ends meet, for there are eight of us and I'm the eldest."

"It's an awful fix altogether," Jack said. "And anyhow, we shall lose our ship and get into a frightful row, and, if somebody won't pay our ransom, I suppose they will knock us on the head finally. The best thing, you know, will be for us to make our escape."

"But how on earth are we to do that?" Hawtry said. "There are ten of them, and I see a lot of guns piled there."

"Oh, I daresay we shall see some chance," Jack said cheerfully. "We must think it over. Jack Easy, Peter Simple, and all those fellows used to get into worse scrapes than this, and they always managed to get out of them somehow; so why shouldn't we? The best thing is, just to think what one of them would have done if he had been in our place. I wish to goodness that we had Mesty prowling about somewhere; he would get us out in no time."

G. A. Henty

Hawtry answered with a grunt, and devoted himself to his kid. Presently Jack spoke again.

"Look here, Hawtry, I vote that to begin with we both pretend to be in an awful funk. If they think that we are only two frightened boys, they won't keep as sharp a watch over us as if they thought we were determined fellows, likely to attempt our escape. There is the sea down there in front of us, and there are sure to be villages on the coast. Therefore we shall know which way to go if we once manage to escape, and, if we can get down there, we can either claim the protection of the head man in the village, or we can take a boat and make off to sea."

When the meal was over, one of the men, who appeared to be the leader, rose and come to the boys. Pointing to himself, he said, "Pedro," to another "Sancho," to a third "Garcia."

"He wants to know our names," Jack said, and pointing to his companion, he said, "Hawtry," and to himself "Archer."

The Spaniard nodded and resumed his seat, when an animated conversation took place. Jack, in the meantime, began to enact the part which he had arranged, turning over upon his face, and at times making a loud, sobbing noise.

Hawtry, after hesitating for some time, seconded his efforts by burying his face in his hands, and appearing also to give way to violent grief.

Chapter III
THE ESCAPE

SHORTLY after the meal was over, the brigands rose. The boys were again bound, and were laid down on the ground near the fire. One of the brigands then took his seat beside them, and the others, rolling themselves in their cloaks, were soon asleep at the fire. The boys, tired as they were by the long and fatiguing day through which they had passed, were some time getting off to sleep. Indeed, with their arms bound by their side, the only way of doing so was by lying flat upon their backs.

With the early dawn they were awake.

"I expect they are getting up steam on board the 'Falcon,'" Hawtry said, "and no doubt there is a nice row over our being missing. I'd give a good sum, if I had it to give, to be back on her decks again."

The band was soon astir, but for some hours nothing was done. They were evidently waiting for the arrival of some one, as one or other of the bandits went frequently to the edge of the plateau and looked down.

At last one of them announced to his comrades that the person expected was in sight, and shortly afterwards the muleteer of the previous day appeared. Over his shoulder hung a heavy skin of wine. In his hand he carried a large basket, in which were several loaves of coarse bread. His arrival was hailed with a shout. A fresh supply of meat had been placed on the fire immediately his coming was reported, and in a short time the meal was prepared, the meat being washed down by horns of the rough wine of the country.

The lads had been again unbound when the band awoke, and were, as before, invited to share the meal. They continued to maintain their forlorn and downcast attitude. The rascally guide of the day before gave the company an account of the proceedings, and roars of laughter were excited by his tragic imitation of the defiant way in which the boys had drawn their dirks, a proceeding which was rendered the more ludicrous from its contrast with their present forlorn attitude.

"But mind," he continued, "they can run like hares. Going up a hill, no doubt, any of you would soon overtake them, but along a straight road, I would back them against the best of us."

"There is no fear of their trying that," the chief said, pointing to the rifles. "They would soon be stopped if they tried it on. However, they are not likely to make any such mad attempt. They are, after all, only young boys, and their spirit has speedily evaporated."

However, as a measure of precaution, he ordered that the man who was acting as sentry over the boys should always keep his rifle in hand.

The meal over, the muleteer produced from his pocket some writing-paper and a pencil. The chief then wrote on a piece of paper the figures 5000, followed by the word "dollars." Then he said to the boys, "Capitan," giving them a pencil and a sheet of note-paper. He pointed to the figures he had written down, then to the sun, marked with his hand its course twice through the sky, and then drew it significantly across his throat.

"Well," Hawtry said, "that's clear enough. We are to write to the captain to say that unless 5000 dollars are paid in two days we are to have our throats cut. Well, I may as well write,—

"Dear Captain Stuart,—We are in an awful mess. We took some mules in the Spanish lines for a ride yesterday, and the fellow who owned them steered us into the middle of a lot of brigands. They were too strong for us to show fight, and here we are. As far as we can make out, they say that, unless 5000 dollars are paid in two days, we are to have our throats cut. We don't expect that you will get this note, as by this time the 'Falcon' was to have sailed. In that case we suppose it will be all up with us. We intend to try to slip our anchors, and make a bolt for it. We are awfully sorry that we have got into this scrape."

To this epistle the boys both signed their names, and as the muleteer had not provided himself with envelopes, the letter was roughly folded and directed,—

"Captain Stuart, H.M.S. 'Falcon.'"

Another letter, embodying the same in the form of a demand, was then written, after much consultation, by the brigands, with postscript stating that if the bearer were in any way molested, the prisoners would at once be put to death. The youngest of the party, a peasant of some twenty years old, was then selected, and to him the letters were given, with full instructions as to his conduct.

During the next two days, the boys maintained their appearance of extreme despondency. They lay on the ground with their faces buried in their arms, and at times strolled listlessly about. They could see that this conduct had lulled to rest any suspicion of their captors that they might attempt an escape. The sentry no longer kept in their immediate vicinity, and although he retained his gun in his hand, did so as a mere form. The others went about their business, several of them absenting themselves for hours together; and at one time but three men, including the guard, remained at the encampment.

The boys kept every faculty on the alert, and were ready to seize the first opportunity, however slight, which might offer itself. They agreed, that however much their guard might be reduced, it would be unsafe to make the attempt in the daytime, as they were wholly ignorant of the way down to the sea, and the shouts of their pursuers would be sure to attract the attention of any of the party who might have gone in that direction.

As to the two days assigned for payment, they did not anticipate that the crisis would arrive at the end of that time, as they felt sure that the "Falcon" would have sailed before the messenger could have arrived, in which case fresh negotiations would probably be set on foot.

So it proved. On the evening of the day after his departure, the messenger returned, and the news that he brought was greeted with an outburst of ejaculations of anger and disappointment on the part of the brigands. They crowded round the boys, shook their fists at them, cuffed and kicked them. When they had somewhat recovered their equanimity, they made signs that the ship had departed.

By using the word "Governor," they made the boys understand that a fresh letter must be written to that officer.

This was done at once, and another of the party started immediately with it.

Late on into the night the boys talked in low voices as to their best plan of attempting an escape. Although free in the daytime, they were tightly bound at night, and the guards, who were changed every two hours, never

Jack Archer

for a moment relaxed their vigilance. Finally, they concluded that their only chance was to endeavor to slip away on the following evening, just as it became dusk, when all the party generally reassembled, and were busy cooking their food, or relating what had happened during the day.

Immediately in front of the encampment the slope was extremely steep. The brigands, in going or coming, always turned to the right or left, and kept along the brow for some distance to points where, as the boys supposed, the slope became more gradual, and paths existed by which they could make their way down to the shore.

At one time the boys thought of rolling down the steep slope, and taking their chance, but this they agreed would be a last resource, as it was probable that the slope ended in an absolute precipice.

"I have an idea," Jack said suddenly in the middle of the day.

"What is it, Jack?"

"You see that heap of rugs in which they wrap themselves when they go to sleep? Now I vote that when it gets dusk, we stand for some time at the edge, looking down into the sea; then, when we see our guard chatting with one of the men who have just arrived, and the others busy round the fire, we will quietly move back towards it. If our guard notices us at all, he won't pay any special attention, as we are going that way. We will steal up to the rear of the blankets, within a few feet of where they are standing, and will crawl quietly under them. When we are missed, they are sure to suppose that we have either made down the slope, or along the brow, and will at once set off in pursuit. The betting is they'll all go, but if only one or two are left, we may take them by surprise. At any rate it seems our best chance."

Hawtry agreed, and it was decided that they should attempt to put the plan into execution that evening.

Late in the afternoon, the brigands, as usual, came dropping in, in twos and threes. One brought in a kid, and two others exhibited to their admiring friends a purse containing some ten or twelve dollars in silver. They related, amid the uproarious laughter of their comrades, the manner in which they had threatened the worthy farmer, its late possessor, into surrendering the proceeds of his day's marketing without resistance. It was already dusk. Jack and Hawtry had a minute before been standing near the edge of the slope. The guard was chatting with the last comer, and keeping one ear open to the narrative told by the fire.

Suddenly he glanced round, and perceived that the figures he had, as he believed, scarcely taken his eye off were missing.

"Madre de Dios!" he exclaimed. "Where are the prisoners?"

At his exclamation, all round the fire started into activity. A hasty glance round the encampment showed that their captives were not within its circle. With an exclamation of fury, the captain seized his gun, and with the butt-end struck the sentry to the ground. Then in furious tones he ordered every man off in instant pursuit. Snatching up their arms, some hurried off one way, some another, shouting threats of vengeance as they went.

As their voices receded, there was a slight movement among the rugs, and the boys' heads peered out from below their hiding-place. The encampment was deserted, save that on the ground lay the form of the prostrate sentinel, while the captain stood, gun in hand, on the edge of the slope, peering down into the gathering darkness.

The boys rose stealthily to their feet, and keeping along by the side of the hill, so as to be out of the direct line of sight should the brigand turn towards the fire, they noiselessly approached him.

He did not look round until they were within five paces, and it was then too late. He turned and threw up his gun, but before he could level it, they both threw themselves upon him.

Taken wholly by surprise, he staggered backwards. He was but a pace from the edge of the steep declivity, and in another moment he fell backward, his gun exploding in the air as he went. The boys heard his body as it rolled and crashed through the slight brushwood on the slope. Fainter and fainter became the sound, and then it suddenly ceased.

As long as it continued the boys stood motionless, and were turning to go, when there was the crack of a rifle, and a ball whizzed between them. Leaping round, they saw the guard, whom they had supposed to be insensible, had risen to his feet. Throwing down the rifle which he had just discharged, and drawing his long knife, he rushed at them.

"Dodge him, Hawtry, dodge him. Get hold of the rifle. I will get a stick from the fire."

The boys separated, one going each way. The Spaniard, still bewildered by the stunning blow he had received, hesitated a moment, and then rushed at Jack, who darted round the fire. Hawtry seized the rifle, and with the butt-end attacked the Spaniard, who turned to defend himself. Jack snatched up a heavy brand from the fire, and coming behind the Spaniard, who was waiting, knife in hand, for an opportunity to rush in between the sweeping blows which Hawtry was dealing at him with the butt-end of the rifle, smote him with all his force across the side of the head.

With a scream of agony the Spaniard fell prostrate and Jack, snatching up his knife, while Hawtry still retained the rifle, they darted off at full speed along the brow.

Presently they heard footsteps of men hastily returning, and drawing aside, threw themselves down among some low bushes. The men were talking eagerly. They had heard the two reports of the guns, and had no doubt that the captain had discovered the fugitives.

When the Spaniards had passed, the boys rose to their feet, and continued their flight at the top of their speed. The men had come from below, and the boys soon discovered traces of a path descending the slope. This they at once took, proceeding with caution now, for the descent was an extremely steep one, and the path little more than a goat track. Fortunately the moon was shining brightly, and by its light they were enabled to follow its windings.

After half an hour's descent, they found themselves in a rough road, along the face of the hill. This they doubted not was the road from one of the coast villages into the interior. They now went more cautiously, for the road was extremely rough, with large stones lying here and there upon it, and a heavy fall or a sprained ankle would be disastrous. They had no fear of pursuit. Once or twice they fancied that they heard shouts far above them, but they considered it likely that the band would be too far paralyzed by the loss of their captain to again take up the pursuit.

Three hours later, they stood by the sea shore, near a tiny fishing village, composed of three or four houses only. They held a consultation as to whether it would be better to rouse the villagers and explain the circumstances, but they had become suspicious of Spaniards, and thought it

Jack Archer

likely that there would be a close relationship between the people here and the band in their neighborhood. No lights were visible in the village, and it was probable that the inhabitants were already in bed.

They sat down for another hour to avoid the chance of their being surprised by any straggler. Then, proceeding to the shore, they launched a small boat. Hawtry stepped the mast and hoisted the sail, and they were soon making their way off the land. The wind was light, and their progress slow. For a time they kept straight out to sea, and then turned the boat's head towards Gibraltar.

The wind presently died quite away, and, lowering the sails, they got out the oars, and set to work. Beyond trying once or twice upon the Stour, Jack had had no experience in rowing, and his clumsiness excited considerable indignation on the part of Hawtry. The boat was heavy, and their progress, in consequence, very slow. They calculated that they must have twenty-five miles to row, as the point at which they were captured was, Hawtry had judged by the sound of the gun, fully fifteen miles distant from it, and they had walked another ten before arriving at the brigands' encampment.

All night they rowed, until the moon sank, this being, as they were aware, about three o'clock. They then lay down in the boat for a nap, and when they awoke it was daylight. They found that the wind had got up, and was blowing steadily off shore, and that they were now distant some five miles from land, the Rock of Gibraltar rising steeply from the sea some ten miles from them in a straight line.

Hawtry at once set the sail again, and the boat was soon slipping fast through the water.

"What a nuisance!" Hawtry said. "The wind is hauling farther round, and we shall not make into the Rock this tack. This tub of a boat makes no end of leeway. We shall have to make right across towards the African shore, and then tack back again."

They were, as Hawtry anticipated, fully three miles to leeward of Europa Point, as they passed the Rock. The wind was now blowing strongly from the west.

"Upon my word," Hawtry said, "I question whether we shall ever be able to make the Rock in this beast of a boat. She won't sail anywhere near the wind, and makes awful leeway. Hurrah! there's a big steamer coming out. We will hail her."

Hawtry now steered the boat till he had placed her as near as possible in the line which the steamer was pursuing, and then lowered the sail, and waited for her to come up.

When she came within a quarter of a mile the sail was again hoisted, and Hawtry so steered the boat that for a moment Jack thought he would put her under the bows of the steamer. This, however, had the effect which Hawtry had intended, of drawing attention to them.

The steamer passed within thirty feet of them. Hawtry lowered the sail, and standing up, shouted,—

"Throw us a rope!"

A number of persons had been attracted to the side, and one of the officers, seeing two young midshipmen in the boat, at once threw a rope to them, while the officer on duty ordered the engines to be stopped. In another two minutes the boat was hauled alongside. The two lads scrambled up the

G. A. Henty

rope, the boat was cast adrift, and the steamer was again ploughing her way eastward.

The boys found that they were on board the transport "Ripon," having the Coldstream Guards on board, the first detachment of the army on its way east.

Considerable excitement was caused by the sudden and unexpected boarding of the ship by the two young officers, and great curiosity was expressed as to how they had got into such a position. As Hawtry said, however, that they had been twenty-four hours without food, they were at once taken to the saloon, where breakfast was on the point of being served. No questions were put to them until they had satisfied their hunger; then they told the story of their adventures, which caused quite an excitement among the officers.

The "Ripon" had sailed from Southampton docks on the 23d of February, in company with the "Manilla" and "Orinoco."

The next four days passed pleasantly, the boys being made a good deal of by the officers of the Coldstream Guards, but they were not sorry when, on Saturday evening, the lights of Malta were seen, and soon after midnight they dropped anchor in Valetta Harbor. The next morning they were delighted at seeing the "Falcon" lying a few cables' length distant, and, bidding good-bye to their new friends, they hailed a shore boat, and were soon alongside the "Falcon." The first lieutenant was on deck.

"Young gentlemen," he said sternly, "you have committed a very serious offence, and are liable to be tried by court-martial for having deserted your ship. I expected better things of you both. Go below immediately, and consider yourselves under arrest. I shall report your coming on board to the captain."

The boys saluted without a word, and went below to the midshipmen's berth where the tale of their adventures was soon related to their comrades, who were at first inclined to believe that the whole story was an invention got up to screen themselves for breaking leave. However, they soon saw that the boys were in earnest, and the truth of the story as to their being picked up at sea by the "Ripon" could, of course, at once be tested.

Presently they were summoned to the captain's cabin, and there Hawtry again recited the story.

The captain told them that they had erred greatly in going away in such a reckless manner, without taking proper precautions to secure their return before gun-fire. But he said they had already been punished so severely for their thoughtlessness that he should overlook the offence, and that he complimented them on the courage and coolness they had displayed in extricating themselves from the dangerous position into which they had fallen.

He then invited them to breakfast, at which meal the first lieutenant was also present, and here they gave much fuller details of their escape than Hawtry had done in his first narration of it.

At ten o'clock, when the boys were below, they heard a loud cheering, and found that the "Orinoco," with the Grenadiers, had just come into harbor, and were being cheered by their comrades on board the "Ripon" and by the blue jackets of the men-of-war.

All through the day the harbor was alive with boats. Before nightfall the Coldstreams were all ashore, and by Monday evening the last of the Grenadiers had also disembarked.

Chapter IV
GALLIPOLI

EVERY day brought fresh troops to Malta, until the brigade of Guards and eleven regiments of infantry of the line were gathered there. The streets of Valetta were like a fair, crowded with soldiery chattering with the vendors of oranges, dates, olives, and apples. Cigars, too, are nowhere cheaper than in Malta, and as, unfortunately, spirits were equally low in price, the British soldier, small as was his daily rate of pay, found but little difficulty in intoxicating himself.

In a few days the French began to put in an appearance, and the crowd in the streets was even more lively and picturesque than before. All this time the great topic of discussion was whether matters would or would not come to the arbitration of war.

During their stay Jack Archer and his comrades enjoyed themselves heartily, but it was by no means all play. The sailors had an immense deal to do in moving stores, preparing fittings, and getting matters ready for the forward despatch of the troops, should war be finally decided upon.

A month after the arrival at Malta, the doubt was put an end to, for upon the 28th of March war was formally declared, and on the 29th the French sailed for Gallipoli, followed, the next day, by Sir George Brown with the advance party of the light division.

The same day the "Falcon" steamed out of harbor, and, although the stay at Malta had been enjoyed, all hands were delighted at the advance towards the scene of future action.

Gallipoli stands near the upper end of the Dardanelles, and is an important military position.

"It looks a nice little town," Delafield said, on returning after his first visit in the captain's gig, to his comrades. "But I can't say much for it when you see it at close quarters. One got tired of Malta, but Malta was a paradise to this place. The confusion seems to be tremendous. But those jolly old Turks are sitting at their doors, smoking like so many old owls, and do not seem to interest themselves in the slightest."

"And did you see any lovely houris?" Simmonds asked, laughing.

"That I did not," Delafield said. "I saw some bundles looking like rolls of dirty white sheets ready for the wash, with a pair of big, yellow shoes underneath them, and I believe that they were women. I did not see any of their faces. I didn't want to, for I'm sure no decently pretty woman would allow herself to be made such an object as that."

The same work of unloading and transporting goods to the shore, which had gone on at Malta, was continued here. Every day fresh troops arrived, English and French, and the whole of the undulating plain round Gallipoli was dotted with their camps. By the end of the month 22,000 French and some 10,000 English were gathered there.

After the day's work was done, the midshipmen often got leave ashore, and enjoyed the scene of bustle and confusion which reigned there. Enormous numbers of pack animals and bullock-carts were at work, and even at this early period of the campaign the immense superiority of the French arrangements over the English was manifest. This was but natural, as the French, like other European nations, had been in the habit in time of peace of regarding the army as a machine which might be required for war, and had therefore kept the commissariat, transport, and other arrangements in a state of efficiency. In England, upon the other hand, the army had been entirely neglected, and had been made the subject of miserable, petty economy in all its branches, and the consequence was that war found us wholly unprepared, except that we possessed an army of seasoned soldiers such as, in the nature of things under the new regulations, England will never see again.

On going ashore the midshipmen would sometimes ramble away to the camp, sometimes stroll through the town, and amuse themselves by chaffing the grave Turkish shopkeepers, by watching the English and French soldiers staggering along with drunken gravity, sometimes with their arms round each other's necks, or by kissing their hands airily to the veiled figures, of whom they got dim glimpses through the closely-latticed windows. The upper part of the town was inhabited principally by Greeks, whose sympathies were, for the most part, with the Russians, and who were as quarrelsome and turbulent as the Turks were placid and good-natured.

One evening Hawtry and Jack had obtained leave to be out later than usual, as they had been asked to dine with some of the officers of the Coldstreams whom they had met on board the "Ripon." The meal was a rough one, for the country had been completely eaten up by this immense accession of strangers. Still, the caterer had succeeded in procuring some tough fowls in addition to the ration beef, and as these were washed down by champagne, there was no reason to grumble.

The boys spent a merry evening, and started at half-past ten for the town. This was already quiet, and for the most part asleep, when they reached it. A few officers, who had been dining with the various generals who had their headquarters there, or with friends on board ship, were the sole people in the streets, although from some of the closed windows of the drinking-shops in the Greek quarter came sounds of singing and noise, for every one was earning high wages, and the place was full of Maltese, Alexandrians, Smyrniotes, and, indeed, the riff-raff of all the Mediterranean cities, who had flocked to the scene of action to make money as petty traders, hucksters, camp-followers, mule-drivers, or commissariat-laborers.

As they were passing through a dark and silent street they suddenly heard a sound of shouting and the clash of weapons, the fall of heavy bodies, and the tramping of feet. Then a window was dashed open, a voice shouted, "Help!" and then the strife continued as before.

"Come on, Archer," Hawtry exclaimed. "There are some of our fellows in a row with these Greeks."

The door was fastened, but the boys burst in a window next to it, leapt into the room, groped their way to the door, and then finding the stairs, hurried up. On the landing a dim oil light was burning, but it needed no light to indicate the room in which the struggle was still proceeding. The door stood ajar, and the boys, with drawn dirks, dashed into the room.

It was a large one. In the centre was a table on which were strewn several packs of cards; some chairs lay on the ground; the oil from an

Jack Archer

overturned lamp was forming a great black stain on the green table-cloth. In the corner by the window, three officers with drawn swords, were defending themselves against the attacks of some twenty Greeks, armed with knives. In the confusion, none had noticed the entry of the boys.

"Pick up a chair, Jack," Hawtry said, recoiling from the idea of rushing with his dirk upon unprepared men.

The two lads each seized one of the strong, but light, chairs scattered on the floor, and, with a sudden hurrah, flung themselves upon the Greeks. Two or three of these were knocked down and the rest, taken by surprise by the sudden attack, recoiled, and the boys were speedily by the side of the assailed officers.

The Greeks drew back, but seeing how slight was the reinforcement, again advanced to the attack. Three of their number lay upon the ground, and several of the others were bleeding freely. Upon the other hand, one of the officers leant against the wall, badly wounded, while both of the others had received nasty cuts. They would, before this, have been overpowered, had they not hastily pulled a small table and a chair or two, so as to form a sort of barricade, across the angle, and so prevented the Greeks from closing upon them. One of the officers was an Englishman, the others were French. All were quite young men. There was scarcely time for the exchange of a word before the Greeks were upon them again.

The boys had again drawn their dirks, but these formed but a poor weapon against the chairs with which several of the Greeks, seeing the inferiority of their knives, had now armed themselves. Hawtry received a crashing blow on the head which sent him staggering back against the wall, and Jack one on his arm which rendered it useless.

"This will never do," the English officer shouted. "Let us make a rush at the scoundrels, and fight our way to the door. It's our only chance."

"Wait a moment," Jack said, a thought striking him. Stooping down behind the others, he pulled out a matchbox from his pocket, struck a light, and applied it to the muslin curtains which hung before the window. In a moment a broad sheet of flame leaped up. The Greeks uttered a shout of terror and surprise.

"Now!" Jack shouted. "All together."

In a moment the five dashed down the table, and flung themselves upon the Greeks. These, taken by surprise, and paralyzed by the great sheet of flame which was already licking the wooden ceiling, recoiled. Some were cut down as they stood. Others were hurled aside. Two or three fell before the dirks of the midshipmen, and in a few seconds the little party had burst through the crowd of their assailants, and had gained the door of the room. Here the Englishman and one of the French officers turned and made a stand, in order to give the midshipmen time to assist their badly-wounded comrade down the narrow stairs, and to open the door of the house. As they flung this open, Jack shouted up that the way was free, and then, half carrying the wounded Frenchman, they hurried down the street, uttering shouts for assistance. The lattice work of the window had already caught fire, and a sheet of flame lit up the street. Before they had gone fifty yards, they heard a noise behind them, as the two officers, followed by the Greeks, issued from the house.

Fortunately, at this moment a party of English officers, who had been dining at the general's, ran up at full speed, attracted by the shouts of the boys and the glare of fire. Upon seeing this accession of strength, the Greeks at once desisted from the attack, and made off. By this time the windows of the various houses were opening, and shouts of affright arose at the sight of the conflagration; for the houses were, for the most part, constructed of wood, and, once begun, there was no saying where a fire would end.

"What is all this about, gentlemen?" one of the officers, a colonel, asked. "Give me your names, for there must be an inquiry into the matter. I see you are all wounded, and 'tis best to get back to camp at once. I fear this will be a serious matter."

In five minutes the street was full of people, and the flames had obtained entire possession of the house, and were rushing high into the air. The wind was blowing briskly, and it was evident that the safety of the whole quarter of the town was menaced. The French officer succeeded in getting four Maltese to carry his comrade to the camp. A door was taken off its hinges, and they were soon upon their way.

Jack and Hawtry, who had only received one or two slight slashes of knives, remained to see what came of it. The Turkish guards were speedily on the spot, but these could do nothing beyond trying to prevent the rabble from commencing a general pillage. From every house the people were throwing out their goods of all descriptions. Every minute the fire spread, and six or seven houses were already in flames when, but a quarter of an hour after the outbreak of the fire, a heavy tramp was heard, and a battalion of French infantry from their nearest camp came up at a double. There was no water, no means whatever of extinguishing the flames, but the active little Frenchmen did not lose a minute. At the word of command, they broke their ranks, and swarmed into the houses, and in a minute a perfect avalanche of goods was thrown from the windows. Some stood along outside the houses, others climbed upon their shoulders, on these again others took their places, and so on until living ladders were formed, up which a score of men climbed the roofs. These set to work with axe and hatchet, tearing off the tiles and hacking down rafters, while their comrades in the houses hewed away at floors and staircases. In less than a quarter of an hour four houses on either side of those in flames were completely gutted, and the fire, thus cut off, speedily burnt itself out, fifteen houses having been consumed.

By this time large numbers of troops, together with sailors from the fleet, had arrived, but the work was fortunately done, and had it not been for the early appearance of the French battalion, and the energetic measures which they adopted, a great portion of the Greek quarter would have been destroyed.

Among those who had landed was a strong party of seamen from the "Falcon," under Mr. Hethcote. The boys joined these, and returned with them on board ship. They reported to the lieutenant the share which they had had in the affair.

"It is an unpleasant business," he said, "but I do not blame you for going to the assistance of those attacked when you heard an Englishman call for help. Still, Mr. Archer, it is clear that you have pretty nearly burnt down the town of Gallipoli, and I don't know the light in which the admiral and Sir George Brown may view the affair. As you say that no one took any notice of you at the time that the names of the military officers were taken, it is

Jack Archer

possible that no inquiry will be made about you. I shall, of course, report the matter to Captain Stuart, and he must act as he thinks fit. But, in the meantime, I should advise you to say nothing of the share which you have had in the matter to any one. You must have those gashes you have got plastered up. But I will speak to the surgeon. Do you know the name of the English officer concerned?"

"Yes, sir, he was Lieutenant Tewson of the Grenadier Guards. We only exchanged a few words before he went away, but he begged us to go and see him."

"I should advise you to keep away from him altogether, until the matter has blown over," Mr. Hethcote said. "Did you give him your names?"

"No, sir, we had no time."

"All the better," Mr. Hethcote said. "It will, of course, come out in the course of the inquiry that two midshipmen were concerned, and it is just as well that he cannot give your names. I expect the ship to be ordered up to Constantinople in a day or two, and I hope we may be off before any inquiries are made. One can never say how these big-wigs may take things. Sir George Brown is a tremendous martinet, and he may consider that it would have been far better that five officers, who chose to go to a gambling-house, should be killed, than that Gallipoli, full as it is of valuable stores, and munitions of war, should run the risk of being destroyed by fire. There, now, go off to the surgeon, and get your faces strapped up, and then ask him to come to me at once. If you two young gentlemen go on as you have begun, you are not likely to live to obtain eminence in your profession. It is but two months since we left England, and we have not yet seen an enemy, yet you have had two as narrow escapes for your lives as one could wish to have."

Very severe was the cross-questioning which the lads had to undergo in the midshipmen's berth as to the manner in which they came by their cut faces, and they were obliged to take refuge under the strict order of the first lieutenant that they were to say nothing about it.

Fortunately the next day the "Falcon" received orders to proceed to the Bosphorus, and got up her anchor and steamed up the Dardanelles before dark. Presently Mr. Hethcote came up to Jack, who was on duty on the quarter-deck.

"I tell you what, Jack," he said quietly, "it is very lucky for you that we are away. The French officer died during the night. I hear that his lungs were pierced. Sir George Brown is said to be furious, and threatens to try Tewson by court-martial, for entering a gambling-house in spite of strict orders to the contrary. Of course it is well known that scores of other officers have done the same, but it is only when a thing is found out that there is a row about it. Tewson had been dining on board a French ship, and was going home with the two French officers, who were also there. None of them had been in a gambling-house before, but it seems they had heard of this place, which was one of the most notorious dens in the town, and agreed to look in for a few minutes to see what it was like. They began to play and had an extraordinary run of luck, winning something like four hundred pounds. The bank was broken, and the Greeks wanted them to stop till some more money was procured. This they would not do, and the Greeks then attacked them. Tewson has strong interest, and the affair will probably, in his case, blow over. The Greeks have made a complaint against them for wilfully setting fire to the house, and this is the most serious part of the affair. I am told that both Tewson and the French officer deny having done so. They say that it was done in order to effect a diversion, by two officers who came in to their assistance in the middle of the fight, and both declare that they do not know who they were or anything about them, as they only saw them for a minute in the middle of the confusion. Some one has said that two young naval officers were seen just at the beginning of the fire, and no doubt inquiries will be set on foot. But now that we are fairly off, they will find out nothing at Gallipoli, and it's likely that it will all blow over. The authorities have plenty to think about at present without troubling themselves very much in following up a clue of this kind."

In all the world there is no more lovely scene than that which greeted Jack Archer's eyes as he went on deck the following morning.

The "Falcon" was anchored about mid-channel. On the left was Constantinople with its embattled wall, its palaces, its green foliage down to the water's edge, its domes and minarets rising thickly. Separated from it by the Golden Horn, crossed by a bridge of boats, are Pera and Galatta, street rising above street. Straight over the bows of the ship was the Bosphorus, with its wooded banks dotted with villas and palaces. To the right was Scutari, with the great barrack standing on the edge of a cliff some fifty feet in height. Little did those who looked at the great square pile of building dream that ere many months it would be crowded from top to bottom with British sick and wounded, and that even its ample corridors would prove wholly insufficient to contain them. The water itself was thronged with shipping of all nations: men-of-war, merchant steamers crowded with stores, troop-ships thronged with red-coats; great barges, laden to the water's edge, slowly made their way between the ships and the shore. The boats of the shipping, filled with soldiers, rowed in the same direction. Men-of-war boats, with their regular, steady swing, went hither and thither, while among all crossed and re-crossed from Constantinople to Scutari, the light caicques with their one or two white-shirted rowers. No boats in the world are more elegant in appearance, none except those built specially for racing can vie with them in speed. The passenger sits comfortably on a cushion in the bottom of the boat, and smokes the long pipe which the boatman, as a matter of course, fills and hands to him as he takes his seat, while the boatmen themselves, generally Albanians, and singularly handsome and athletic men, lay themselves down to their work with a vigor and a heartiness which would astound the boatmen of an English watering-place.

A scene so varied, so beautiful, and so busy could not be equalled elsewhere.

Chapter V
A BRUSH WITH THE ENEMY

TWO days later Jack obtained leave to go on shore. He hesitated for a moment whether to choose the right or left bank. The plateau of Scutari was covered with the tents of the British army, which were daily being added to, as scarce an hour passed without a transport coming in laden with troops. After a little hesitation, however, Jack determined to land at Constantinople. The camps at Scutari would differ but little from those at Gallipoli, while in the Turkish capital were innumerable wonders to be investigated. Hailing a caicque which was passing, he took his seat with young Coveney, who had also got leave ashore, and accepted with dignity the offer of a long pipe. This, however, by no means answered his expectations; the mouthpiece being formed of a large piece of amber of a bulbous shape, and too large to be put into the mouth. It was consequently necessary to suck the smoke through the end, a practice very difficult at first to those accustomed to hold a pipe between the teeth.

In ten minutes the boat landed them at Pera, close to the bridge of boats across the Golden Horn. For a time the lads made no motion to advance, so astonished were they at the crowd which surged across the bridge: Turkish, English, and French soldiers, Turks in turbans and fezes, Turkish women wrapped up to the eyes in white or blue clothes; hamals or porters staggered past under weights which seemed to the boys stupendous; pachas and other dignitaries riding on gayly-trapped little horses; carriages, with three or four veiled figures inside and black guards standing on the steps, carried the ladies of one harem to visit those of another. The lads observed that for the most part these dames, instead of completely hiding their faces with thick wrappings as did their sisters in the streets, covered them merely with a fold of thin muslin, permitting their features to be plainly seen. These ladies evidently took a lively interest in what was going on, and in no way took it amiss when some English or French officer stared unceremoniously at their pretty faces; although their black guards gesticulated angrily on these occasions, and were clearly far more indignant concerning the admiration which their mistresses excited than were those ladies themselves.

At last the boys moved forward across the bridge, and Jack presently found himself next to two young English officers proceeding in the same direction. One of these turned sharply round as Jack addressed his companion.

"Hallo, Jack!"

"Hallo, Harry! What! you here? I had no idea you had got your commission yet. How are you, old fellow, and how are they all at home?"

"Every one is all right, Jack. I thought you would have known all about it. I was gazetted three days after you started, and was ordered to join at once. We wrote to tell you it."

"I have never had a letter since I left home," Jack said. "I suppose they are all knocking about somewhere. Every one is complaining about the post. Well, this is jolly; and I see you are in the 33d too, the regiment you wanted to get into. When did you arrive?"

G. A. Henty

"We came in two days ago in the 'Himalaya.' We are encamped with the rest of the light division who have come up. Sir George Brown commands us, and will be here from Gallipoli in a day or two with the rest of the division."

The boys now introduced their respective friends to each other, and the four wandered together through Constantinople, visited the bazaars, fixed upon lots of pretty things as presents to be bought and taken home at the end of the war, and then crossed the bridge again to Pera, and had dinner at Missouri's, the principal hotel there, and the great rendezvous of the officers of the British army and navy. Then they took a boat and rowed across to Scutari, where Harry did the honors of the camp, and at sundown Jack and his messmate returned on board the "Falcon."

The next three weeks passed pleasantly, Jack spending all his time, when he could get leave, with his brother, and the latter often coming off for an hour or two to the "Falcon." Early in May the news arrived that the Russians had advanced through the Dobrudscha and had commenced the siege of Silistria. A few hours later the "Falcon" and several other ships of war were on their way up the Dardanelles, convoying numerous store-ships bound to Varna. Shortly afterwards the generals of the allied armies determined that Varna should be the base for the campaign against the Russians, and accordingly towards the end of May the troops were again embarked.

Varna is a seaport, surrounded by an undulating country of park-like appearance, and the troops were upon their arrival delighted with their new quarters. Here some 22,000 English and 50,000 French were encamped, together with 8,000 or 10,000 Turks. A few days after their arrival Jack obtained leave for a day on shore, and rowed out to Alladyn, nine miles and a half from Varna, where the light division, consisting of the 7th, 19th, 23d, 33d, 77th, and 88th regiments, was encamped. Close by was a fresh-water lake, and the undulated ground was finely wooded with clumps of forest timber, and covered with short, crisp grass. No more charming site for a camp could be conceived. Game abounded, and the officers who had brought guns with them found for a time capital sport. Everyone was in the highest spirits, and the hopes that the campaign would soon open in earnest were general. In this, however, they were destined to be disappointed, for on the 24th of June the news came that the Turks had unaided beaten off the Russians with such heavy loss in their attack upon Silistria that the latter had broken up the siege, and were retreating northward.

A weary delay then occurred while the English and French home authorities, and the English and French generals in the field were settling the point at which the attack should be made upon Russia. The delay was a disastrous one, for it allowed an enemy more dangerous than the Russians to make his insidious approaches. The heat was very great; water bad, indeed almost undrinkable, the climate was notoriously an unhealthy one, and fruit of all kinds, together with cucumbers and melons, extremely cheap, and the soldiers consequently consumed very large quantities of these.

Through June and up to the middle of July, however, no very evil consequences were apparent. On the 21st of July two divisions of French troops under General Canrobert marched into the Dobrudscha, in search of some bodies of Russians who were said to be there. On the night of the 28th cholera broke out, and before morning, in one division no less than 600 men lay dead. The other divisions, although situated at considerable distances, were simultaneously attacked with equal violence, and three days later the expedition returned, having lost over 7000 men. Scarcely less sudden or less fatal was the attack among the English lines, and for some time the English camps were ravaged by cholera.

Jack was extremely anxious about his brother, for the light division suffered even more severely than did the others. But he was not able to go himself to see as to the state of things, for the naval officers were not allowed to go on shore more than was absolutely necessary. And as the camp of the light division had been moved some ten miles farther away on to the slopes of the Balkans, it would have been impossible to go and return in one day. Such precautions as were taken, however, were insufficient to keep the cholera from on board ship. In a short time the fleet was attacked with a severity almost equal to that on shore, and although the fleet put out to sea, the flagship in two days lost seventy men.

Fortunately the "Falcon" had left Varna before the outbreak extended to the ships. The Crimea had now been definitely determined upon as the point of assault. Turkish vessels with heavy siege guns were on their way to Varna, and the "Falcon" was ordered to cross to the Crimea and report upon the advantages of several places for the landing of the allied army. The mission was an exciting one, as beside the chance of a brush with shore batteries, there was the possibility that they might run against some of the Russian men-of-war, who still held that part of the Black Sea, and whose headquarters were at Sebastopol, the great fortress which was the main object of the expedition to the Crimea.

The "Falcon" started at night, and in the morning of the second day the hills of the Crimea were visible in the distance. The fires were then banked up and she lay-to. With nightfall she steamed on until within a mile or two of the coast, and here again anchored. With the early dawn steam was turned on, and the "Falcon" steamed along as close to the shore as she dare go, the lead being constantly kept going, as but little was known of the depth of water on these shores. Presently they came to a bay with a smooth beach. The ground rose but gradually behind, and a small village stood close to the shore.

"This looks a good place," Captain Stuart said to the first lieutenant. "We will anchor here and lower the boats. You, Mr. Hethcote, with three boats, had better land at that village, get any information that you can, and see that there are no troops about. If attacked by a small force, you will of course repel it; if by a strong one, fall back to your boats, and I will cover your retreat with the guns of the ship. The other two boats will be employed in sounding. Let the master have charge of these, and make out, as far as he can, a perfect chart of the bay."

In a few minutes the boats were lowered, and the men in the highest glee took their places. Jack was in the gig with the first lieutenant. The order was given, and the boats started together towards the shore. They had not gone fifty yards before there was a roar of cannon, succeeded by the whistle of shot. Two masked batteries, one upon each side of the bay, and mounting each six guns, had opened upon them. The cutter, commanded by the second lieutenant, was smashed by a round shot and instantly sunk. A ball struck close to the stroke-oar of the gig, deluging its occupants with water and ricochetting over the gunwale of the boat, between the stroke-oar and Mr. Hethcote. Two shot hulled the "Falcon," and others whistled through her rigging.

"Pick up the crew of the cutter, Mr. Hethcote, and return on board at once," Captain Stuart shouted; the engines of the "Falcon" at once began to move, and the captain interposed the ship between the nearest battery and the boats, and a few seconds later her heavy guns, which had previously been got ready for action, opened upon the forts. In two minutes the boats were alongside with all hands, save one of the cutter's crew who had been cut in two by the round shot. The men, leaving the boats towing alongside, rushed to the guns, and the heavy fire of the "Falcon" speedily silenced her opponents. Then, as his object was to reconnoitre, not to fight, Captain Stuart steamed out to sea. He was determined, however, to obtain further information respecting the bay, which appeared to him one adapted for the purpose of landing.

"I will keep off till nightfall, Mr. Hethcote. We will then run in as close as we dare, showing no lights, and I will then ask you to take a boat with muffled oars to row to the village. Make your way among the houses as quietly as possible, and seize a couple of fishermen and bring them off with you. Our interpreter will be able to find out from them at any rate, general details as to the depth of water and the nature of the anchorage."

"Who shall I take with me, sir?"

"The regular gig's crew and Mr. Simmonds. He has passed, and it may give him a chance of promotion. I think, by the way, you may as well take the launch also; it carries a gun. Do not let the men from it land, but keep her lying a few yards off shore to cover your retreat if necessary. Mr. Pascoe will command it."

There was a deep but quiet excitement among the men when at nightfall the vessel's head was again turned towards shore, and the crews of the gig and launch told to hold themselves in readiness. Cutlasses were sharpened and pistols cleaned. Not less was the excitement in the midshipmen's berth, where it was known that Simmonds was to go in the gig; but no one knew who was to accompany the launch. However, Jack turned out to be the lucky one, Mr. Pascoe being probably glad to please the first lieutenant by selecting his relation, although that officer would not himself have shown favoritism on his behalf.

It was about eleven o'clock when the "Falcon" approached her former position, or rather to a point a mile seaward of it as nearly as the master could bring her, for the night was extremely dark and the land scarcely visible. Not a light was shown, not a voice raised on board, and the only sound heard was the gentle splash of the paddles as they revolved at their slowest rate of speed. The falls had been greased, the rowlocks muffled, and the crew took their places in perfect silence.

"You understand, Mr. Hethcote," were Captain Stuart's last words, "that you are not to attempt a landing if there is the slightest opposition."

Very quietly the boats left the "Falcon's" side. They rowed abreast and close to each other, in order that the first lieutenant could give orders to Mr. Pascoe in a low tone. The men were ordered to row quietly, and to avoid any splashing or throwing up of water. It was a longer row than they had expected, and it was evident that the master, deceived by the uncertain light, had brought the vessel up at a point considerably farther from the shore than he had intended. As they got well in the bay they could see no lights in the village ahead; but an occasional gleam near the points at either side showed that the men in the batteries were awake and active. As the boat neared the shore the men rowed, according to the first lieutenant's orders, more and more gently, and at last, when the line of beach ahead became distinctly visible, the order was given to lie upon their oars. All listened intently, and then Mr. Hethcote put on his helm so that the boat which had still some way on it drifted even closer to the launch.

"Do you hear anything, Mr. Pascoe?"

"I don't know, sir. I don't seem to make out any distinct sound, but there certainly appears to be some sort of murmur in the air."

"So I think, too."

Again they listened.

"I don't know, sir," Jack whispered in Mr. Pascoe's ear, "but I fancy that at times I see a faint light right along behind those trees. It is very faint, but sometimes their outline seems clearer than at others."

Mr. Pascoe repeated in a low voice to Mr. Hethcote what Jack had remarked.

"I fancied so once or twice myself," he said. "There," he added suddenly, "that is the neigh of a horse. However, there may be horses anywhere. Now we will paddle slowly on. Lay within a boat's length of the shore, Mr. Pascoe, keep the gun trained on the village, and let the men hold their arms in readiness."

In another minute the gig's bow grated on the beach. "Quietly, lads," the first lieutenant said. "Step into the water without splashing. Then follow me as quickly as you can."

The beach was a sandy one, and the footsteps of the sailors were almost noiseless as they stole towards the village. The place seemed hushed in quiet, but just as they entered the little street a figure standing in the shade of a house rather larger than the rest, stepped forward and challenged, bringing, as he did so, his musket to the present. An instant later he fired, just as the words, "A Russian sentry," broke from the first lieutenant's lips. Almost simultaneously three or four other shots were fired at points along the beach. A rocket whizzed high in the air from each side of the bay, a bugle sounded the alarm, voices of command were heard, and, as if by enchantment, a chaos of sounds followed the deep silence which had before reigned, and from every house armed men poured out.

"Steady, lads, steady!" Mr. Hethcote shouted. "Fall back steadily. Keep together, don't fire a shot till you get to the boat; then give them a volley and jump on board. Now, retire at the double."

For a moment the Russians, as they poured from the houses, paused in ignorance of the direction of their foes, but a shout from the sentry indicated this, and a scattering fire was opened. This, however, was at once checked by the shout of the officer to dash forward with all speed after the enemy. As the mass of Russians rushed from the village, the howitzer in the bows of the launch poured a volley of grape into them, and checked their advance. However, from along the bushes on either side fresh assailants poured out.

G. A. Henty

"Jump on board, lads, jump on board!" Mr. Hethcote shouted, and each sailor, discharging his musket at the enemy, leapt into his place. "Give them a volley, Mr. Pascoe. Get your head round and row. Don't let the men waste time in firing."

The volley from the launch again momentarily checked the enemy, and just as she got round, another discharge from the gun further arrested them. The boats were not, however, thirty yards from the shore before this was lined with dark figures who opened a tremendous fire of musketry.

"Row, lads, row!" Mr. Pascoe shouted to his men. "We shall be out of their sight in another hundred yards."

Chapter VI
THE ALMA

DESPERATELY the men bent to their oars, and the heavy boat surged through the water. Around them swept a storm of musket balls, and although the darkness and their haste rendered the fire of the Russians wild and uncertain, many of the shot took effect. With a sigh, Mr. Pascoe fell against Jack, who was sitting next to him, just at the moment when Jack himself experienced a sensation as if a hot iron had passed across his arm. Several of the men dropped their oars and fell back, but the boats still held rapidly on their way, and in two or three minutes were safe from anything but random shot. At this moment, however, three field pieces opened with grape, and the iron hail tore up the water near them. Fortunately they were now almost out of sight, and although the forts threw up rockets to light the bay, and joined their fire to that of the field guns, the boat escaped untouched.

"Thank God we are out of that!" Mr. Hethcote said, as the fire ceased and the boats headed for a light hung up to direct then.

"Have you many hurt, Mr. Pascoe?"

"I'm afraid, sir, Mr. Pascoe is either killed or badly wounded. He is lying against me, and gives no answer when I speak to him."

"Any one else hurt?" Mr. Hethcote asked in a moment.

The men exchanged a few words among themselves.

"There are five down in the bottom of the boat, sir, and six or seven of us have been hit more or less."

"It's a bad business," Mr. Hethcote said. "I have two killed and three wounded here. Are you hit yourself, Mr. Archer?"

"I've got a queer sensation in my arm, sir, and don't seem able to use it, so I suppose I am, but I don't think it's much."

"Pull away, lads," Mr. Hethcote said shortly. "Show a light there in the bow to the steamer."

The light was answered by a sharp whistle, and they heard the beat of the paddles of the "Falcon" as she came down towards them, and five minutes later the boats were hoisted to the davits. "No casualties, I hope, Mr. Hethcote?" Captain Stuart said, as the first lieutenant stepped on board. "You seem to have got into a nest of hornets."

"Yes, indeed, sir. There was a strong garrison in the village, and we have suffered, I fear heavily. Some eight or ten killed and as many wounded."

"Dear me, dear me!" Captain Stuart said. "This is an unfortunate circumstance, indeed. Mr. Manders, do you get the wounded on board and carried below. Will you step into my cabin, Mr. Hethcote, and give me full details of this unfortunate affair?"

Upon mustering the men, it was found that the total casualties in the two boats of the "Falcon" amounted to, Lieutenant Pascoe killed, Midshipman Archer wounded; ten seamen killed, and nine wounded. Jack's wound was more severe than he had at first thought. The ball had gone

G. A. Henty

through the upper part of the arm, and had grazed and badly bruised the bone in its passage. The doctor said he would probably be some weeks before he would have his arm out of a sling. The "Falcon" spent another week in examining the Crimean coast, and then ran across again to Varna. Here everything was being pushed forward for the start. Over six hundred vessels were assembled, with a tonnage vastly exceeding that of any fleet that had ever sailed the seas. Twenty-seven thousand English and twenty-three thousand French were to be carried in this huge flotilla; for although the French army was considerably larger than the English, the means of sea-transport of the latter were vastly superior, and they were able to take across the whole of their army in a single trip; whereas, the French could convey but half of their force. Unfortunately, between Lord Raglan, the English Commander-in-Chief, and Marshal Saint Arnaud, the French commander, there was little concert or agreement. The French, whose arrangements were far better, and whose movements were prompter than our own, were always complaining of British procrastination; while the English General went quietly on his own way, and certainly tried sorely the patience of our allies. Even when the whole of the allied armies were embarked, nothing had been settled beyond the fact that they were going to invade the Crimea, and the enormous fleet of men-of-war and transports, steamers with sailing vessels in tow, extending in lines farther than the eye could reach, and covering many square miles of the sea, sailed eastward without any fixed destination. The consequence was, as might be expected, a lamentable waste of time. Halts were called, councils were held, reconnaissances sent forward, and the vast fleet steamed aimlessly north, south, east, and west, until, when at last a landing-place was fixed upon, near Eupatoria, and the disembarkation was effected, fourteen precious days had been wasted over a journey which is generally performed in twenty-four hours, and which even the slowly moving transports might have easily accomplished in three days.

The consequence was the Russians had time to march round large bodies of troops from the other side, and the object of the expedition—the capture of Sebastopol by a *coup de main*—was altogether thwarted. No more imposing sight was ever seen than that witnessed by the bands of Cossacks on the low shores of the Crimea, when the allied fleets anchored a few miles south of Eupatoria. The front extended nine miles in length, and behind this came line after line of transports until the very topmasts of those in the rear scarce appeared above the horizon. The place selected for the landing-place was known as the Old Fort, a low strip of bush and shingle forming a causeway between the sea and a stagnant fresh-water lake, known as Lake Saki.

At eight o'clock in the morning of the 14th of September, the French admiral fired a gun, and in a little more than an hour six thousand of their troops were ashore, while the landing of the English did not commence till an hour after. The boats of the men-of-war and transports had already been told off for the ships carrying the light division, which was to be the first to land, and in a wonderfully short time the sea between the first line of ships and the shore was covered with a multitude of boats crowded with soldiers. The boats of the "Falcon" were employed with the rest, and as three weeks had elapsed since Jack had received his wound, he was able to take his share

Jack Archer

of duty, although his arm was still in a sling. The ship to which the "Falcon's" boats were told off lay next to that which had carried the 33d, and as he rowed past, he exchanged a shout and a wave of the hand with Harry, who was standing at the top of the companion-ladder, seeing the men of his company take their seats in the boats. It was a day of tremendous work. Each man and officer carried three days' provisions, and no tents or other unnecessary stores were to be landed. The artillery, however, had to be got ashore, and the work of landing the guns on the shingly beach was a laborious one indeed. The horses in vain tugged and strained, and the sailors leaped over into the water and worked breast high at the wheels, and so succeeded in getting them ashore. Jack had asked permission from Captain Stuart to spend the night on shore with his brother, and just as he was going off from the ship for the last time. Simmonds, who had obtained his acting commission in place of Mr. Pascoe, said, "Archer, I should advise you to take a tarpaulin and a couple of bottles of rum. They will be useful before morning, I can tell you, for we are going to have a nasty night."

Indeed the rain was already coming down steadily, and the wind was rising. Few of those who took part in it will ever forget their first night in the Crimea. The wind blew pitilessly, the rain poured down in torrents, and twenty-seven thousand Englishmen lay without shelter in the muddy fields, drenched to the skin. Jack had no trouble in finding his brother's regiment, which was in the advance, some two or three miles from the landing-place. Harry was delighted to see him, and the sight of the tarpaulin and bottles did not decrease the warmth of his welcome. Jack was already acquainted with most of the officers of the 33d.

"Hallo, Archer," a young ensign said, "if I had been in your place, I should have remained snugly on board ship. A nice night we are in for!"

So long as the daylight lasted, the officers stood in groups and chatted of the prospects of the campaign. There was nothing to do—no possibility of seeing to the comforts of their men. The place where the regiment was encamped was absolutely bare, and there were no means of procuring any shelter whatever.

"How big is that tarpaulin, Jack?"

"About twelve feet square," Jack said, "and pretty heavy I found it, I can tell you."

"What had we better do with it?" asked Harry. "I can't lie down under that, you know, with the colonel sitting out exposed to this rain."

"The best thing," Jack said after a minute's consideration, "would be to make a sort of tent of it. If we could put it up at a slant, some six feet high in front with its back to the wind, it would shelter a lot of fellows. We might hang some of the blankets at the sides."

The captain and lieutenant of Harry's company were taken into consultation, and with the aid of half a dozen soldiers, some muskets bound together and some ramrods, a penthouse shelter was made. Some sods were laid on the lower edge to keep it down. Each side was closed with two blankets. Some cords from one of the baggage carts were used as guy ropes to the corners, and a very snug shelter was constructed. This Harry invited the colonel and officers to use, and although the space was limited, the greater portion of them managed to sit down in it, those who could not find room taking up their places in front, where the tent afforded a considerable shelter from the wind and rain. No one thought of sleeping. Pipes were lighted, and Jack's two bottles of rum afforded a tot to each. The night could scarcely be called a comfortable one, even with these aids; but it was luxurious, indeed, in comparison with that passed by those exposed to the full force of the wind.

The next morning Jack said good-bye to his brother and the officers of the regiment, to whom he presented the tarpaulin for future use, and this was folded up and smuggled into an ammunition cart. It was not, of course, Jack's to give, being government property, but he would be able to pay the regulation price for it on his return. Half an hour later, Jack was on the beach, where a high surf was beating. All day the work of landing cavalry and artillery went on under the greatest difficulties. Many of the boats were staved and rendered useless, and several chargers drowned. It was evident that the weather was breaking up, and the ten days of lovely weather which had been wasted at sea were more bitterly regretted than ever. No tents were landed, and the troops remained wet to the skin, with the additional mortification of seeing their French allies snugly housed under canvas, while even the 4000 Turks had managed to bring their tents with them. The natural result was that sickness again attacked the troops, and hundreds were prostrated before, three days later, they met the enemy on the Alma. The French were ready to march on the 17th, but it was not until two days later, that the British were ready; then at nine o'clock in the morning the army advanced. The following is the list of the British force. The light division under Sir George Brown—2d Battalion Rifle Brigade, 7th Fusiliers, 19th Regiment, 23d Fusiliers, under Brigadier Major-General Codrington; 33d Regiment, 77th Regiment, 88th Regiment, under Brigadier-General Butler. First division, under the Duke of Cambridge—The Grenadier, Coldstream and Scots Fusilier Guards, under Major-General Bentinck; the 42d, 79th and 93d Highlanders, under Brigadier-General Sir C. Campbell. The second division, under Sir De Lacy Evans—The 30th, 55th, and 95th, under Brigadier-General Pennefather; the 41st, 47th and 49th, under Brigadier-General Adams. The third division under Sir R. England—The 1st, 28th and 38th under Brigadier-General Sir John Campbell; the 44th, 50th, and 68th Regiments under Brigadier-General Eyre. Six companies of the fourth were also attached to this division. The fourth division under Sir George Cathcart consisted of the 20th, 21st, 2d Battalion Rifle Brigade, 63d, 46th and 57th, the last two regiments, however, had not arrived. The cavalry division under Lord Lucan consisted of the Light Cavalry Brigade under Lord Cardigan, composed of the 4th Light Dragoons, the 8th Hussars, 11th Hussars, 13th Dragoons and 17th Lancers; and the Heavy Cavalry Brigade under Brigadier-General Scarlett, consisting of the Scots Greys, 4th Dragoon Guards, 5th Dragoon Guards, and 6th Dragoons. Of these the Scots Greys had not yet arrived.

It was a splendid sight, as the allied army got in motion. On the extreme right, and in advance next the sea, was the first division of the French army. Behind them, also by the sea, was the second division under General Canrobert, on the left of which marched the third division under Prince Napoleon. The fourth division and the Turks formed the rearguard. Next to the third French division was the second British, with the third in its rear in support. Next to the second division was the light division, with the

Jack Archer

Duke of Cambridge's division in the rear in support. The Light Cavalry Brigade covered the advance and left flank, while along the coast, parallel with the march of the troops, steamed the allied fleet, prepared, if necessary, to assist the army with their guns. All were in high spirits that the months of weary delay were at last over, and that they were about to meet the enemy. The troops saluted the hares which leaped out at their feet at every footstep as the broad array swept along, with shouts of laughter and yells, and during the halts numbers of the frightened creatures were knocked over and slung behind the knapsacks to furnish a meal at the night's bivouac. The smoke of burning villages and farmhouses ahead announced that the enemy were aware of our progress.

Presently, on an eminence across a wide plain, masses of the enemy's cavalry were visible. Five hundred of the Light Cavalry pushed on in front, and an equal number of Cossacks advanced to meet them. Lord Cardigan was about to give the order to charge when masses of heavy cavalry made their appearance. Suddenly one of these extended and a battery of Russian artillery opened fire upon the cavalry. Our artillery came to the front, and after a quarter of an hour's duel the Russians fell back; and soon after the army halted for the night, at a stream called the Boulyanak, six miles from the Alma, where the Russians, as was now known, were prepared to give battle. The weather had now cleared again, and all ranks were in high spirits as they sat round the bivouac fires.

"How savage they will be on board ship," Harry Archer said to Captain Lancaster, "to see us fighting a big battle without their having a hand in it. I almost wonder that they have not landed a body of marines and blue-jackets. The fleets could spare 4000 or 5000 men, and their help might be useful. Do you think the Russians will fight?"

"All soldiers will fight," Captain Lancaster said, "when they've got a strong position. It needs a very different sort of courage to lie down on the crest of a hill and fire at an enemy struggling up it in full view, to that which is necessary to make the assault. They have too all the advantage of knowing the ground, while we know absolutely nothing about it. I don't believe that the generals have any more idea than we have. It seems a happy-go-lucky way of fighting altogether. However, I have no doubt that we shall lick them somehow. It seems, though, a pity to take troops direct at a position which the enemy have chosen and fortified, when by a flank march, which in an undulating country like this could be performed without the slightest difficulty, we could turn the position and force them to retreat, without losing a man."

Such was the opinion of many other officers at the time. Such has been the opinion of every military critic since. Had the army made a flank march, the enemy must either have retired at once, or have been liable to an attack upon their right flank, when, if beaten, they would have been driven down to the sea-shore under the guns of the ships, and killed or captured, to a man. Unfortunately, however, owing to the jealousies between the two generals, the illness of Marshal Arnaud, and the incapacity of Lord Raglan, there was neither plan nor concert. The armies simply fought as they marched, each general of division doing his best and leading his men at that portion of the enemy's position which happened to be opposite to him. The sole understanding arrived at was that the armies were to march at six in the morning; that General Bosquet's division, which was next to the sea, was, covered by guns of the ships, to first carry the enemy's position there; and that when he had obtained a footing upon the plateau, a general attack was to be made. Even this plan, simple as it was, was not fully carried out, as Lord Raglan did not move his troops till nine in the morning. Three precious hours were therefore wasted, and a pursuit after the battle which would have turned the defeat into a rout was therefore prevented, and Sebastopol saved, to cost tens of thousands of lives before it fell. The Russian position on the Alma was along a crest of hills. On their left by the sea these rose precipitously, offering great difficulties for an assault. Further inland, however, the slope became easy, and towards the right centre and right against which the English attack was directed, the hill was simply a slope broken into natural terraces, on which were many walls and vineyards. Near the sea the river ran between low banks, but inland the bank was much steeper, the south side rising some thirty or forty feet, and enabling its defenders to sweep the ground across which the assailants must advance. While on their left the Russian forces were not advanced in front of the hill which formed their position, on the lower ground they occupied the vineyards and inclosures down to the river, and their guns were placed in batteries on the steps of the slope, enabling them to search with their fire the whole hill-side as well as the flat ground beyond the river.

The attack, as intended, was begun by General Bosquet. Bonat's brigade crossed the river by a bar of sand across the mouth where the water was only waist-deep, while D'Autemarre's brigade crossed by a bridge, and both brigades swarmed up the precipitous cliffs which offered great difficulties, even to infantry. They achieved their object, without encountering any resistance whatever, the guns of the fleet having driven back the Russian regiment appointed to defend this post. The enemy brought up three batteries of artillery to regain the crest, but the French with tremendous exertions succeeded in getting up a battery of guns, and with their aid maintained the position they had gained.

When the sound of Bosquet's guns showed that his part of the programme was carried into effect, the second and third divisions of the French army crossed the Alma, and were soon fiercely engaged with the enemy. Canrobert's division for a time made little way, as the river was too deep for the passage of the guns, and these were forced to make a detour. Around a white stone tower some 800 yards on their left, dense masses of Russian infantry were drawn up, and these opened so tremendous a fire upon the French that for a time their advance was checked. One of the brigades from the fourth division, which was in reserve, advanced to their support, and joining with some of the regiments of Canrobert's division, and aided by troops whom General Bosquet had sent to their aid, a great rush was made upon the dense body of Russians, who, swept by the grape of the French artillery, were unable to stand the impetuous attack, and were forced to retire in confusion. The French pressed forward and at this point also of the field, the day was won.

In the mean time the British army had been also engaged. Long before they came in sight of the point which they were to attack they heard the roar of cannon on their right, and knew that Bosquet's division were engaged. As the troops marched over the crest of the rounded slopes they caught glimpses of the distant fight. They could see masses of Russian infantry threatening the French, gathered on the height, watch the puffs of smoke as the guns on either side sent their messengers of death, and the white smoke which hung over the fleet as the vessels of war threw their shells far over the heads of the French into the Russian masses. Soon they heard the louder roar which proclaimed that the main body of the French army were in action, and burning with impatience to begin, the men strode along to take their share in the fight. Until within a few hundred yards of the river the troops could see nothing of it, nor the village on its banks, for the ground dipped sharply. Before they reached the brow twelve Russian guns, placed on rising ground some 300 yards beyond the river, opened upon them.

"People may say what they like," Harry Archer said to his captain, "but a cannon-ball makes a horribly unpleasant row. It wouldn't be half as bad if they would but come silently."

As he spoke a round shot struck down two men a few files to his right. They were the first who fell in the 33d.

"Steady, lads, steady," shouted the officers, and as regularly as if on field-day, the English troops advanced. The Rifles, under Major Northcote, were ahead, and, dashing through the vineyards under a rain of fire, crossed the river, scaled the bank, and pushed forward to the top of the next slope. It was on the plateau beyond that the Russian main body were posted, and for a time the Rifles had hard work to maintain themselves. In the meantime, the Light Division were advancing in open order, sometimes lying down, sometimes advancing, until they gained the vineyards. Here the regular order which they had so far maintained was lost, as the ground was broken up by hedges, stone walls, vines and trees. The 19th, 7th, 23d and 33d were then led, at a run, right to the river by General Codrington, their course being marked by killed and wounded, and crossing they sheltered themselves under the high bank. Such was the state of confusion in which they arrived there that a momentary pause was necessary to enable the men of the various regiments to gather together, and the enemy, taking advantage of this, brought down three battalions of infantry, who advanced close to the bank, and, as the four regiments dashed up it, met them with a tremendous fire. As hotly it was answered, and the Russians retired while their batteries again opened fire.

There was but little order in the British ranks as they struggled forward up the hill. Even under this tremendous fire the men paused to pick grapes, and all the exertions of their officers could not maintain the regular line of advance. From a rising ground a Russian regiment kept up a destructive fire upon them, and the guns in the batteries on their flank fired incessantly. The slaughter was tremendous, but the regiments held on their way unflinchingly. In a few minutes the 7th had lost a third of their men, and half the 23d were down. Not less was the storm of fire around the 33d. Confused, bewildered and stunned by the dreadful din, Harry Archer struggled on with his company. His voice was hoarse with shouting, though he himself could scarce hear the words he uttered. His lips were parched with excitement and the acrid smell of gunpowder. Man after man had fallen beside him, but he was yet untouched. There was no thought of fear or danger now. His whole soul seemed absorbed in the one thought of getting into the battery. Small as were the numbers who still struggled on, their determined advance began to disquiet the Russians. For the first time a doubt as to victory entered their minds. When the day began they felt assured of it. Their generals had told them that they would annihilate their foes, their priests had blessed them, and assured them of the protection and succor of the saints. But the British were still coming on, and would not be denied. The infantry behind the battery began to retire. The artillery, left unprotected, limbered up in haste, and although three times as numerous as the men of the Light Division, the Russians, still firing heavily, retired up the hill, while, with a shout of triumph the broken groups of the 23d, the 19th, and 33d burst into the battery, capturing a gun which the Russians had been unable to withdraw.

Chapter VII
BEFORE SEBASTOPOL

NOT long were the Light Division to enjoy the position they had won. Breathless, exhausted, bleeding, they were but a handful; and the Russians, looking down upon them and seeing that they were unsupported, again advanced in heavy masses, and the Light Division fell back.

Had their division had the whole of their strength they might have been enabled to hold the position they had won. But just as they crossed the river, there was an unfounded alarm of a cavalry attack on the flank, and the 77th and 88th were halted to repel this, and took no share in the advance by the rest of the division.

As the shattered regiments fell back before the Russians in a state of disorder, they saw advancing up the slope behind them the brigade of Guards in as regular order as if on parade. For a moment the splendid formation was broken as the disordered troops came down upon them. But opening their files they allowed the Light Division to pass through them, and then closing up again moved forward in splendid order, the Highland Brigade keeping pace with them on their left, while the regiments of the Light Division reformed in their rear and followed after.

Steadily, under a storm of fire, the Guards advanced. Grape, canister, round shot, shell, and shot, swept through them but they kept forward till nigh crossing bayonets with the Russian infantry.

At this moment, however, two British guns mounted on a knoll opened upon the Russians, the victorious French threatened their flank, the Russian gunners limbered up and retired, and their infantry suddenly fell back.

On the right of the Light Division, General Sir De Lacy Evans had also been fighting sternly. The second division had advanced side by side with that of Prince Napoleon. The resistance which he encountered was obstinate, but more skilled in actual warfare than his brother generals, he covered his advance with the fire of eighteen guns, and so bore forward, suffering far less than the division on his left. He had, however, very heavy fighting before he gained the river. The village had been set on fire by the Russians, and the smoke and flames greatly incommoded the men as they fought their way through it. The 95th, however, dashed across the bridge under a storm of missiles, while the 55th and 30th waded through the river, and step by step won their way up the hill. Then the firing ceased, and the battle of Alma was won.

The force under the Russians consisted of some 37,000 men, of whom 3500 were cavalry. They had eighty guns, besides two light batteries of horse artillery. Inferior in number as they were, the discrepancy was more than outbalanced by the advantage of position, and had the troops on both sides been of equally good material, the honor of the day should have rested with the defenders.

The British loss consisted of 26 officers killed and 73 wounded, 327 men killed and 1557 wounded. The French had only 3 officers killed and 54 wounded, 253 men killed and 1033 wounded. The Turks were not engaged. The Russians lost 45 officers killed and 101 wounded, 1762 men killed and

2720 wounded. The Allied Army had 126 guns against 96 of the Russians; but the former, owing to the nature of the ground, played but a small part in the fight.

The whole of the loss fell upon a comparatively small number of the English regiments, and as the French had 9000 men in reserve who had not fired a shot, there was no season why the greater portion of the army, with all the cavalry, should not at once have followed on the track of the beaten Russians. Had they done so, the war in the Crimea would have been over in three days. That time, however, elapsed before a move was made. The reason assigned was the necessity of caring for the wounded and burying the dead. But this might have been committed to the hands of sailors and marines, of whom 5000 might have been landed at night; in which case the whole Allied Army could have marched at day break.

It was a sad sight when the four regiments of the Light Division mustered after their work was done. Hitherto in the confusion and fierce excitement of the fight, men marked not who stood and who fell. But now as the diminished regiments paraded, mere skeletons of the fine corps which had marched gayly from their camping-ground of the night before, the terrible extent of their losses was manifest. Tears rolled down the cheeks of strong men who had never flinched in the storm of fire, as they saw how many of their comrades were absent, and the glory of the victory was dimmed indeed by the sorrow for the dead.

"I wanted to see a battle," Harry Archer said to Captain Lancaster, who, like him, had gone through the fight without a scratch, "but this is more than I bargained for. To think of half one's friends and comrades gone, and all in about two hours' fighting. It has been a deadly affair, indeed."

"Yes, as far as we are concerned, Archer. But not for the whole army. I heard Doctor Alexander say just now that the casualties were about 1500, and that out of 27,000 men is a mere nothing to the proportion in many battles. The French have, I hear, lost rather less."

"I thought in a battle," Harry said, "one would see something of the general affair, but I certainly did not. In fact, from the time when we dashed up the river bank till the capture of the battery, I saw nothing. I knew there were some of our men by the side of me, and that we were all pushing forward, but beyond that I knew absolutely nothing. It was something like going through a tremendous thunder shower with one's head down, only a thousand times more so."

After parade the men scattered in groups; some went down to the river to fill their canteens, others strolled through the vineyards picking grapes, and in spite of the fact that in many places the dead lay thickly together, a careless laugh was sometimes heard. The regiments which had not been engaged were at work bringing in the wounded, and Doctor Alexander and his assistants were busy at the ghastly task of amputating limbs and extracting balls.

The next day a few officers from the fleet came up; among these was Hawtry, who was charged with a special mission from Jack, who could not again ask for leave, to inquire after his brother. The wounded were sent down in arabas and litters to the ships, a painful journey of three miles. The French wounded fared better, as they had well-appointed hospital vans. Seven hundred and fifty Russian wounded were collected and laid together, and were given in charge of the inhabitants of a Tartar village near; Dr. Thomson, of the 44th

Jack Archer

Regiment with a servant volunteering to remain in charge of them, with the certain risk of capture when the Russian troops returned after our departure.

On the morning of the 23d the army started, continuing its march along the road to Sebastopol, the way being marked not only by debris thrown away by the retreating Russians, but by the cottages and pretty villas having been sacked by the Cossacks as they retired.

The troops halted for the night at Katcha, where the French were reinforced by 8000 men who were landed from transports just arrived, and the English by the Scots Greys and the 57th. As it was found that the enemy had batteries along the northwest of the harbor of Sebastopol which would cause delay and trouble to invest, while the army engaged in the operation would have to draw all its provisions and stores from the harbor at the mouth of the Katcha River, it was determined to march round Sebastopol, and to invest it on the southern side, where the Russians, not expecting it, would have made but slight preparations for a resistance.

Towards the sea-face, Sebastopol was of immense strength, mounting seventeen guns at the Telegraph Battery, 104 at Fort Constantine, eighty at Fort Saint Michael, forty at battery No. 4, and some fifty others in smaller batteries. All these were on the north side of the harbor. On the southern side were the Quarantine Fort with fifty-one guns, Fort Alexander with sixty-four, the Arsenal Battery with fifty, Fort Saint Nicholas with 192, and Fort Paul with eighty. In addition to these tremendous defences, booms had been fixed across the mouth of the harbor, and a three-decker, three two-deckers, and two frigates sunk in a line, forming a formidable barrier against the entry of hostile ships. Besides all this, the whole of the Russian Black Sea fleet were in harbor, and prepared to take part in the defence against an attack by sea. Upon the other hand, Sebastopol was naturally weak on the land side. It lay in a hollow, and guns from the upper ground could everywhere search it.

At the time when the Allied Armies arrived before it the only defences were an old loop-holed wall, a battery of fourteen guns and six mortars, and one or two batteries which were as yet scarcely commenced.

The march from the Katcha to the south side was performed without interruption, and on the 26th, six days after the battle of Alma, the Allied Army reached their new position. According to arrangements, the British occupied the harbor of Balaklava, while the French took possession of Kamiesch and Kaznatch, as bases for the supply of their armies. At the mouth of Balaklava Harbor are the ruins of a Genoese fort standing 200 feet above the sea. This was supposed to be unoccupied. As the staff, however, were entering the town, they were astonished by four shells falling close to them.

The "Agamemnon," which was lying outside, at once opened fire, and the fort immediately hung out a flag of truce. The garrison consisted only of the commandant and sixty men. The officer, on being asked why he should have opened fire when he knew that the place could not be held, replied that he did so as he had not been summoned to surrender, and felt bound in honor to fire until he did so.

The British ships at once entered the harbor, and the disembarkation of the stores and siege-train commenced. The harbor of Balaklava was but ill-suited for the requirements of a large army. It was some half mile in length and a few hundred yards broad, and looked like a little inland lake, for the rocks rose precipitously at its mouth, and the passage through them made a

G. A. Henty

bend, so that the outlet was not visible from a ship once fairly inside. The coast is steep and bold, the rocky cliff rising sheer up from the water's edge to heights varying from 400 to 2000 feet. A vessel coasting along it would not notice the narrow passage, or dream—on entering—that a harbor lay hidden behind. On either side of the harbor inside the hills rose steeply, on the left hand, so steeply, that that side was useless for the purposes of shipping. On the right hand there was a breadth of flat ground between the water and the hill, and here and upon the lower slopes stood the village of Balaklava. The valley extended for some distance beyond the head of the harbor, most of the ground being occupied with vineyards. Beyond was the wide rolling plain upon which the battles of Balaklava and Inkerman were to be fought. Taken completely by surprise, the inhabitants of Balaklava had made no attempt to escape, but upon the arrival of the British general, a deputation received him with presents of fruit and flowers.

By this time the fleet had come round, and the sailors were soon hard at work assisting to unload the transports and get the stores and siege materials on shore. It was reported that a marine battery was to be formed, and there was eager excitement on board as to the officers who would be selected. Each of the men-of-war contributed their quota, and Lieutenant Hethcote found that he had been told off as second in command, and that he was to take a midshipman and twenty men of the "Falcon."

The matter as to the midshipman was settled by Captain Stuart.

"You may as well take Archer," he said. "You won't like to ask for him because he's your cousin; but I asked for his berth, you know, and don't mind doing a little bit of favoritism this once."

And so, to Jack's intense delight, he found that he was to form a portion of the landing party.

These were in all 200 in number, and their work was, in the first place, to assist to get the heavy siege guns from the wharf to the front.

It is necessary that the position occupied by the Allies should be perfectly comprehended, in order to understand the battles and operations which subsequently took place. It may be described as a triangle with one bulging side. The apex of the triangle were the heights on the seashore, known as the Marine Heights.

Here, at a point some 800 feet above the sea, where a ravine broke the line of cliffs, was the camp of the marines, in a position almost impregnable against any enemy's force, following the seashore. On the land-slopes of the hills, down towards Balaklava, lay the Highland Brigade, guarding the approach from the plains from the Marine Heights to the mouth of Balaklava Valley, at the mouth of which were the camps of the cavalry, and not far off a sailor's camp with heavy guns and 800 men.

This side of the triangle continued along over the undulating ground, and some three miles farther, reached the right flank of the position of the Allies above Sebastopol, which formed the base of our imaginary triangle.

This position was a plateau, of which one side sloped down to Sebastopol; the end broke steeply off down into the valley of Inkerman, while behind the slopes were more gradual. To the left it fell away gradually towards the sea. This formed the third side of the triangle. But between Balaklava and Sebastopol the land made a wide bulge outwards, and in this bulge lay the French harbor of Kamiesch.

Jack Archer

From the Marine Heights to the crest looking down upon Sebastopol was a distance of some seven miles. From the right of our position above Inkerman Valley to Kamiesch was about five miles.

A glance at the map will enable this explanation to be understood.

At the commencement of the siege the British were posted on the right of the Allies. This, no doubt, was the post of honor, but it threw upon them an enormous increase of work. In addition to defending Balaklava, it was upon them that the brunt of any assault by a Russian army acting in the field would fall. They would have an equal share of the trench-work, and had five miles to bring up their siege guns and stores; whereas the French harbor was close to their camp.

It was tremendous work getting up the guns, but soldiers and sailors willingly toiled away, pushing, and hauling, and aiding the teams, principally composed of bullocks, which had been brought up from Constantinople and other Turkish ports. Long lines of arabas, laden with provisions and stores, crawled slowly along between Balaklava and the front. Strings of mules and horses, laden with tents, and driven by men of every nationality bordering the Mediterranean, followed the same line.

Parties of soldiers, in fatigue suits, went down to Sebastopol to assist unloading the ships and bringing up stores. Parties of officers on ponies brought from Varna or other ports on the Black Sea, cantered down to make purchases of little luxuries on board the ships in the harbor, or from the Levantines, who had set up little shops near it. All was life and gayety.

"It is all very well, Mr. Archer," growled Dick Simpson, an old boatswain, as the men paused after helping to drag a heavy gun up one of the slopes, "in this here weather, but it won't be no laughing matter when the winter comes on. Why, these here fields would be just a sheet of mud. Why, bless you, last winter I was a staying with a brother of mine what farms a bit of land down in Norfolk, and after a week's rain they couldn't put the horses on to the fields. This here sile looks just similar, only richer and deeper, and how they means to get these big carts laden up through it, beats me altogether."

"Yes, Dick," Jack Archer answered, "but they expect to take the place before the winter comes on."

"They expects," the old tar repeated scornfully. "For my part, I don't think nothing of these soldier chaps. Why, I was up here with the first party as come, the day after we got here, and there warn't nothing in the world to prevent our walking into it. Here we've got 50,000 men, enough, sir, to have pushed those rotten old walls down with their hands, and here we be a-digging and a-shovelling on the hillside nigh a mile from the place, and the Russians are a-digging and a-shovelling just as hard at their side. I see 'em last night after we got back to camp. It seems to me as if these here generals wanted to give 'em time to make the place so strong as we cannot take it, before they begins. Why, it stands to reason that the Rooshians, who've got their guns all stored close at hand, their soldiers and their sailors handy, and no trouble as to provisions and stores, can run up works and arm them just about three times as fast as we can; and where shall we be at the end of three months? We shall be just a-shivering and a-shaking, and a-starving with cold, and short of grub on that 'ere hill; and the Rooshians will be comfortable in the town a-laughing at us. Don't tell me, Mr. Archer; my opinion is, these 'ere soldiers are no better than fools. They don't seem to have no common sense."

G. A. Henty

"I hope it's not as bad as all that, Dick," Jack laughed. "But it certainly does seem as if we were purposely giving the Russians time to strengthen themselves. But you'll see when we go at them we shall make short work of them."

"Well, I hope so, Mr. Archer," Dick Simpson said, shaking his head ominously, "but I'm dubious about it."

By this time the oxen and men had recovered their breath, and they again set to at their tiresome work. Although the weather was fine and the position of the camps high and healthy, the cholera which had ravaged their ranks at Varna still followed them, and during the three first weeks in the Crimea, the Allies lost as many men from this cause as they had done in the Battle of Alma.

By the 4th of October forty pieces of heavy artillery had been brought up to the front, and the work of the trenches began in earnest.

On the morning of the 10th the Russian batteries for the first time opened a heavy fire upon us. But the distance was too great for much harm to be done. On the 11th the Russians made their first sortie, which was easily repulsed.

On the 17th of October the bombardment commenced. The French and English had 117 guns in position, the Russians 130. The fire commenced at half-past six. By 8.40 a French magazine at the extreme right blew up, killing and wounding 100 men, while the French fire at this part was crushed by that of the Russians opposed to them. All day, however, the cannonade continued unabating on both sides, the men-of-war aiding the land forces by engaging the forts.

During the night the Russians, having plenty of guns at hand, and labor in abundance, mounted a larger number of guns, and their superiority was so marked that the bombardment was gradually discontinued, and even the most sanguine began to acknowledge that an enormous mistake had been made in not attacking upon our arrival, and that it was impossible to say how long the siege would last. Ammunition, too, was already running short.

For the next day or two, however, our guns continued their fire. But the French had been so completely overpowered by the heavy Russian metal that they were unable to assist us. The sailors had had their full share of work during the bombardment. Captain Peel, who commanded the party, was just the man to get the greatest possible amount of work from them. Always in high spirits, taking his full share in all the work, and exposing himself recklessly in the heaviest fire, he was almost idolized by his men.

Jack Archer lived in a tent with five other midshipmen, and was attended upon by one of the fore-top men, who, not having been told off for the party, had begged permission to go in that capacity.

Tom Hammond was the most willing of servants, but his abilities were by no means equal to his good will. His ideas of cooking were of the vaguest kind. The salt junk was either scarcely warm through, or was boiled into a soup. The preserved potatoes were sometimes burned from his neglect of putting sufficient water, or he had forgotten to soak them beforehand, and they resembled bits of gravel rather than vegetables. Sometimes the boys laughed, sometimes they stormed, and Tom was more than once obliged to beat a rapid retreat to escape a volley of boots and other missiles.

At first the tent was pitched in the usual way on the ground; but one of the boys, in a ramble through the camp, had seen an officer's tent prepared in a way which added greatly to its comfort, and this they at once adopted. Tom Hammond was set to dig a hole of eighteen inches smaller diameter than the circle of the tent. It was three feet in depth, with perpendicular sides. At nine inches from the edge a trench a foot deep was dug. In the centre was an old flour barrel filled with earth. Upon this stood the tent-pole. The tent was brought down so as to extend six inches into the ditch, the nine-inch rim of earth standing inside serving as a shelf on which to put odds and ends. A wall of sods, two feet high, was erected round the outside of the little ditch. Thus a comfortable habitation was formed. The additional three feet of height added greatly to the size of the tent, as the occupants could now stand near the edges instead of in the centre only. It was much warmer than before at night, and all draught was excluded by the tent overlapping the ditch, and by the wall outside. A short ladder at the entrance enabled them to get in and out.

Tom Hammond had grumbled at first at the labor which this freak of his masters entailed. But as the work went on and he saw how snug and comfortable was the result, he took a pride in it, and the time was not far off when its utility was to become manifest. Indeed, later on in the winter the greater portion of the tents were got up in this manner.

The camp of the Light Division was not far from that of the sailors, and the two brothers were often together. Fortunately both of them had so far escaped the illnesses which had already decimated the army.

Chapter VIII
BALAKLAVA

ON the morning of the 25th Harry ran into Jack's tent.

"Wake up, Jack, there is a row down near Balaklava. The Russians are coming on in force. You're off duty, are you not? So am I. We only came out of the trenches half an hour ago. Hurry on your things and come along."

Jack was only a minute or two getting into his clothes, the other midshipmen off duty also hurrying up. Tom Hammond brought in four cups of hot coffee, which they drank hastily, and then munching their hard biscuits as they went, the party of four hurried off.

On reaching the edge of the plateau the whole scene was visible. On four knolls in the plain, redoubts had been erected, and these were garrisoned by the Turks. Some two miles out ran the little river called the Tchernaya, which runs through the valley of Inkerman into the head of the harbor of Sebastopol, and upon this a body of Russian troops had been for some time encamped. Large bodies of the enemy were known to be gathered on the Mackenzie heights, a range of hills which bounded the plain upon the opposite side. These had been strongly reinforced, and at daybreak the Russian army, having gathered at the Tchernaya, advanced upon the Turkish redoubts. The scene when the boys reached the edge of the plateau was a stirring one. Great bodies of infantry were marching across the undulating plain. Strong regiments of cavalry swept hither and thither, and two batteries of light guns had already opened on the redoubts. Lines of British infantry could be seen drawn up at the foot of the slopes from Balaklava to the Marine Heights, where the marines were getting the guns in a position to command the plain. Solid bodies of British cavalry were drawn up near the mouth of the valley. The drums and bugles were sounding all over the plateau behind the group, and the troops were already forming up, and staff-officers were dashing about with orders.

"There goes my regimental call," Harry said. "I must go back again, Jack."

"I shall push on," Jack said. "Come along, you fellows, we're too far off to see much of it here. Let us get down as near Balaklava as we can."

So saying, the midshipmen set off at a run. For a few minutes the guns of No. 1 redoubt, the farthest out of all, replied to the Russian fire, and then the Turks, menaced by overwhelming forces, and beyond the possibility of any assistance, left their guns and bolted across the plain towards the second redoubt. Few of them, however, reached it, for the Russian cavalry swooped down on them and nearly all were sabred as they ran. As soon as the Russians obtained possession of the redoubt they turned its guns upon the British, and the 93d Highlanders who were drawn up in front of the entrance to the Balaklava valley, were forced to fall back. Our cavalry, which were formed up in a slight dip of the ground, were invisible to the enemy. As the Russians advanced, the Turks in the second redoubt fled towards the third, but the Russian cavalry were too quick for them, and but few escaped. The guns were turned by the Russians upon the third redoubt, and, untaught by the fate of their comrades that it was safer to stand than to run, the Turks here also bolted, and ran for the town. Again did the Russian cavalry sweep down. The naval guns from the Marine Heights, the French and Turkish batteries on the road up to the camp in vain spoke out, and sent their shot and shell far out on the plain. The distance was too great, and many of the Turks were cut down, the rest reaching our lines where they formed up behind the 93d.

By this time the whole sweep from the Sebastopol plateau to Balaklava was alive with spectators. The British infantry were drawn up ready to defend their position or to march down and take part in a general battle. Heavy columns of the French were marching from their distant camps, while groups of generals and mounted officers watched the progress of the fight. Lord Raglan and General Canrobert, who now commanded the French (Marshal St. Arnaud having gone on board ship a day or two after the battle of the Alma, where he died two days later), had taken up their position on some rising ground above Kadikoi, a village which lay near the mouth of the Balaklava valley.

As the Russian cavalry on the left of their advance crowned the slope they saw the Highlanders drawn up in line across the plain. They halted till joined by numbers of other squadrons. Then they dashed at the Highlanders. As they came sweeping in magnificent array the Turks fired a volley and bolted. The Highlanders stood firm and immovable. When the Russians came within 600 yards, a long flash of fire ran along the British front. The distance, however, was too great, and the Russians came steadily on, although the shot from the British batteries were plunging thick among them.

When within 250 yards of the Highlanders another flash of fire swept out along the line, and this time so great was the effect that the Russian squadrons recoiled, and in another minute were galloping back towards their main body, while a cheer ran along the heights from the marine battery to Sebastopol.

Lord Raglan now sent orders to Lord Lucan to advance, and the Heavy Brigade moved forward just as a large body of Russian cavalry came over the brow in front of them. The British trumpets rang out the charge, and the Scots Greys and Inniskillings, who formed the first line of the Heavy Brigade, dashed at the enemy. Gathering speed as they went, these two splendid regiments rode at the heavy masses of Russian cavalry. Faster and faster grew their speed till, with a mighty shout, they flung themselves upon the foe. For a moment all seemed wild confusion to the spectators. Redcoats and black were inextricably mixed together, and over them like a play of rapid lightning was the flash of steel as the swords rose and fell. Presently the Redcoats were seen emerging from the rear, having cut their way through the surging mass. The flanks of the Russian column, however, were lapping them in, and it seemed that the little body would be annihilated, when the 4th and 5th Dragoon Guards, forming the second line of the Heavy Brigade, burst upon them like a torrent. Smitten, as if by a thunderbolt, the Russian cavalry, men and horses, rolled over before the stroke, and the column, shattered and broken into fragments, galloped away to the shelter of their infantry, while a roar of triumph arose from long lines of the allies.

By this time the French infantry had arrived upon the ground, and Balaklava was safe. Then came the episode by which the battle of Balaklava is best known, the famous charge of the Six Hundred. An order was sent from

G. A. Henty

Lord Raglan to Lord Lucan to advance the light cavalry farther. Captain Nolan, who bore the order, was himself a light cavalry officer of great enterprise and distinction, and who had an unlimited faith in the powers of British light cavalry. Excited probably by the sight of the glorious feat achieved by the "heavies," and burning to see it emulated by his comrades of the light regiments, he so gave the order to Lord Lucan that the latter conceived it to be his duty to charge. The order was simply to advance, but when Lord Lucan asked him, "How far are we to advance?" he replied, pointing to the Russians, "There are the enemy and there are the guns."

Lord Lucan, conceiving that his orders were absolute, ordered Lord Cardigan to advance upon the guns. Lord Cardigan saw at once the desperate nature of the enterprise. The guns were a mile and a half distant, backed by the whole Russian army. The line to be ridden over was swept not only by the fire of the guns he was about to charge, but by those of other batteries on the flank. No support was possible, for the heavy cavalry were at this time far away, executing a movement which had been ordered. Lastly, even if successful, the charge could be attended with no great results, as it would be impossible either to hold or carry away the guns.

The enterprise was indeed a desperate one. Lord Cardigan gave the order, and the Light Brigade, numbering in all but the strength of a single regiment, set out at a trot towards the distant Russians. As they approached they quickened their speed, and the spectators saw with feelings of mixed horror and admiration, the enterprise on which they had embarked. When at the distance of 1200 yards from the Russians, thirty pieces of artillery opened fire upon them. Men and horses rolled over before the iron shower, but the squadrons closed up their gaps and rode straight forward, with sabres flashing in the sun, leaving the plain behind them dotted with killed and wounded.

Again, as they neared the battery, the iron shower swept through their ranks; then with a mighty shout they dashed upon the guns. Brief was the struggle here. The Russian gunners were cut down, and gathering together, boot to boot, the British cavalry rode straight at a Russian line of infantry which formed up 100 yards behind the guns, poured a volley into them. There was no pause, but straight, and with the shock of an avalanche, they hurled themselves at the Russians. There was a yell, a crash, the clash of sabre on bayonet, the shout of the victor, the scream of the dying, and the British horsemen burst through the Russian line. Their work was done. They were conquerors, but alone in an army of enemies. Turning now, they swept back again through the guns on their homeward way. The flank batteries belched their fire upon them, the rattle of musketry sounded round them, a regiment of cavalry was hurled upon their flanks, but these, weak as they were, they dashed aside, and wounded and bleeding, the remnant of the gallant band rode on until met by the Heavy Brigade, advancing to assist them and cover their retreat.

Our infantry now made a forward movement. The Russians fell back, and at half-past eleven the battle of Balaklava was over. While the British charge was going on, 200 of the French cavalry made a brilliant charge on the left and carried a battery, but had to retreat with a loss of two captains, and fifty men killed and wounded. Our loss in all was thirteen officers killed or taken, and twenty-seven officers wounded, 162 men killed or taken, and 224 men wounded. There were 394 horses killed or missing, and 126 horses wounded. The Russians carried off some ten guns from the redoubts which they captured in the morning.

Jack and his friends returned at the conclusion of the fight to camp, where, as they had rather expected, they met with a severe reprimand for their absence, being told that upon such an occasion, whether off duty or not, their duty was to remain in camp. Captain Peel indeed, was nearly sending them back to their ships again. But after a very severe reprimand he allowed them to remain. The boys went back to their tent somewhat crestfallen, but agreed that such a sight as they had witnessed was worth anything.

October ended, and the batteries of besieged and besiegers continued to play, the Russians causing much annoyance by the heavy shell which they threw up from their mortars; the battery worked by the blue-jackets suffering particularly. The Russians had now 240 guns in their new works, a number far superior to those of the allies. As yet no damage whatever had been inflicted on the enemy's works. Each day their faces were pitted with shot, each night the Russians repaired the damages. In the mean time the Russians had received very large reinforcements. Two of the Imperial Grand Dukes had also arrived, and they were preparing for an attempt to sweep the allies into the sea. The weather had set in wet; the soldiers were weakened by their incessant work in the trenches, by wet and exposure, and the strength of many of the regiments was greatly reduced by disease. All hopes of capturing the fortress and returning to Constantinople to winter were now at an end, and the roads having become mere quagmires, the supplies of food and of fuel were growing scanty. On the 3d, Jack had been sent down to Balaklava with a despatch from Captain Peel to Admiral Lyons. Mr. Hethcote lent him his pony, and having delivered his message in the guard-ship in the harbor, whence it would be taken out to the "Agamemnon," Jack went on board some of the transports, and discharged a number of commissions with which he had been intrusted by his comrades. So numerous were they that he was obliged to get a couple of sacks which were completely filled with hams, bottled stout, fresh bread, potted meats, brandy, matches, and tobacco. He had, too, succeeded in purchasing several waterproof sheets and tarpaulins, and these being fastened on the top of the sacks, were placed upon the pony's back, and, taking his bridle, Jack started through the mud for his long tramp back to camp, for it was quite out of the question that the pony could carry him in addition to these burdens. Not a little laughter was excited on his arrival, and there was quite a rush of the various officers to procure their share of Jack's purchases, for no officer had been down to Balaklava for a fortnight, and the stores of luxuries were completely exhausted.

Next night Jack and his messmates gave a grand entertainment. Harry and two other lieutenants of the 33d—for the battle of the Alma had made so many death vacancies in the regiment that he had obtained his promotion—were there, and two young officers of the 30th who were cousins of one of Jack's tentmates. It certainly was a close pack. Tom Hammond had obtained some planks, and, laying these on the flour barrel, had contrived a sort of circular table, round which the parties sat with their backs to the wall, on boxes, empty preserved potato tins, rum kegs, and portmanteaus. There was no room for Tom to enter the tent, so the full dishes were handed in through the entrance, and the empty ones passed out. Each guest of course brought his own plate, knife, fork, spoon, and drinking tin. As for a change of plates, no one dreamed of such a thing.

G. A. Henty

Outside, the night set in wet and gloomy, but four tallow candles stuck in bottles threw a grand illumination.

The first course was pea-soup. It smelt good, but it had a suspicious appearance, globules of grease floated upon its surface. All fell to with a will, but with the first spoonful there was a general explosion.

"What on earth is this, Jack?" Harry exclaimed.

"What the deuce is it?" another said. "It is filthy!"

While one of the young officers of the 30th exclaimed to his cousin, "Confound it, Ned! you haven't brought us here to poison us, have you?"

This explosion was followed by a simultaneous shout for Tom by his six angry masters.

The top-man put his head in at the slit.

"What the deuce have you been doing to this soup?" roared the indignant chorus.

"Soup, your honors? Nothing."

"Nothing! Don't tell me, you ruffian!" exclaimed Allison, the oldest of the midshipmen. "It's poison! What have you been doing to it?"

"Well, your honor, the only way I can account for it is that a while ago I took off the lid to see if it was boiling nicely, when a bit of tallow candle I had in my fingers slipped and fell into it. I couldn't get it out, though I scalded my fingers in trying, and it just melted away in no time. I skimmed the fat off the top, your honors, and didn't think it would make no matter."

The shout of laughter which greeted the explanation was loud and general.

"You're a scoundrel, Tom!" Allison said, "and I shall have to ask Mr. Hethcote to disrate you, and get some one here who is not a born idiot. Here, take this horrible mess away! Pour the contents of your plates back into the pot, boys, and put the plates together. You must wash them, Tom, or the tallow will taste in everything we have."

The things were passed out of the tent, and after five minutes the plates were returned, and with them a great tin piled up with Irish stew, the contents of five tins. A cheer rose as the smell of the food greeted their nostrils.

"Hurrah! This is something like! I don't think there's any mistake this time."

Nor was there. The stew was unanimously voted to be perfect, and Tom was again called to the tent-door, and solemnly forgiven.

Then came fried rashers of ham, eaten with hard biscuit. Then came the great triumph of the banquet—a great plum-pudding, which had been sent out from England in a tin, ready cooked, and which had only required an hour's boiling to warm it through.

In order to eat this in what the midshipmen called proper style, a tin pannikin half filled with brandy was held over the candles, and the brandy being then ignited, was poured over the pudding. Not a scrap of this was left when the party had finished, and the table being cleared, pipes were brought out and lighted; the drinking-cups refilled with grog, and the party set-to to enjoy a long evening.

"It is a beastly night," the one sitting next to the door said, peering out into the darkness. "It is a fine rain, or rather a Scotch mist, so thick I can hardly see the next tent. It will be as much as you fellows will be able to do to find your way back to your camps.

Jack Archer

"Now," Allison said, "let us make ourselves comfortable. It is only seven o'clock yet, and you've got three hours before 'lights out.' It's my duty as president of the mess to call upon some one for a song, but as I'm a good fellow I will set the example myself. Upon the present occasion we can't do better than begin with 'The Red, White, and Blue,' and, mind, a good chorus every one. Any one shirking the chorus will have no share of the next round of grog, and any one who does not sing when called upon, or who attempts to make any base explanations or excuses, will have to drink his tin full of salt and water."

Without further delay Allison began his song, one very popular at that time. There was no occasion for him to use his authority as president in the infliction of fines, for every one in turn, when called upon, did his best, and the choruses were heard over the whole of the naval camp.

"Hullo! What's all this noise about?" said a cheery voice presently, as a head was put through the opening of the tent.

The midshipmen all jumped to their feet.

"We are having a jollification, sir," Allison said, "on the things Archer brought up from Balaklava yesterday. Are we making too much noise, sir?"

"Not a bit, lads," the first lieutenant said. "It's cheerful to hear you. It isn't much enjoyment that we get on this bleak plateau. Well, good-night. You mustn't keep it up after 'lights out,' you know."

"That's something like a first lieutenant," Allison said, when Mr. Hethcote had retired. "Most of them look as if they'd swallowed a ramrod, and treat middies as if they were the dust of the earth. I'm quite sure that a man who is genial and nice gets his work done ever so much better than do those stand-off fellows. I see in your camp," he said to the officers, "colonels and majors standing and chatting to the young officers just as pleasantly and freely as a party of gentlemen on shore. Why the captain of a ship should hold himself as if he were a little god, is a thing I have never been able to make out. I'm sure you fellows obey orders on parade none the less promptly and readily because the colonel has been chatting with you in the mess-room half an hour before. But don't let us waste time. Archer, it's your turn for a song."

And so merrily the hours passed away, until it was time to break up and put out the lights. And as the young fellows laughed and sung, while the mist and rain came down pitilessly outside, they little thought what was preparing for the morrow, or dreamed that the churches in Sebastopol were crowded with Russian soldiers praying the saints to give them victory on the morrow, and to aid them to drive the enemies of the Czar into the sea.

Chapter IX
INKERMAN

IT was soon after five in the morning when the pickets of the second division, keeping such watch as they were able in the misty light, while the rain fell steadily and thickly, dimly perceived a gray mass moving up the hill from the road at the end of the harbor. Although this point was greatly exposed to attack, nothing had been done to strengthen the position. A few lines of earthworks, a dozen guns in batteries, would have made the place secure from a sudden attack. But not a sod had been turned, and the steep hillside lay bare and open to the advance of an enemy.

Although taken by surprise, and wholly ignorant of the strength of the force opposed to them, the pickets stood their ground, but before the heavy masses of men clambering up the hill, they could do nothing, and were forced to fall back, contesting every foot.

Almost simultaneously, the pickets of the light division were also driven in, and General Codrington, who happened to be making his rounds at the front, at once sent a hurried messenger to the camp with the report that the Russians were attacking in force. The second division was that encamped nearest to the threatened spot. General Pennefather, who, as Sir De Lacy Evans was ill on board ship, was in command, called the men who had just turned out of their tents, and were beginning as best they could to light their fires of soaked wood, to stand to their arms, and hurried forward General Adam's brigade, consisting of the 41st, 47th, and 49th, to the brow of the hill to check the advance of the enemy by the road from the valley, while with his own brigade, consisting of the 30th, 55th, and 95th, he took post on their flank. Already, however, the Russians had got their guns on to the high ground, and these opened a tremendous fire on the British troops.

Sir George Cathcart brought up such portions of the 20th, 21st, 46th, 57th, 63d, and 68th regiments as were not employed in the trenches, and occupied the ground to the right of the second division. General Codrington, with part of the 7th, 23d, and 33d, took post to cover the extreme of our right attack. General Buller's brigade was to support the second division on the left, while Jeffrey's brigade, with the 80th regiment, was pushed forward into the brushwood. The third division, under Sir R. England, was held in reserve. The Duke of Cambridge, with the Guards, advanced on the right of the second division to the edge of the plateau overlooking the valley of the Tchernaya, Sir George Cathcart's division being on his right.

There was no manoeuvring. Each general led his men forward through the mist and darkness against an enemy whose strength was unknown, and whose position was only indicated by the flash of his guns and the steady roll of his musketry. It was a desperate strife between individual regiments and companies scattered and broken in the thick brushwood, and the dense columns of gray-clad Russians, who advanced from the mist to meet them. Few orders were given or needed. Each regiment was to hold the ground on which it stood, or die there.

Sir George Cathcart led his men down a ravine in front of him, but the

Jack Archer

Russians were already on the hillside above, and poured a terrible fire into the 63d. Turning, he cheered them on, and led them back up the hill; surrounded and enormously outnumbered, the regiments suffered terribly on their way back, Sir George Cathcart and many of his officers and vast numbers of the men being killed. The 88th were surrounded, and would have been cut to pieces, when four companies of the 77th charged the Russians, and broke a way of retreat for their comrades.

The Guards were sorely pressed; a heavy Russian column bore down upon them, and bayonet to bayonet, the men strove fiercely with their foes. The ammunition failed, but they still clung to a small, unarmed battery called the Sand-bag battery, in front of their portion, and with volleys of stones tried to check their foes. Fourteen officers and half the men were down, and yet they held the post till another Russian column appeared in their rear. Then they fell back, but, reinforced by a wing of the 20th, they still opposed a resolute front to the Russians.

Not less were the second division pressed; storms of shot and bullets swept through them, column after column of grey-clad Russians surged up the hill and flung themselves upon them; but, though suffering terribly, the second division still held their ground. The 41st was well-nigh cut to pieces, the 95th could muster but sixty-four bayonets when the fight was over, and the whole division, when paraded when the day was done, numbered but 800 men.

But this could not last. As fast as one assault was repulsed, fresh columns of the enemy came up the hill to the attack, our ammunition was failing, the men exhausted with the struggle, and the day was well-nigh lost when, at nine o'clock, the French streamed over the brow of the hill on our right in great force, and fell upon the flank of the Russians. Even now the battle was not won. The Russians brought up their reserves, and the fight still raged along the line. For another three hours the struggle went on, and then, finding that even the overwhelming numbers and the courage with which their men fought availed not to shake the defence, the Russian generals gave up the attack, and the battle of Inkerman was at an end.

On the Russian side some 35,000 men were actually engaged, with reserves of 15,000 more in their rear; while the British, who for three hours withstood them, numbered but 8500 bayonets. Seven thousand five hundred of the French took part in the fight. Forty-four British officers were killed, 102 wounded; 616 men killed, 1878 wounded. The French had fourteen officers killed, and thirty-four wounded; 118 men killed, 1299 wounded. These losses, heavy as they were, were yet small by the side of those of the Russians. Terrible, indeed, was the destruction which the fire of our men inflicted upon the dense masses of the enemy. The Russians admitted that they lost 247 officers killed and wounded, 4076 men killed, 10,162 wounded. In this battle the British had thirty-eight, the French eighteen guns engaged. The Russians had 106 guns in position.

Jack Archer and his comrades were still in bed, when the first dropping shots, followed by a heavy roll of musketry, announced that the Russians were upon them. Accustomed to the roar or guns, they slept on, till Tom Hammond rushed into the tent.

"Get up, gentlemen, get up. The Russian army has climbed up the hill, and is attacking us like old boots. The bugles are sounding the alarm all over the camps."

G. A. Henty

In an instant the lads were out of bed, and their dressing took them scarce a minute.

"I can't see ten yards before me," Jack said, as he rushed out. "By Jove, ain't they going it!"

Every minute added to the din, till the musketry grew into one tremendous roar, above which the almost unbroken roll of the cannon could scarce by heard. Along the whole face of the trenches the batteries of the allies joined in the din; for it was expected that the Russians would seize the opportunity to attack them also.

In a short time the fusillade of musketry broke out far to the left, and showed that the Russians were there attacking the French lines. The noise was tremendous, and all in camp were oppressed by the sound which told of a mighty conflict raging, but of which they could see absolutely nothing.

"This is awful," Jack said. "Here they are pounding away at each other, and we as much out of it as if we were a thousand miles away. Don't I wish Captain Peel would march us all down to help!"

But in view of the possible sortie, it would have been dangerous to detach troops from their places on the trenches and batteries, and the sailors had nothing to do but to wait, fuming over their forced inaction while a great battle was raging close at hand. Overhead the Russian balls sang in swift succession, sometimes knocking down a tent, sometimes throwing masses of earth into the air, sometimes bursting with a sharp detonation above them; and all this time the rain fell, and the mist hung like a veil around them. Presently a mounted officer rode into the sailor's camp.

"Where am I?" he said. "I have lost my way."

"This is the marine camp." Captain Peel said, stepping forward to him as he drew rein. "How is the battle going, sir?"

"Very badly, I'm afraid. We are outnumbered by five to one. Our men are fighting like heroes, but they are being fairly borne down by numbers. The Russians have got a tremendous force of artillery on to the hills, which we thought inaccessible to guns. There has been gross carelessness on our part, and we are paying for it now. I am looking for the third division camp; where is it?"

"Straight ahead, sir; but I think they have all gone forward. We heard them tramping past in the mist."

"I am ordered to send every man forward; every musket is of value. How many men have you here in case you are wanted?"

"We have only fifty," Captain Peel said. "The rest are all in the battery, and I dare not move forward without absolute orders, as we may be wanted to reinforce them, if the enemy makes a sortie."

The officer rode on, and the sailors stood in groups behind the line of piled muskets, ready for an instant advance, if called upon.

Another half-hour passed, and the roll of fire continued unabated.

"It is certainly nearer than it was," Captain Peel said to Mr. Hethcote. "No orders have come, but I will go forward myself and see what is doing. Even our help, small as it is, may be useful at some critical point. I will take two of the midshipmen with me, and will send you back news of what is doing."

"Mr. Allison and Mr. Archer, you will accompany Captain Peel," Mr. Hethcote said.

Jack Archer

And the two youngsters, delighted at being chosen, prepared to start at once.

"If they send up for reinforcements from the battery, Mr. Hethcote, you will move the men down at once, without waiting for me. Take every man down, even those on duty as cooks. There is no saying how hard we may be pressed."

Followed by the young midshipmen, Captain Peel strode away through the mist, which was now heavy with gunpowder-smoke. They passed through the camp of the second division, which was absolutely deserted, except that there was a bustle round the hospital marquées, to which a string of wounded, some carried on stretchers, some making their way painfully on foot, was flowing in.

Many of the tents had been struck down by the Russian shot; black heaps showed where others had been fired by the shell. Dimly ahead, when the mist lifted, could be seen bodies of men, while on a distant crest were the long lines of Russian guns, whose fire swept the British regiments.

"I suppose these regiments are in reserve?" Jack said, as he passed some of Sir R. England's division, lying down in readiness to move to the front when required, most of the battalions having already gone forward to support the troops who were most pressed.

Presently Captain Peel paused on a knoll, close to a body of mounted officers.

"There's Lord Raglan," Allison said, nudging Jack. "That's the headquarter staff."

At that moment a shell whizzed through the air, and exploded in the centre of the group.

Captain Gordon's horse was killed, and a portion of the shell carried away the leg of General Strangeway. The old general never moved, but said quietly,—

"Will any one be kind enough to lift me off my horse?"

He was laid down on the ground, and presently carried to the rear, where an hour afterwards he died.

Jack and his comrades, who were but a few yards away, felt strange and sick, for it was the first they had seen of battle close at hand. Lord Raglan, with his staff, moved slowly forward. Captain Peel asked if he should bring up his sailors, but was told to hold them in reserve, as the force in the trenches had already been fearfully weakened.

"Stay here," Captain Peel said to the midshipmen. "I shall go forward a little, but do you remain where you are until I return. Just lie down behind the crest. You will get no honor if you are hit here."

The lads were not sorry to obey, for a perfect hail of bullets was whistling through the air. The mist had lifted still farther, and they could obtain a sight of the whole line along which the struggle was raging, scarce a quarter of a mile in front of them. Sometimes the remnants of a regiment would fall back from the front, when a fresh battalion from the reserves came up to fill its place, then forming again, would readvance into the thick belt of smoke which marked where the conflict was thickest. Sometimes above the roll of musketry would come the sharp rattle which told of a volley by the British rifles.

Well was it that two out of the three divisions were armed with Minies, for these created terrible havoc among the Russians, whose smooth-bores were no match for these newly-invented weapons.

With beating hearts the boys watched the conflict, and could mark that the British fire grew feebler, and in some places ceased altogether, while the wild yells of the Russians rose louder as they pressed forward exultingly, believing that victory lay within their grasp.

"Things look very bad, Jack," Allison said. "Ammunition is evidently failing, and it is impossible for our fellows to hold out much longer against such terrible odds. What on earth are the French doing all this time? Our fellows have been fighting single-handed for the last three hours. What in the world can they be up to?"

And regardless of the storm of bullets, he leaped to his feet and looked round.

"Hurrah, Jack! Here they come, column after column. Ten more minutes and they'll be up. Hurry up, you lubbers," he shouted in his excitement; "every minute is precious, and you've wasted time enough, surely. By Jove, they're only just in time. There are the Guards falling back. Don't you see their bearskins?"

"They are only just in time," Jack agreed, as he stood beside his comrade. "Another quarter of an hour and they would have had to begin the battle afresh, for there would have been none of our fellows left. Hurrah! hurrah!" he cried, as, with a tremendous volley and a ringing shout, the French fell upon the flank of the Russians.

The lads had fancied that before that onslaught the Russians must have given way at once. But no. Fresh columns of troops topped the hill, fresh batteries took the place of those which had suffered most heavily by the fire of our guns, and the fight raged as fiercely as ever. Still, the boys had no fear of the final result. The French were fairly engaged now, and from their distant camps fresh columns of troops could be seen streaming across the plateau.

Upon our allies now fell the brunt of the fight, and the British, wearied and exhausted, were able to take a short breathing-time. Then, with pouches refilled and spirits heightened, they joined in the fray again, and, as the fight went on, the cheers of the British and the shouts of the French rose louder, while the answering yell of the Russians grew fainter and less frequent. Then the thunder of musketry sensibly diminished. The Russian artillery-men were seen to be withdrawing their guns, and slowly and sullenly the infantry fell back from the ground which they had striven so hard to win.

It was a heavy defeat, and had cost them 15,000 men; but, at least, it had for the time saved Sebastopol; for, with diminished forces, the British generals saw that all hopes of carrying the place by assault before the winter were at an end and that it would need all their effort to hold their lines through the months of frost and snow which were before them.

When the battle was over, Captain Peel returned to the point where he had left the midshipmen, and these followed him back to the camp, where, however, they were not to stay, for every disposable man was at once ordered out to proceed with stretchers to the front to bring in wounded.

Terrible was the sight indeed. In many places the dead lay thickly piled on the ground, and the manner in which Englishmen, Russians, and Frenchmen lay mixed together showed how the tide of battle had ebbed and flowed, and how each patch of ground had been taken and retaken again and again. Here Russians and grenadiers lay stretched side by side, sometimes with their bayonets still locked in each other's bodies. Here, where the shot and shell swept most fiercely, lay the dead, whose very nationality was scarcely distinguishable, so torn and mutilated were they.

Here a French Zouave, shot through the legs, was sitting up, supporting on his breast the head of his dying officer. A little way off, a private of the 88th, whose arm had been carried away, besought the searchers to fill and light his pipe for him, and to take the musket out of the hand of a wounded Russian near, who, he said, had three times tried to get it up to fire at him as he lay.

In other cases, Russians and Englishmen had already laid aside their enmity, and were exchanging drinks from their water-bottles.

Around the sand-bag battery, which the Guards had held, the dead lay thicker than elsewhere on the plateau; while down in the ravine where Cathcart had led his men, the bodies of the 63d lay heaped together. The sailors had, before starting, fill their bottles with grog, and this they administered to friend and foe indiscriminately, saving many a life ebbing fast with the flow of blood. The lads moved here and there, searching for the wounded among the dead, awed and sobered by the fearful spectacle. More than one dying message was breathed into their ears; more than one ring or watch given to them to send to dear ones at home. All through the short winter day they worked, aided by strong parties of the French who had not been engaged; and it was a satisfaction to know that, when night fell, the greater portion of the wounded, British and French, had been carried off the field. As for the Russians, those who fell on the plateau received equal care with the allies; but far down among the bushes that covered the hillside lay hundreds of wounded wretches whom no succor, that day at least, could be afforded.

The next day the work of bringing in the Russian wounded was continued, and strong fatigue parties were at work, digging great pits, in which the dead were laid those of each nationality being kept separate.

The British camps, on the night after Inkerman, afforded a strong contrast to the scene which they presented the night before. No merry laugh arose from the men crouched round the fires; no song sounded through the walls of the tents. There was none of the joy and triumph of victory; the losses which had been suffered were so tremendous as to overpower all other feeling. Of the regiments absolutely engaged, fully one-half had fallen; and the men and officers chatted in hushed voices over the good fellows who had gone, and of the chances of those who lay maimed and bleeding in the hospital tents.

To his great relief, Jack had heard, early in the afternoon, that the 33d had not been hotly engaged, and that his brother was unwounded. The two young officers of the 30th, who had, a few hours before, been spending the evening so merrily in the tent, had both fallen, as had many of the friends in the brigade of Guards whose acquaintance he had made on board the "Ripon," and in the regiments which, being encamped near by the sailors, he had come to know.

Midshipmen are not given to moralizing, but it was not in human nature that the lads, as they gathered in their tent that evening, should not talk over the sudden change which so few hours had wrought. The future of the siege, too, was discussed, and it was agreed that they were fixed where they were for the winter.

The prospect was a dreary one, for if they had had so many discomforts to endure hitherto, what would it be during the next four months on that bleak plateau? For themselves, however, they were indifferent in this respect, as it was already known the party on shore would be shortly relieved.

Chapter X
THE GREAT STORM

TWO days after the battle of Inkerman, the party of sailors who manned the batteries before Sebastopol were relieved by a fresh set from on board the men-of-war. Some of those who had been away at the front returned on board ship, while others, among whom was Jack Archer, were ordered to join the camp at the marine heights above Balaklava, to fill the places of some men invalided on board ship.

The change was, in some respects, an agreeable one; in others, the reverse. The position was very high and exposed to wind; but, on the other hand, the men, being able to obtain materials at Balaklava, had constructed warm shelters. The ravines below were well wooded, and they were consequently enabled to keep up cheerful fires; whereas at the front the supply of fuel barely sufficed to cook the food, and was almost useless for any purposes of warmth. There was far less privation here, for Balaklava lay within twenty minutes' walk, and stores of all kinds could be bought on board the ships. There was, too, an entire absence of the heavy and continuous work in the wet trenches. The great drawback to the position was, indeed, the absence of excitement and change, and the quiet seemed almost preternatural after the almost continual boom of cannon at the front.

Jack was pleased to find his chum Hawtry on duty at the height.

"This is a grand view, Hawtry," he said, as he stood at the edge of the cliff the morning after his arrival.

Below at his feet lay a great fleet of transports. To the left the cliffs stretched away, wild and precipitous, rising to heights far greater than the point at which they stood, some 600 feet above the sea. On his right the hill sloped gradually down to the old Genoese castle, and then sharply to the harbor, in which lay several men-of-war. In Balaklava, lines of wooden huts had been erected for a hospital, and their felt-covered roofs contrasted with the red tiles of the Tartar houses, and with the white walls and tower of the church. Along the valley at the foot of the harbor long lines of arabas and pack-animals, looking like mere specks from the point where the lads were standing, could be seen making their way to the front; while seven miles distant, on the plateau above Sebastopol, rose, like countless white dots, the tents of the Allied Army. Turning still farther round, they saw the undulating plain across which the light cavalry had charged upon the Russian guns, while standing boldly against the sky was the lofty table-land extending from above the village of Inkerman, right across the line of sight to the point known as Mackenzie Heights, from a farm belonging to an Englishman situated there. On these heights were encamped a large body of Russian troops.

"It's a splendid view, Dick," Jack Archer said; "but," he added, turning to look at the fleet of transports again, "I shouldn't like to be on board one of those ships if it came on to blow. It must be a rocky bottom and no holding-ground."

"That's what every one is saying, Jack. No one can make out why they don't let them all go inside. Of course they could not all unload at once, but there is room for them to shelter, if laid in tiers, as they would be in a crowded port. Yes, if we get a storm, and they say in the Black Sea they do have terrific gales during the winter, I fear we shall have a terrible business here."

Two days later they had a taste of what a storm in the Black Sea was. On the afternoon of Friday, the 10th, the wind got up, blowing straight into the bay. Very rapidly the sea rose. As dusk came on the sailors on the marine heights gathered on the edge of the cliff, and looked anxiously down upon the sea. Already great waves were tumbling in, dashing against the foot of the cliff, and sending clouds of spray half-way up to the old castle, 200 feet above them. The ships were laboring heavily, tugging and straining on their cables. From the funnels of the steamers volumes of black smoke were pouring, showing that they were getting up steam to keep the screws or paddles going, and relieve the strain upon their anchors.

"I wouldn't be aboard one of them craft," an old sailor said, "not for enough money to find me in grog and 'bacca for the rest of my life. If the gale gets stronger, half them ships will be ashore afore morning, and if they do, God help those on board!"

Happily the storm did not increase in violence, and when morning broke it was found that although many of the vessels had dragged their anchors, and some damage had been done by collisions, none had gone ashore. The knowledge, however, of how heavy a sea got up in a gale of even moderate force, and how frightfully dangerous was the position of the vessels, would, it might be thought, have served as a lesson, but unhappily it did not do so. The naval officer who was in charge of the harbor was obstinate, and again refused the request of the masters of many of the transports that the shipping might all be allowed to enter the harbor. He refused, and upon him is the responsibility of the terrible loss of life which ensued. On the 14th the wind again began to rise, and the sailors, as night came on, looked over the sea.

"We are going to have a bad night of it again," the officer in command of the post said, as he gazed seaward. "It looks as wild a night as ever I saw. Look how fast the scud is flying overhead. Last week's gale was a stiff one, but, unless I'm mistaken, it will be nothing to that which is upon us."

Louder and louder roared the wind, till men could scarce keep their feet outside shelter. The tents shook and rocked. Men could hardly hear each other's voices above the storm, and even in the darkness of night the sheets of foam could be seen dashing up to the very walls of the castle.

Jack Archer and Dick Hawtry, who with two other midshipmen occupied a tent, sat listening awe-struck to the fury of the gale. There was a gust fiercer than usual, accompanied by a crack like the sound of a pistol, followed by a stifled shout.

"There's a tent down!" Hawtry exclaimed, "and I shouldn't wonder—"

He did not finish, for at the moment the pole of their own tent broke asunder like a pipe, and in an instant the four were buried beneath the folds of the canvas. With much shouting and laughter they struggled to the entrance and made their way out. Half the tents were already levelled to the ground, and ten minutes later not one remained standing. The midshipmen crowded into the turf huts which some of the officers had had erected. Scarcely had they entered, when there was the boom of a heavy gun.

"I thought so," Dick Hawtry said. "There's the first of them. How many more will there be before morning?"

G. A. Henty

The door opened, and a sailor put in his head.

"Gentlemen, the captain says you are to turn out. He's going to take a party down to the castle with ropes."

In a few minutes a hundred men mustered, and moved down the hill. So fierce was the gale that, during the squalls, it was impossible to keep themselves on their feet, and all had to lie down till the fury of the gust had passed. It was pitch dark, and they groped rather than made their way along. Fast now, one after another, came the sound of the signal guns.

"There must be a dozen of them adrift," Dick shouted into his friend's ear during one of the lulls. "God help them all; what will become of them? A ship would be dashed to pieces like an eggshell against these cliffs."

When they reached the lowest point of the cliff, the party were halted and told to lie down and keep themselves in readiness, in case their services should be required. The officers struggled forward to the edge, and tried to see what was going on down in the bay below; but little could be seen, save the mighty sheets of spray, as the waves struck the cliffs. Here and there in the wild waters they fancied occasionally that they could see the dark forms of the ships, but even of this they could not have been certain, save for the twinkling lights which rose and fell, and dashed to and fro like fire-flies in their flight. Now and then the flash of a cannon momentarily showed some ship laboring in the trough of the mountainous sea.

"I believe that is the 'Black Prince,'" Jack shouted to his friend. "That big steamer which has been lying there the last week. If it is, she's ever so much nearer to shore than she was."

Suddenly a blue light threw its glare on the sea. It came from almost under their feet.

"Good heavens, Dick, there is a vessel on the rocks already; and look, a dozen more close in!"

The example was followed, and several other blue lights were burned showing plainly the terrible nature of the scene. The vessels were wallowing in the tremendous waves. Many had cut away their masts to relieve the strain on their anchors. The paddles and screws of the steamers were working at full speed, for the lines of white foam behind them could be plainly seen. But even this availed them but little, for almost every ship lay nearer to the line of cliffs than she did when night fell; several were close to the foot of the rocks, and the lookers-on noticed that some which had lain near the shore were missing. On the decks of the ships could be seen numbers of persons holding on to ropes and bulwarks. Sometimes from the deck of a vessel a rocket soared up, the wind catching it as it rose, and carrying it far inland.

By the captain's orders several blue lights, which the party had brought down, were burned, to show those on board that their position was perceived, but beyond this nothing could be done. Presently even above the noise of the gale a tremendous crash was heard, and they fancied that they heard a wild shout come faintly up.

"Can nothing be done?" Jack shouted to his friend.

"Nothing, sir," an old sailor said close by. "They are all doomed. There were over thirty ships there this morning, for I counted them, and I doubt if one will live out the night."

By this time the sailors, unable to lie inactive, had joined the officers, and all were scattered in groups along the cliff.

"Is there no possible way of getting down near the water?" Jack said.

Jack Archer

"I don't think so, sir; but if it were daylight we might make a shift to try."

"Let us try, anyhow," Jack said.

"Oh, there is another!" as another crash was heard above the gale.

"Anything is better than standing here. I don't think the cliff goes quite sheer down everywhere. Let us try, Dick; it would be a relief to be doing something."

"All right, Jack. Let you and I stick together. Do you lads," he said, turning to three or four sailors who were standing by, "keep close to us, and lend a hand." At the point where they were standing, it was clearly impossible to get down, for the rock sloped straight from, their feet. Farther to the left, however, it went down more gradually, and here the boys began to try to descend.

"There is a sort of hollow here," Jack shouted, "a sort of ravine. This is our best place."

Cautiously, step by step, holding on to such bushes as grew among the rocks pausing sometimes flattened against the rocks by the force of the gust, and drenched every moment by the sheets of spray, the boys made their way down, till they paused at a spot where the rock fell away sheer under their feet. They could go no farther. At the moment they heard a wild scream. A vessel appeared through the darkness below, and crashed with a tremendous thud against the rocks. The masts, which were so close that the boys seemed almost able to jump upon them, as they reached nearly to the level on which they were standing, instantly going over the side. Peering over, they could see the black mass in the midst of the surging white waters at their feet. The sailors had paused some way up the ascent, appalled by the difficulties which the boys, lighter and more active, had accomplished.

"Go up to the top again," Hawtry said, climbing back to them. "Bring down one of those spars we brought down, a block, a long rope, and a short one to serve as a guy. Get half-a-dozen more hands. You'd better fix a rope at the top firmly, and use it to steady you as you return. There's a ship ashore just underneath us, and I think we can get down."

In a few minutes the sailors descended again, carrying with them a spar some twenty feet long. With immense difficulty this was lowered to the spot which the boys had reached. One of the sailors had brought down a lantern, and by its light a block was lashed to the end, and a long rope roved through it. Then a shorter rope was fastened to the end as a guy, and the spar lowered out, till it sloped well over the edge. The lower edge was wedged in between two rocks, and others piled round it.

"Now," Dick said, "I will go down."

"You'll never get down alive, sir," one of the sailor said. "The wind will dash you against the cliff. I'll try, sir, if you like; I'm heavier."

"Let me go down with you," Jack said. "The two of us are heavier than a man, and we shall have four legs to keep us off the cliff. Besides, we can help each other down below."

"All right," Dick said. "Fasten us to the rope, Hardy. Make two loops so that we shall hang face to face, and yet be separate, and give me a short rope of two or three fathoms long, so that we can rope ourselves together, and one hold on in case the other is washed off his feet when we get down. Look here, Hardy, do you lie down and look over the edge, and when you hear me yell, let them hoist away. Now for it!"

The boys were slung as Dick had ordered. "Lower away steadily," Dick said. "Stop lowering if we yell."

G. A. Henty

In another minute the lads were swinging in space, some ten feet out from the face of the cliff. For the first few yards they descended steadily, and then, as the rope lengthened, the gusts of wind flung them violently against the face of the cliff.

"Fend her off with your legs, Jack; that's the way. By Jove, that's a ducking!" he said, as a mighty rush of spray enveloped them as a mountainous sea struck the rock below. "I think we shall do it. There's something black down below, I think some part of her still holds together; slowly!" he shouted up, in one of the pauses of the gale, and Hardy's response of "Aye, aye, sir," came down to them.

It was a desperate three minutes; but at the end of that time, bruised, bleeding, half-stunned by the blows, half-drowned by the sheets of water which flew over them, the lads' feet touched the rocks. These formed a sloping shelf of some thirty feet wide at the foot of the cliff.

The wreck which had appeared immediately under them was forty feet away, and appeared a vague, misshapen black mass. They had been seen, for they had waved the lantern from the edge of the cliff before starting, and they had several times shouted as they descended, and as they neared the ground, they were delighted at hearing by an answering shout that their labors had not been in vain, and that some one still survived.

"Throw us a rope," Dick shouted at the top of his voice; and in a moment they heard a rope fall close to them. Groping about in the darkness, they found it, just as a wave burst below them, and, dashing high over their heads, drove them against the rock, and then floated them off their feet. The rope from above held them, however. "Lower away!" Dick yelled, as he regained his feet, and then, aided by the rope from the ship, they scrambled along, and were hauled on to the wreck before the next great sea came.

"I've broken my arm, Dick," Jack said; "but never mind me now. How many are there alive?"

There were sixteen men huddled together under the remains of the bulwark. The greater portion of the ship was gone altogether, and only some forty feet of her stern remained high on the rocky ledge on which she had been cast. The survivors were for the most part too exhausted to move, but those who still retained some strength and vigor at once set to work. In pairs they were fastened in the slings, and hauled up direct from the deck of the vessel, another rope being fastened to them and held by those on the wreck, by which means they were guided and saved somewhat from being dashed against the cliff in the ascent.

When those below felt, by the rope no longer passing between their hands, that the slings had reached the top, they waited for a minute to allow those in them to be taken out, and then hauling upon the rope, pulled the slings down again for a fresh party. So, slowly and painfully, the whole party were, two by two, taken up from the wreck.

Several times while the operation was being performed great crashes were heard, followed by loud shouts and screams, as vessel after vessel drove ashore to the right or left of them. But Jack and his friend, who consulted together, agreed that by no possibility could these be aided, as it was only just at the point where the wreck lay that the rocks at the foot of the cliff were high enough to be above all but exceptionally high waves, and any one adventuring many yards either to the right or left would have been dashed to pieces against the cliff by the first wave.

Jack Archer

The midshipmen were the last to leave the ship. Dick had in vain begged his messmate to go up in one of the preceding batches, as the last pair would necessarily be deprived of the assistance from the lower rope, which had so materially aided the rest. Jack, however, refused to hear of it. When the slings came down to them for the last time, they put them on, and stood on the wreck watching till a great wave came. When it had passed, they slipped down the side of the ship by a rope, and hurried over the rocks till immediately under the spar, whose position was indicated by a lantern held there. Then, in answer to their shout, the rope tightened, and they again swung in the air.

The wind blew no more fiercely than before; indeed, it was scarce possible it could do so; but they were now both utterly exhausted. During the hour and a half which they had stood upon the remains of the wreck, they had been, every minute or two, deluged with water. Sometimes, indeed, the sea had swept clean over them, and had it not been that they had lashed themselves with ropes, they must have been swept away.

Every great wave had swept away some plank or beam of the wreck, and when they left it, scarce a fragment of the deck remained attached to the rudder-post. Terrible was the buffeting they received as they ascended, and time after time they were dashed with immense force against the face of the cliff.

To Jack the noise and confusion seemed to increase. A strange singing sounded in his ears, and as the slings reached the top, and a burst of cheering broke from the seamen there, all consciousness left him.

The officer in command of the party was himself at the spot; he and many others having made their way down, when the news spread that a rescue was being attempted. Dick, too, was unable to stand, and both were carried by the sailors to the top of the slope. Here a cup of strong rum-and-water was given to Dick, while some pure spirits poured down his throat soon recalled Jack to consciousness. The latter, upon opening his eyes, would have got up, but this his officer would not allow; and he was placed on a stretcher and carried by four tars up to the heights, where he was laid in one of the sod huts, and his arm, which was badly fractured, set by the surgeon.

The sixteen rescued men had, as they gained the top, been at once taken down into Balaklava, the sole survivors of the crews of over twenty ships which had gone to pieces in that terrible hurricane.

Of the fleet of transports and merchantmen which, trim and in good order, had lain in the bay the afternoon before, some half-dozen only had weathered the hurricane. The "City of London" alone had succeeded in steaming out to sea when the gale began. The "Jason" and a few others had ridden to their anchors through the night. The rest of the fleet had been destroyed, victims to the incompetence and pig-headedness of the naval officer in charge of the harbor. That there was ample room for all within it, was proved by the fact that, later on, a far larger number of ships than that which was present on the day of the gale lay comfortably within it.

The largest ship lost was the "Prince," with whom nearly 300 men went down. Even inside the harbor vessels dragged their anchors and drifted ashore, so terrible was the gale, which, indeed, was declared by old sailors and by the inhabitants of the town to be the most violent that they ever experienced. Enormous quantities of stores of all kinds, which would have been of immense service to the troops in the winter, were lost in the gale, and even in the camps on shore the destruction was very great.

Chapter XI
TAKEN PRISONERS

"THAT arm of yours always seems to be getting itself damaged, Jack," Hawtry said next morning, as he came into the hut. "You put it in the way of a bullet last time, and now you've got it smashed up. How do you feel altogether?"

"I am awfully bruised, Dick, black and blue all over, and so stiff I can hardly move."

"That's just my case," Dick said, "though, as you see, I can move. The doctor's been feeling me all over this morning, and he said it was lucky I was a boy and my bones were soft, for if I had been a man, I should have been smashed up all over. As to my elbows and my knees, and all the projecting parts of me, I haven't got a bit of skin on them, and my uniform is cut absolutely to ribbons. However, old boy, we did a good night's work. We saved sixteen lives, we got no end of credit, and the chief says he shall send a report in to the Admiral; so we shall be mentioned in despatches, and it will help us for promotion when we have passed. The bay is a wonderful sight. The shores are strewn with floating timber, bales of stores, compressed hay, and all sorts of things. Fellows who have been down to the town told me that lots of the houses have been damaged, roofs blown away, and those gingerbread-looking balconies smashed off. As for the camps, even with a glass there is not a single tent to be seen standing on the plateau. The gale has made a clean sweep of them. What a night the soldiers must have had! I am put on the sick list for a few days so I shall be able to be with you. That's good news, isn't it?"

"Wonderfully good," Jack laughed, "as if I haven't enough of your jaw at other times. And how long do you suppose I shall be before I am out?"

"Not for some little time, Jack. The doctor says you've got four ribs broken as well as your arm."

"Have I?" Jack said, surprised. "I know he hurt me preciously while he was feeling me about this morning; but he didn't say anything about broken ribs."

A broken rib is a much less serious business than a broken arm, and in ten days Jack was up and about again, feeling generally stiff and sore, and with his arm in a sling. The surgeon had talked of sending him on board ship, but Jack begged so hard for leave to remain with the party ashore, that his request was granted.

Winter had now set in in earnest. The weather was cold and wet, sometimes it cleared up overhead, and the country was covered with snow. A month after the accident, Jack was fit for duty again. Seeing what chums the lads were, the officer in command had placed them in the same watch, for here on land the same routine was observed as on board ship. The duties were not severe. The guns were kept bright and polished, the arms and accoutrements were as clean as if at sea. Each day the tars went through a certain amount of drill, and fatigue parties went daily down to the harbor to bring up stores, but beyond this there was little to do. One of the occupations of the men was chopping wood for fuel. The sides of the ravine immediately below the battery had long since been cleared of their brushwood, and each day the parties in search of fuel had to go farther away. Upon the day after Jack returned to duty, he and Hawtry were told off with a party of seamen to go down to cut firewood. Each man carried his rifle in addition to his chopper, for, although they had never been disturbed at this occupation, the Russians were known not to be far away. The sailors were soon at work hacking down the undergrowth and lopping off branches of trees. Some were making them up into faggots as fast as the others cut them, and all were laughing and jesting at their work.

Suddenly there was a shout, and looking up, they saw that a party of Russians had made their way noiselessly over the snowclad ground, and were actually between them and the heights. At the same moment a volley of musketry was poured in from the other side, and three or four men fell.

"Form up, form up," Hawtry shouted. "Well together, lads. We must make a rush at those beggars ahead. Don't fire till I tell you, then give them a volley and go at them with the butt-end of your muskets, then let every one who gets through make a bolt for it."

The sailors, some twenty strong, threw themselves together, and, headed by the midshipmen, made a rush at the Russians. These opened fire upon them, and several dropped, but the remainder went on at the double until within twenty yards of the enemy, when pouring in a volley and clubbing their muskets, they rushed upon them.

For a moment there was a sharp *mèlèe*; several of the sailors were shot or bayoneted, but the rest, using the butt-ends of their muskets with tremendous execution, fought their way through their opponents. Jack had shot down two men with his revolver, and having got through, was taking his place at the rear of the men—the proper place for an officer in retreat?—when he saw Hawtry fall. A Russian ran up to bayonet him as he lay, when Jack, running back, shot him through the head. In a moment he was surrounded, and while in the act of shooting down an assailant in front, he was struck on the back of the head with the butt of a musket, and fell stunned across the body of his friend. When he recovered consciousness, he found that he was being carried along by four Russians. He could hear the boom of cannon and the rattle of musketry, and knew that the defenders on the heights were angrily firing at the retreating party, who had so successfully surprised them. As soon as his bearers perceived that Jack had opened his eyes, they let him drop, hauled him to his feet, and then holding him by his collar, made him run along with them.

When they had mounted the other side of the slope, and were out of fire of the guns, the party halted, and Jack, hearing his own name called, looked round, and saw Hawtry in the snow, where his captors had dropped him.

"Hullo, Dick! old fellow," Jack shouted joyfully; "so there you are. I was afraid they had killed you."

"I'm worth a lot of dead men yet, Jack. I've been hit in the leg, and went down, worse luck, and that rascally Russian would have skewered me if you hadn't shot him. You saved my life, old fellow, and made a good fight for me and I shall never forget it; but it has cost you your liberty."

"That's no great odds," Jack said. "It can't be much worse stopping a few months in a Russian prison, than spending the winter upon the heights.

G. A. Henty

Besides, with two of us together, we shall be as right as possible, and maybe, when your leg gets all right again, we'll manage to give them the slip."

The Russian officer in command of the party, which was about 200 strong, now made signs to the boys that they were to proceed.

Dick pointed to his leg, and the officer examined the wound. It was a slight one, the ball having passed through the calf, missing the bone.

He was, however, unable to walk. A litter was formed of two muskets with a great-coat laid between them, and Dick, being seated on this, was taken up by four men, and Jack taking his place beside him, the procession started. They halted some four miles off at a village in a valley beyond the Tchernaya.

The next day the boys were placed on ponies, and, under the escort of an officer and six troopers, conducted to Sebastopol. Here they were taken before a Russian general who, by means of an interpreter, closely examined them as to the force, condition, and position of the army.

The lads, however, evaded all questions by stating that they belonged to the fleet, and were only on duty on the heights above Balaklava, and were in entire ignorance of the force of the army and the intentions of its general. As to the fleet, they could tell nothing which the Russians did not already know.

The examination over, they were conducted to one of the casemates of Fort St. Nicholas. Here for a fortnight they remained, seeing no one except the soldier who brought them their food. The casemate was some thirty feet long by eighteen wide, and a sixty-eight-pounder stood looking out seaward. There the boys could occasionally see the ships of war of the allies as they cruised to and fro.

It was very cold, for the opening was of course unglazed. They had each a heap of straw and two blankets, and these in the daytime they used as shawls, for they had no fire, and it was freezing sharply.

Dick's leg had been examined and dressed by a surgeon upon his first arrival; but as the wound was not serious, and the surgeons were worked night and day with the enormous number of wounded at Inkerman, and in the various sorties, with which the town was crowded, he did not again come near his patient. The wound, however, healed rapidly.

As Jack remarked, the scanty rations of black bread and tough meat—the latter the produce of some of the innumerable bullocks which arrived at Sebastopol with convoys, too exhausted and broken down for further service—were not calculated to cause any feverish excitement to the blood, nor, had it been so, would the temperature have permitted the fever to rise to any undue height.

Their guards were kind to them so far as was in their power, and upon their using the word "tobacco," and making signs that they wanted to smoke, furnished them with pipes and with tobacco, which, although much lighter and very different in quality from that supplied on board ship, was yet very smokable, and much mitigated the dulness from which the boys suffered. A few days after their captivity the boys heard the church bells of Sebastopol ringing merrily.

"I wonder what all this is about?" Dick said; "not for a victory, I'll be bound."

"Why, bless me," Jack exclaimed, "if it isn't Christmas day, and we had forgotten all about it! Now, that is hard, monstrously hard. The fellows on the heights will just be enjoying themselves to-day. I know they were talking

Jack Archer

about getting some currants and raisins from on board ship, and there will be plum-duff and all sorts of things. I wonder how they're all getting on at home? They're sure to be thinking often enough of us, but it will never enter their minds that here we are cooped up in this beastly hole."

The day, however, did not pass unnoticed, for a Russian officer who spoke English called upon them, and said that he came at the request of the governor himself to express to them his regret that their quarters were so uncomfortable and their fare so bad. "But," he said, "we cannot help ourselves. Every barrack in the town is crowded; every hospital, every private house even, filled with wounded. We have fifty or sixty thousand troops, and near twenty thousand sick and wounded. Your people are very good not to fire at the town, for if they did, I do not know what the poor fellows would do. For to-day the governor has sent you down a dinner from his own table, together with a few bottles of wine and spirits—and what you will not prize less, for I see you smoke, a box of cigars. It is very cold here. I will see that you have some more blankets."

Two soldiers came in with baskets, the one with tin-covered dishes, the other with wines. These were set out on the ground, and the boys, after sending a message expressing their cordial thanks to the general for his thoughtfulness, sat down, when alone, in the highest spirits to their unexpected feast.

"This is a glorious spread, Jack. I wonder what all these dishes are? I don't recognize any of them. However, this is soup, there is no doubt about that, so let's fall to on that to begin with. But first of all, get out the cork of one of those champagne bottles. Now fill up your tin, Jack, and let's drink 'God bless all at home, and a merry Christmas to them.' We'll have our other toasts after dinner. I couldn't begin till we drank that. Now set to."

The dishes were not as cold as might have been expected, for each had been enveloped in flannel before placing it in the basket. The soup was pronounced excellent, and the unknown meats, prime—better than anything they had tasted since they left England. There were sweets, too, which they made a clean sweep of. Then they called their guard, to whom they gave the remains of their dinner, together with a strong pannikin of water and spirits, to his extreme delight.

Then, making themselves snug in the straw, wrapping themselves well in their blankets, fencing in their candle, so that it was sheltered from the draughts, they opened a bottle of brandy, drank a variety of toasts, not forgetting the health of the governor, who they agreed was a brick, they sang a song or two, then blew out the light, and, thoroughly warm and comfortable, were asleep in a minute or two.

A few days later, an officer came in, signed to them to make their blankets into a bundle, and to follow him.

The boys slipped four bottles of spirits which they had still remaining, and also the stock of cigars, into the rolls. Then, holding the bundles on their shoulders, they followed him.

Dick, although still weak on his legs, was now able to walk.

Presently they came to a large party of men, some of whom had their arms in slings, some were bandaged on the head, some lay in stretchers on the ground.

"It is a convoy of wounded," Jack said. "I suppose we're going to be taken into the interior."

G. A. Henty

An officer, evidently in charge, saluted the boys as they came up, and said something in Russian.

They returned the salute. He was a pleasant-looking fellow with light-blue eyes, and yellowish moustache and beard. He looked at them, and then gave orders to a soldier, who entered the building, and returned with two peasants' cloaks lined with sheep-skin, similar to the one he himself wore.

These were handed to them, and the midshipmen expressed their warmest gratitude to him; their meaning, if not their words, being clearly intelligible.

"These are splendid," Jack said. "They've got hoods too, to go over the head. This is something like comfort. I wish our poor fellows up above there had each got one. It must be awful up on the plateau now. Fancy twelve hours in the trenches, and then twelve hours in the tents, with no fires, and nothing but those thin great-coats, and scarcely anything to eat. Now there's a move."

A strong party of soldiers came down, lifted the stretchers, and in a few minutes the whole convoy were at the water's edge. Other similar parties were already there, and alongside were a number of flat barges. Upon these the invalids walked, or were carried, and the barges were then taken in tow by ships' boats, and rowed across the harbor to the north side.

"I hope to goodness," Jack said, looking up at the heights behind them, along which the lines of entrenchments were clearly visible against the white snow, "that our fellows won't take it into their heads to have a shot at us. From our battery we often amused ourselves by sending a shell from one of the big Lancaster guns down at the ships in the harbor. But I never dreamed that I was likely to be a cockshy myself."

The usual duel was going on between the batteries, and the puffs of white smoke rose from the dark line of trenches and drifted up unbroken across the deep blue of the still wintry sky.

But happily the passage of the flotilla of boats attracted no attention, and they soon arrived at the shore close to the work known as Battery No. 4.

Here they were landed. Those who could not walk were lifted into carts, of which some hundreds stood ranged alongside. The rest fell in on foot, and the procession started. The boys, to their satisfaction, found that the officer who had given them the coats was in charge of a portion of the train, and as they started he stopped to speak a word or two to them, to which they replied in the most intelligible manner they could by offering him a cigar, which a flash of pleasure in his face at once showed to be a welcome present.

It took some time to get the long convoy in motion, for it consisted of some 700 or 800 carts and about 5,000 sick and wounded, of whom fully three-fourths were unable to walk. It mounted to the plateau north of the harbor, wound along near the great north fort, and then across undulating land parallel with the sea. They stopped for the night on the Katcha, where the allied army had turned off for their flank march to the southern side.

The boys during the march were allowed to walk as they liked, but two soldiers with loaded muskets kept near them. They discussed the chances of trying to make their escape, but agreed that although they might be able to slip away from the convoy, the probability of their making their way through the Russian troops to their own lines at Balaklava or Sebastopol was so slight that the attempt would be almost madness. Their figures would be everywhere conspicuous on the snow, their footsteps, could be followed, they had no food,

Jack Archer

and were ignorant of the language and country. Altogether they determined to abandon any idea of escaping for the present.

There were but a dozen soldiers with the convoy, the officers being medical men in charge of the wounded. A halt was made in a sheltered spot near the river, and close to the village of Mamaschia, which was entirely deserted by its inhabitants.

The worst cases of sickness were carried into the houses, and the rest prepared to make themselves as comfortable as they could in or under the wagons. Stores of forage were piled by the village for the use of the convoys going up and down, and the drivers speedily spread a portion of this before their beasts.

The guard and such men as were able to get about went off among the orchards that surrounded the village, to cut fuel. The boys' special guard remained by them. When the doctor whom they regarded as their friend came up to them, he brought with him another officer as interpreter, who said in broken French,—

"Voulez-vous donner votre parole pas essayez echapper?"

Jack was as ignorant of French as of Russian, but Dick knew a little. He turned to Jack and translated the question.

"Tell him we will give our words not to try and escape during the march, or till we tell him to the contrary." This was almost beyond Dick.

"Nous donnons notre parole pour le prèsent," he said, "pour la marche, vous comprenez. Si nous changons notre—I wonder what mind is," he grumbled to himself—"intention, nous vous dirons."

This was intelligible, although not good French, and their friend, having shaken hands with them as if to seal the bargain, told the soldiers that they need no longer keep a watch on the prisoners, and then beckoned them to accompany him. The boys had, at starting, placed their bundles upon a cart to which they had kept close during the march. Putting these on their shoulders, they accompanied their friend to a cart which was drawn up three or four feet from the wall of a house. They set to work at once, and with the aid of some sticks and blankets, of which there was a good supply in the wagon, made a roof covering the space between it and the house, hung others at the end and side, and had soon a snug tent erected.

One of the soldiers brought a large truss of straw, and another a bundle of firewood. The blanket at the end of the tent sheltered from the wind, was drawn aside, and a great fire speedily blazed up at the entrance. The straw was shaken out to form a soft seat, just inside the tent. All three produced their pipes and lit them, while the doctor's servant prepared over the fire a sort of soup with the rations. This turned out to be by no means bad, and when after it the boys produced one of their bottles of brandy and three cigars, the Russian doctor patted them on the back, and evidently told them that they were first-rate fellows.

For half-an-hour he smoked his cigar and sipped his tin of brandy and water, then, explaining by signs that he must go and look after his wounded, left them.

The boys chatted for another half-hour, and then stowing their brandy carefully away, they shook up the straw into a big bed, and, wrapping themselves in their sheepskins, were soon soundly asleep; but it was long after midnight before the doctor returned from his heavy work of dressing wounds and administering medicine, and stretched himself on the straw beside them.

Chapter XII
PRISONERS ON PAROLE

DAY after day the convoy made its way northward without any incident of importance happening. The midshipmen were glad to find that, thanks to their sheepskin cloaks and pointed hoods, they passed through the towns without attracting any attention whatever.

The convoy lessened in length as it proceeded. The animals broke down in great numbers and died by the road, under the task of dragging the heavy wagons through the deep snow.

At a town of some size, where they halted for two days, relief was afforded by the wheels being taken off the wagons, and rough runners affixed, the wheels being placed on the carts, as that they could be put on again in case of a thaw.

Famine, however, did more that fatigue in destroying the animals; for although good exertions had been made to form depots of forage along the roads, these were exhausted faster than they could be collected by the enormous trains, which, laden with provisions and warlike stores, were making their way to Sebastopol from the interior of Russia. There was no lack of food for the men, for ample stores of black bread were carried, and a supply of meat was always obtainable at the end of the day's journey by the carcase of some bullock which had fallen and then been shot during the day's march.

But though the train diminished in length, its occupants diminished even more rapidly. Every morning, before starting, a burying party were busy interring the bodies of those who had died during the previous day's march or in the night.

When the halt was made at a village, the papa or priest of the place performed a funeral mass; when, as was more common, they encamped in the open, the grave was filled in, a rough cross was erected over it, and the convoy proceeded on its march.

The midshipmen found the journey dreary and uninteresting in the extreme.

After leaving the Crimea the country became a dead flat; which, though bright in summer, with a wide expanse of waving grain, was inexpressibly mournful and monotonous as it lay under its wide covering of snow. Here and there, far across the plain, could be seen the low, flat-roofed huts of a Russian village, or the massively-built abode of some rich landed proprietor.

Scarce a tree broke the monotony of the wide plain, and the creaking of the carts and the shouts of the drivers seemed strangely loud as they rose in the dense silence of the plain.

From the first day of starting, the midshipmen set themselves to learn something of the language. The idea was Jack's and he pointed out to Hawtry, who was rather disinclined to take the trouble, that it would in the first place give them something to think about, and be an amusement on the line of march; in the second, it would render their captivity less dull, and, lastly, it would facilitate their escape if they should determine to make the attempt.

As they walked, therefore, alongside their friend the doctor, they asked him the names of every object around them, and soon learned the Russian words for all common objects. The verbs were more difficult, but thanks occasionally to the doctor (who spoke French) joining them at their encampment at night, they soon learned the sentences most commonly in use.

As they had nothing else to do or to think about, their progress was rapid, and by the end of a month they were able to make themselves understood in conversations upon simple matters.

They had been much disappointed, when, upon leaving the Crimea, the convoy had kept on north instead of turning west; for they had hoped that Odessa would have been their place of captivity.

It was a large and flourishing town, with a considerable foreign population, and, being on the sea, might have offered them opportunities for escape. The Russians, however, had fears that the allied fleets might make an attack upon the place, and for this reason, such few prisoners as fell into their hands were sent inland.

The journeys each day averaged from twelve to fifteen miles, twelve, however, being the more ordinary distance. The sky was generally clear and bright, for when the morning was rough and the snow fell, the convoy remained in its halting-place.

The cold was by no means excessive during the day, and although the snow was deep and heavy, there was no difficulty in keeping up with the convoy, as the pace of the bullocks was little over a mile and a half an hour. At night they were snug enough, for the doctor had adapted an empty wagon as their sleeping-place, and this, with a deep bed of straw at the bottom, blankets hung at the sides and others laid over the top, constituted as comfortable a shelter as could be desired.

At last, after a month's travelling, the doctor pointed to a town rising over the plain, and signified that this was their halting-place.

It was a town of some seven or eight thousand inhabitants, and the mosque-like domes of the churches shining, brightly in the sun, and the green-painted roofs and bright colors of many of the houses, gave it a gay and cheerful appearance.

The convoy made its way through the streets to large barracks, now converted into a hospital. When the sick had been taken into the wards, the doctor proceeded with the midshipmen to the residence of the governor.

The boys had laid aside the sheepskin cloaks which had proved so invaluable during their journey, and as they walked through the streets, in their midshipman's uniform, attracted a good deal of attention.

They were at once shown in to the governor, an officer of some five-and-thirty years old, with a fierce and disagreeable expression of countenance. He was a member of a high Russian family; but as a punishment for various breaches of discipline, arising from his quarrelsome disposition and misconduct, he had been appointed governor to this little town, instead of going with his regiment to the front.

Saluting him, the doctor delivered to him an order for the safe guardianship of the two English officers.

"Ah," he said, as he perused the document, and glanced at the midshipmen, "if these are British officers, I can scarcely understand the trouble they are giving us. They are mere boys. I thought their uniform was red. The soldiers who were brought here a month ago were all in red."

G. A. Henty

"These are young naval officers," the doctor said. "I understand that some of the sailors are serving on shore, and these were captured, I am told, when out with a party of their men cutting fuel."

"A wonderful capture, truly," the governor said sneeringly. "Two boys scarce out of the nursery."

"It cost us some men," the doctor said calmly, "for I hear from the officer who brought them in that we lost altogether fifteen men, and the sailors would all have got away had it not been that one of these young officers was shot in the leg and the other stood by him, and shot several men with his revolver before he was captured."

"A perfect St. George," the commandant sneered. "Well, sir, your duty is done, and I will see to them. Are they on parole?"

"They gave me their parole not to try to escape during the journey, and have expressed their willingness to renew it."

"It matters little one way or the other," the governor said. "Unless they could fly, they could not make their way through the country. There, sir, that will do."

The doctor bowed, shook hands with the boys, and without a word went out, touching his lips with his fingers to them as he turned his back to the governor, a movement which the lads understood at once as a hint that it would be as well to say nothing which might show that they had any knowledge of Russian.

The governor rang a hand-bell, and a sergeant entered. The governor wrote a few words on a piece of paper.

"Take these prisoners to Count Preskoff's," he said, "and deliver this order to him."

The sergeant motioned the lads to follow him. With a bow to the governor, which he passed unacknowledged, they followed the soldier.

"A disagreeable brute, that," Jack said. "A little work in the trenches would do him good, and take some of his cockiness out of him. That was a good idea of the doctor, not saying good-bye in Russian. I don't suppose we shall run against that fellow again, but if we did, he might make it so disagreeable that we might be driven to show him a clean pair of heels."

"He didn't ask for our parole," Dick said, "so we shall be justified in making a bolt if we see a chance."

Passing through the streets the sergeant led them through the town and out into the country beyond.

"Where on earth is he taking us to?" Jack wondered. "I would bet that he has quartered us on this Count Preskoff from pure spite. I wonder what sort of chap he is."

After half an hour's walking they approached a large chateau, surrounded by smaller buildings.

"He's a swell evidently," Dick said. "We ought to have comfortable quarters here."

They entered a large courtyard, across one side of which stood the house; and the sergeant, proceeding to the main entrance, rang the bell. It was opened by a tall man dressed in full Russian costume.

"I have a message for the count from the commandant," the sergeant said.

"The count is absent," the servant answered; "but the countess is in."

"I will speak to her."

Jack Archer

Leaving them standing in the hall, the man ascended a wide staircase, and in a minute or two returned and motioned to the sergeant to follow him.

They ascended the stairs and entered a large and handsome room, in which sat a lady of some forty years old, with three younger ones of from sixteen to twenty years old.

Countess Preskoff was a very handsome woman, and her daughters had inherited her beauty.

The sergeant advanced and handed to her the order. She glanced at it, and an expression of displeasure passed across her face.

"The commandant's orders shall be obeyed," she said coldly; and the sergeant, saluting, retired.

The countess turned to her daughters.

"The commandant has quartered two prisoners, English officers, upon us," she said. "Of course he has done it to annoy us. I suppose these are they." And she rose and approached the lads, who were standing by the door. "Why, they are boys," she said in surprise, "and will do for playfellows for you, Olga. Poor little fellows, how cruel to send such boys to fight!"

Then she came up to the boys and bade them welcome with an air of kindness which they both felt.

"Katinka," she said, turning to her eldest daughter, "you speak French, and perhaps they do also. Assure them that we will do our best to make them comfortable. Come here, my dears."

Then she formally, pointing to each of them, uttered their names,—

"Katinka, Paulina, Olga."

Dick, in reply, pointed to his companion,—

"Jack Archer,"—and to himself—"Dick Hawtry."

The girls smiled, and held out their hands.

"Mamma says," the eldest said in French, "that she is glad to see you, and will do all in her power to make you comfortable."

"You're very good," Dick said. "I can speak very little French, and cannot understand it at all unless you speak quite slow. I wish now I hadn't been so lazy at school. But we both speak a few words of Russian, and I hope that we shall soon be able to talk to you in your own language."

Bad as Dick's French was, the girls understood it, and an animated conversation in a mixed jargon of French and Russian began. The girls inquired how they had come there, and how they had been taken, and upon hearing they had been in Sebastopol, inquired more anxiously as to the real state of things there, for the official bulletins were always announcing victories, and they could not understand how it was that the allies, although always beaten, were still in front of Sebastopol, when such huge numbers of troops had gone south to carry out the Czar's orders, to drive them into the sea.

The lads' combined knowledge of French and Russian proved quite insufficient to satisfy their curiosity, but there was so much laughing over their wonderful blunders and difficulty in finding words to explain themselves, that at the end of half an hour the boys were perfectly at home with their hostesses.

"You will like to see your rooms," the countess said; and touching a hand-bell, she gave some orders to a servant who, bowing, led the way along a corridor and showed the boys two handsomely-furnished rooms opening out of each other, and then left them, returning in a minute or two with hot water and towels.

G. A. Henty

"We're in clover here," Jack said, "and no mistake. The captain's state cabin is a den by the side of our quarters; and ain't they jolly girls?"

"And pretty, too, I believe you; and the countess, too. I call her a stunner!" he exclaimed enthusiastically; "as stately as a queen, but as friendly and kind as possible. I don't think we ought to go to war with people like this."

"Oh, nonsense!" Jack said. "We've seen thousands of Russians now, and don't think much of them; and 'tisn't likely we're going to let Russia gobble up Turkey just because there's a nice countess with three jolly daughters living here."

Dick laughed.

"No, I suppose not," he said. "But, Jack, what on earth are we going to do about clothes? These uniforms are getting seedy, though it is lucky that we had on our best when we were caught, owing to our having had the others torn to pieces the night of the wreck. But as for other things, we have got nothing but what we have on. We washed our flannel shirts and stockings as well as we could whenever we halted, but we can't well do that here; and as for money, we haven't a ha'penny between us. It's awful, you know."

At this moment there was a knock at the door, and the servant entered, bringing in a quantity of linen and underclothing of all kinds, which he laid down on the bed with the words,—

"With the countess's compliments."

"Hurrah!" shouted Dick. "The countess is a brick. This is something like. Now for a big wash, Jack, and a clean white shirt. We shan't know ourselves. Here is a brush, too. We shall be able to make our uniforms presentable."

It was nearly an hour before the boys again joined the ladies, looking, it must be owned, a great deal more like British officers and gentlemen than when they left the room. They were both good-looking lads, and the Russian girls were struck with their bright and cheerful faces.

Dick hastened to express their warm thanks to the countess for the welcome supply of clothes, and said that Jack and himself were ashamed indeed at not only trespassing on their hospitality, but being obliged to rely upon their wardrobe.

As Dick had carefully thought out this little speech, translated it into French, and said it over half-a-dozen times, he was able to make himself understood, utterly defective as were his grammar and pronunciation.

Katinka explained that the clothes had belonged to her brother, who was now a lieutenant in a regiment stationed in Poland, and that they had long been outgrown; he being now, as she signified by holding up her hand, over six feet in height.

A quarter of an hour later the dinner was announced, and the countess in a stately way took Dick's arm, and Jack, not without blushing, offered his to the eldest of the girls. The dinner was, in the boys' eyes, magnificent. Several domestics stood behind the chairs and anticipated their wants. The girls continued their Russian lessons by telling them the names of everything on the table, and making them repeat them after them, and there was so much laughter and merriment, that long as the meal was, it was by no means formal or ceremonious. They learnt that the Count Preskoff was absent at some estates in the north of Russia, and that he was not likely to return for some little time.

After dinner Dick asked Katinka to tell the countess that they did not wish to be troublesome, and that they would be out and about the place, and

Jack Archer

would not intrude upon them except when they wished to have them. The countess replied through her daughter that they would be always glad to have them in the room.

"You will really be a great amusement to us. We were very dull before, and instead of being a trouble, as Count Smerskoff no doubt intended when he quartered you upon us, you will make a very pleasant break. It is dreadfully dull here now," she said. "There is no longer any gayety, many of our neighbors are away, and nobody talks of anything but that horrid war. Count Smerskoff is almost the only person we see, and," and she shrugged her pretty shoulders, "he's worse than nothing. And now, mamma says, would you like to ride or to go out in a sledge? If you would like some shooting, there is plenty in the neighborhood. But of course for that you will want a whole day, and it must be arranged beforehand. I wish my brother Orloff had been at home. He could have looked after you nicely."

Delighted at the prospect, the boys said that they should like a drive, and a few minutes later, descending to the courtyard, they found a sledge with three horses at the door.

"What a stunning turn-out!" Jack exclaimed, delighted. "We shall fancy we are princes, Dick, and get spoiled altogether for a midshipman's berth."

The sledge was of graceful form, painted deep blue. The seats were covered with furs, while an apron of silver fox-skin was wrapped round their legs. The driver sat perched up on a high seat in front. He was a tall, stately figure, with an immense beard. On his head was the cap of black sheep-skin, which may be considered the national head-dress. He wore a long fur-lined coat of dark blue, fitting somewhat tightly, and reaching to his ankles. It was bound by a scarlet sash round his waist. It had a great fur collar and cuffs. His feet were encased in untanned leather boots, reaching above the knees.

The horses were harnessed in a manner quite different to anything the lads had before seen. They were three abreast; the middle one was in shafts, those on either side ran free in traces, and by dint, as the boys supposed, of long training, each carried his head curved round outwards, so that he seemed to be looking half-backwards, giving them a most peculiar effect, exactly similar to that which may be seen in ancient Greek bas-reliefs, and sculptures of horses in ancient chariots. This mode of harnessing and training the horses is peculiarly Russian, and is rigidly adhered to by all the old Russian families. Over each horse was a blue netting reaching almost to the ground, its object being to prevent snow or dirt being thrown up in the faces of those sitting in the low sledge.

Cracking his whip with a report as loud as that of a pistol, the driver set the horses in motion, and in a minute the sledge was darting across the plain at a tremendous pace; the centre horse trotting, the flankers going at a canter, each keeping the leg next to the horse in the shafts in front. The light snow rose in a cloud from the runners as the sledge darted along, and as the wind blew keenly in their faces, and their spirits rose, the boys declared to each other that sledging was the most glorious fun they had ever had.

They had been furnished with fur-lined coats, whose turned-up collars reached far above their ears, and both felt as warm as toast, in spite of the fact that the thermometer was down at zero.

The country here differed in its appearance from that over which they had been travelling, and great forests extended to within two or three miles of the town.

G. A. Henty

"I suppose," Dick said, "that's where the shooting is, for I can't fancy any birds being fools enough to stop out on these plains, and if they did, there would be no chance of getting a shot at them. How pretty those sledge-bells are, to be sure! I wonder they don't have them in England."

"I've seen wagons down in the country with them," Jack said, "and very pretty the bells sounded on a still night. But the bells were not so clear-toned as these."

From one shaft to another, in a bow, high over the horses' necks, extended an arch of light wood, and from this hung a score of little bells, which tinkled merrily as the sledge glided along.

"It's a delicious motion," Jack said; "no bumping or jolting, and yet, even when one shuts one's eyes, he feels that he is going at a tremendous pace."

The boys were amused at the driver, who frequently cracked his whip, but never touched the horses, to whom, however, he was constantly talking, addressing them in encouraging tones, which, as Jack said, they seemed to understand just like Christians.

After an hour-and-a-half's drive, in which they must have traversed some eighteen miles, they returned to the chateau. The servant at the door relieved them of their warm cloaks and of the loose, fur-lined boots, with which they had also been furnished, and then, evidently in accordance with orders, conducted them upstairs to the room where the countess and two of her daughters were working, while the third was reading aloud. It was already getting dusk, and lighted lamps burned on the tables, and the room, heated by a great stove in the corner, felt pleasantly warm and comfortable.

Chapter XIII
A NOMINAL IMPRISONMENT

THE evening passed pleasantly. There was some music, and the three girls and their mother sang together, and Jack (who had learnt part-singing at home, for his family were very musical, and every night were accustomed to sing glees and catches) also, at their request, joined in, taking the part which their brother, when at home, had been accustomed to fill.

In the course of the evening the boys explained that they had said nothing to the commandant about their having picked up a little Russian, as they had thought that it was better to allow him to remain in ignorance of it, as they had had some idea of making their escape.

"Why, you foolish boys," Paulina said, "where would you escape to? However, perhaps it is as well that you said nothing about it, for he only sent you here because he thought it would annoy mamma; and if he had thought you had known any Russian, he might have lodged you somewhere else."

"We don't want to escape now, you know," Jack said in his broken Russian. "We are much more comfortable here than we should be in the cold before Sebastopol."

The next few days passed pleasantly; sometimes the countess was not present, and then the girls would devote themselves to improving the boys' Russian.

Sometimes two sledges would come to the door, and two of the girls accompanied the boys on their drive. On the fourth evening, Count Smerskoff called, and a cloud fell upon the atmosphere.

The countess received him ceremoniously, and maintained the conversation in frigid tones. The girls scarcely opened their lips, and the midshipmen sat apart, as silent as if they understood no word of what was passing.

"I am sorry, countess," the commandant said, "that I was obliged to quarter these two English boys upon you, but every house in the town is full of sick and wounded; and as they were given over to me as officers, though they look to me more like ship-boys, I could not put them in prison with the twenty or thirty soldiers whom we captured at the victory on the heights above Inkerman."

"It is my duty to receive them," the countess said very coldly, "and it therefore matters little whether it is pleasant or otherwise. Fortunately one of them speaks a few words of French, and my daughters can therefore communicate with them. So you have twenty or thirty English prisoners in the jail? Where are all the rest; for, of course, in such a great victory, we must have taken, some thousands of prisoners?"

The count glanced angrily at her.

"They have, no doubt, been sent to Odessa and other places," he said. "You do not doubt, countess, surely, that a great victory was gained by the soldiers of his Majesty?"

"Doubt," the countess said, in a tone of slight surprise. "Have I not read the official bulletins describing the victory? Only we poor women, of course, are altogether ignorant of war, and cannot understand how it is that, when they are always beaten, these enemies of the Czar are still in front of Sebastopol."

"It may be," said the count, "that the Archdukes are only waiting until all the reinforcements arrive to drive them into the sea, or capture them to the last man."

"No doubt it is that," said the countess blandly, "but from the number of sick and wounded who arrive here, to say nothing of those taken to Odessa and the other towns among which, as you say, the prisoners are distributed, it is to be wished that the reinforcements may soon be up, so as to bring the fighting to an end."

"The enemy are suffering much more than we are," the governor said, "and before the spring comes we may find that there are none left to conquer. If the soldiers of the Czar, accustomed to the climate as they are, feel the cold, although they have warm barracks to sleep in, what must be the case with the enemy on the bleak heights? I hear that the English newspapers are full of accounts of the terrible sufferings of their troops. They are dying like sheep."

"Poor creatures!" the countess said gravely. "They are our fellow-beings, you know, Count Smerskoff, although they are our enemies, and one cannot but feel some pity for them."

"I feel no pity for the dogs," the count said fiercely. "How dare they set foot on the soil of Holy Russia?"

"Hating them as you do," the countess said, "it must be annoying for you indeed, count, to occupy even so exalted a position as that of governor of this town, instead of fighting against the English and French."

The count muttered something between his teeth, which was certainly not a blessing. Then turning to Katinka, he changed the subject by asking her if she would favor him with some music.

Without a word, the girl seated herself at the piano and played. When she had finished the piece, she began another without stopping, and continued steadily for an hour. The countess leaned back in her chair, as if she considered that conversation would be out of place while her daughter was playing.

Count Smerskoff sat quietly for a quarter of an hour. Then he began to fidget in his chair, but he stoically sat on until, when at the end of an hour Katinka showed no signs whatever of leaving off, he rose, and ceremoniously regretting that his duties prevented him from having the pleasure of hearing the conclusion of the charming little piece which the young countess was playing (for in Russia all children bear the title of their parents) he took his leave.

When the door had closed behind him, and the sound of his footsteps along the corridor ceased, the girls burst into a fit of laughter, in which the midshipmen joined heartily.

"Well done, Katinka!" Olga said, clapping her hands. "That was a splendid idea of yours, and you have routed the governor completely. Oh, dear, how cross he did look, and how he fidgeted about as you played on and on without stopping! I thought I must have laughed out-right."

"It was a clever thought," the countess said, "and yet the count cannot complain of want of courtesy. He is a disagreeable man, and a bad man; but he is powerfully connected, and it will not do to offend him. We have enemies enough, heaven knows."

Jack Archer

The boys at the time could not gather the drift of the conversation; but a month later, when their knowledge of the language had greatly increased, Olga, when driving in a sledge with Jack, enlightened him as to the position in which they stood.

"Papa," she said, "is a Liberal, that is to say, he wants all sorts of reform to be carried out. If he had his way, he would free the serfs and would have the affairs of the nation managed by a parliament, as you do in England, instead of by the will of the Czar only. I don't pretend to know anything about it myself, but papa has perhaps expressed his opinions too openly, and some enemy has carried them to the ears of the Czar. Nicholas is, you know, though it is treason to say so, very autocratic and absolute. Papa was never in favor, because mamma was a Pole, but these terrible opinions finished it. Papa was forbidden to appear at court, and ordered to live upon his estates, and it is even possible," she said anxiously, "that this will not be all. You don't know Russia, or how dreadful it is to be looked upon as disaffected here. Papa is so good and kind! His serfs all love him so much, and every one says that no estates in Russia are better managed. But all this will avail nothing, and it is only because we have powerful friends at court that worse things have not happened."

"Unless you are very fond of gayety and society," Jack said, "I don't think it can matter much being sent away from St. Petersburg, when you have such a nice place here."

"Oh, no," the girl said. "It would not matter at all, only, you see, when any one gets into disgrace there is no saying what may happen. An enemy misrepresents some speech, some evil report gets to the ears of the Czar, and the next day papa might be on his way to Siberia," she dropped her voice as she uttered the dreadful word, "and all his estates confiscated."

"What?" said Jack indignantly, "without any trial, or anything? I never heard such a shame."

The girl nodded.

"It is dreadful," she said, "and now, to make matters worse, that odious Count Smerkoff wants to marry Katinka. She will be rich, as she will inherit large estates in Poland. Of course, papa and mamma won't consent, and Katinka hates him, but, you see, he has got lots of powerful relations at court. If it hadn't been for that, I hear that he would have been dismissed from the army long since; and, worst of all, he is governor here, and can send to headquarters any lying report he likes, and do papa dreadful harm."

Jack did not understand anything like all that Olga said, but he gleaned enough to understand the drift of her conversation, and he and Dick chatted over the matter very seriously that night.

Both agreed that something ought to be done. What that something was to be, neither could offer the remotest suggestion. They were so happy in the family now, were so kindly treated by the countess and her daughters, that they felt their troubles to be their own, and they would have done anything which could benefit them.

"We must think it over, Jack," Dick said, as he turned into bed. "It's awful to think of all these nice people being at the mercy of a brute like that. The idea of his wanting to marry the pretty Katinka! Why, he's not good enough to black her boots. I wish we had him in the midshipmen's berth on board the 'Falcon'; we would teach him a thing or two."

G. A. Henty

The lads had not availed themselves of the offer of riding-horses, as they were neither of them accustomed to the exercise, and did not like the thought of looking ridiculous. But they had eagerly accepted the offer to have some wolf-shooting.

One night, everything having been prepared, they took their seats in a sledge drawn by two of the fastest horses in the stables of the countess. A whole battery of guns was placed in the seat with them. The sledge was larger than that which they were accustomed to use, and held four, besides the driver. Two woodmen—experienced hunters—took their places on the seat facing the midshipmen. A portion of the carcase of a horse, which had broken its leg and been shot the previous day, was fastened behind the sledge.

A drive of an hour took them far into the heart of the forest, although the coachman drove much slower than usual, in order that the horses might be perfectly fresh when required. Presently the woodmen told the driver that they had gone far enough, and the sledge was turned, the horses facing homeward. The great lump of meat was then unfastened from behind the sledge, and a rope some forty yards long attached to it, the other end being fastened to the sledge. The horses were next moved forward until the rope was tight.

They were then stopped, rugs were laid across their backs to keep them warm, and the party awaited the result.

The young moon was shining in the sky, and dark objects showed clearly over the white snow for a considerable distance. Half an hour passed without a word being spoken, and without a sound breaking the silence that reigned in the forest. Presently a low whimpering was heard, and the boys fancied that they could see dark forms moving among the trees. The horses became restless and excited, and it was as much as the man standing at their heads could do to quiet them.

The coachman sat looking back, whip in hand, ready for an instant start.

All at once a number of dark objects leaped from among the trees on to the broad line of snow which marked the road.

"Jump in, Ivan!" the coachman exclaimed. "Here they come. Keep a sharp look-out on both sides. We can leave those fellows behind standing still. The only danger is from a fresh pack coming from ahead."

The peasant leaped into the car, and in an instant the horses dashed off at a speed which would have taken them far away from the wolves had not their driver reined them in and quieted them with his voice.

They soon steadied down into a long sweeping gallop, the coachman at times looking back and regulating their speed so as to keep the bait gliding along just ahead of the wolves.

The peasant now gave the signal to the midshipmen, who with their guns cocked were standing up with one knee on the seat to steady themselves, ready to fire, and the two barrels at once rang out.

One of the leading wolves, who was but a few yards from the bait, dropped and rolled over, while a sharp whimpering cry told that another was wounded.

The boys had an idea that the wolves would stop to devour their fallen comrade, but the smell of the meat was, it appeared, more tempting, for without a pause they still came on. Again and again the lads fired, the woodmen handing them spare guns and loading as fast as they discharged them.

Jack Archer

Suddenly the driver gave an exclamation, and far ahead on the white road, the boys, looking round, could see a dark mass. The peasant, with a stroke of his knife, cut the rope which held the bait.

The coachman drove forward with increased speed for fifty yards or so, and then suddenly drew up the horses. The peasants in an instant leaped out, each with a rug in his hand, and running to the horses' heads, at once blindfolded the animals by wrapping these around them. Then the men jumped into the sledge again.

A hundred and fifty yards behind, their late pursuers, in a mass, were growling, snarling, and fighting over the meat, but already many, finding themselves unable to obtain a share, had set off in pursuit of the prize ahead, which promised to be ample for all.

To these, however, the peasants paid no attention, but each taking a double-barrel gun, poured heavy charges of shot in above the bullets. Handing them to the boys, they performed the same operation to the other two guns, which they intended this time to use themselves.

Standing on the seat, the men prepared to fire at the wolves directly ahead, signing to the boys to lean over, one on each side, and take those on the flanks of the horses. All this was done in a very few seconds, as the sledge glided steadily along towards the fast-approaching foes. When these came within fifty yards, the horses were sent forward at full gallop. In another second or two the four barrels of the woodmen poured their contents into the mass of wolves. The boys waited until the horses were fairly among them, and then they fired.

A hideous chorus of yells arose, and the horses at full speed dashed in upon the pack. Already a lane had been prepared for them, and, trampling over dead and dying, they rushed through. In spite of the execution done by the heavy charges of the midshipmen's double-barrel guns, several wolves tried to spring into the sledge as it went past, and one of them succeeded in leaping upon one of the horses. The animal made a wild plunge, but in an instant one of the woodmen sprang to the ground, and buried his long knife in the beast; then, as the sledge swept on again, he caught at the side and clambered into the car before the wolves, who had already turned in pursuit, could come up to him.

The guns were quickly loaded again, and another volley poured into the wolves. Then the coachman, knowing that one of the horses was hurt, and both nearly mad with fright, let them have their heads, and the sledge darted away at a pace which soon left the wolves far in the rear. So rapid was the motion indeed, that the boys held on to the sides, expecting every moment that the sledge would be dashed against the trees which lined the road. The coachman, however, kept the horses straight, and, quieting them down, again brought them to a standstill, when the cloths were taken off their heads, and the journey to the chateau completed at a steady pace.

"That's sharp work," Jack said, when the wolves had been fairly left in the rear. "They call that wolf-hunting. I call it being hunted by wolves. These are fine fellows; they were as cool as cucumbers."

"I've nearly broken my shoulder," Dick grumbled, "The gun with those tremendous charges kicked like a horse. Well, it's fine fun anyhow, but its rather too risky to be often repeated. If two or three of those fellows had got hold of the horses' heads, they would all have been upon us, and very short work they would have made of us if they had."

G. A. Henty

"Ugh!" Jack said with a shudder. "What teeth they have! and what mouths! It seemed like a sort of nightmare for a moment with those great open mouths and shining teeth, as they leaped towards us, as we rushed past. I hope I shan't dream about them."

"No fear of that," Dick said laughing. "The countess said that some supper should be ready for us when we got back. I feel tremendously peckish. After the night air, and plenty of hot tea and a good tuck-in, we shall sleep without dreaming, I can venture to say."

The countess and her daughters had gone to bed long before the return of the sportsmen. At breakfast next morning the boys attempted to relate their adventures, but their vocabulary being wholly insufficient, the coachman was sent for, and requested to give a full account of the proceedings. This he did, and added on his own account that the little lords had been as cool and collected as if they had been wolf-hunting all their lives.

After breakfast, the letter-bag arrived, and the countess, having opened her correspondence, said that her husband would return the next day. Great as was the pleasure of the ladies, the boys hardly felt enthusiastic over the news; they were so jolly as they were, that they feared any change would be for the worse.

Next day the count arrived, and the boys soon felt that they had no cause for apprehension. He greeted them with much cordiality, and told them that he had heard from the countess that he had to thank them for having made the time of his absence pass so cheerfully, and that she had said she did not know how they would have got through the dull time without them. The boys, after the manner of their kind, were bad hands at compliment; but they managed to express in their best Russian their thanks for the extreme kindness which they had received.

The days went on after the count's arrival much as they had done before, except that the boys now took to horse exercise, accompanying their host as he rode round his estate, and visited the various villages upon it.

The houses in these villages astonished the boys. Built of mud, of one story only and flat-roofed, they each occupied a large extent of ground; for here whole families lived together. As the sons grew up and married, instead of going into separate houses, and setting up life on their own account, they brought their wives home, as did their children when their turn came also to marry, so that under one roof resided as many as four generations, counting some forty or fifty souls altogether.

Each village had its headman, who settled all disputes, but against whose decision, if it failed to give satisfaction, there was an appeal to the master. The serfs worked, the count told the boys, without pay, but they had so many days in each month when they cultivated the land which was common to the village. They could, the count said, be sold, but in point of fact never were sold except with the land.

"It's a bad system, and I wish that they were as free is your laborers are in England."

"Of course our people cannot be sold," Jack said, "but after all there's not so much difference in that respect, for if an estate changes hands, they work for the new owner just as yours do."

"Yes, but your laborers cannot be killed or even flogged by their masters with impunity."

"No, I should think not," Jack exclaimed. "We should have a revolution in no time, if masters were to try that sort of thing."

"I fear that we shall have one too, some day," the count said, "unless the serfs are emancipated. The people are terribly ignorant, but even among them some sort of enlightenment is going on, and as they know better they will refuse to live and to work as mere beasts of burden."

"Will they be better off, sir, than before?" Dick Hawtry asked. "I have heard my father say that the negroes in the West Indian islands are worse off than they were in the days when they were slaves. They will not work except just enough to procure themselves means of living, and they spend the rest of their lives lying about and smoking."

"It would no doubt be the same thing here," the count said, "for a time. The Russian peasant is naturally extremely ignorant and extremely fond of 'vodka.' Probably at first he would be far worse off than at present. He would be content to earn enough to live and to get drunk upon, and wide tracts of land would remain untilled. But it is of the future we must think; and who can doubt that in the future, Russia, with a free people and free institutions, with her immense resources and enormous population, must become the grandest empire on earth?"

Chapter XIV
A SUSPECTED HOUSEHOLD

CHEERFUL though their hosts were, the midshipmen could see that a cloud of anxiety hung over them. To be "suspected" in Russia is equivalent to being condemned. Secret police spies in the very bosom of the household may be sending denunciations. The man who meets you and shakes hands with you in the street may have reported on your conduct. The letters you write are opened, those you should receive stopped in the post. At any moment the agent of the authorities may appear and conduct you to a prison which you may leave only for the long journey to Siberia.

Count Preskoff did not think that matters had yet reached this point. He was in disgrace at court, and had enemies who would injure him to the utmost with the emperor, but he believed that no steps would be taken until Count Smerskoff had received his final refusal of Katinka's hand. He had already once proposed for it, but would not consider the answer which her father then gave him as final.

"I cannot accept your refusal, count," he had said. "The marriage would be for the advantage of all parties concerned. My family is, as you are aware, not without influence at court, and they would, were I the husband of your daughter, do all in their power to incline the emperor favorably towards you; while, were I rejected, they would probably view your refusal to accept my offers as a slight to the family, and resent it accordingly. I cannot but think that when you have given the matter calm consideration, you will see the advantages which such an alliance would offer. I shall therefore do myself the honor to renew my proposals at some future date."

This conversation took place in the beginning of December; Count Preskoff had shortly afterwards left for his estates in the north, and he felt sure that upon his return the subject would be renewed, and that upon his announcement of his continued determination to refuse his daughter's hand to this pressing suitor, the latter would use every means in his power to ruin him, and that the cloud which had so long threatened would burst over his head.

From Olga, who, being about his own age, a little under sixteen, was his special chum in the family, Jack gathered a general idea of the situation. Olga was an adept at pantomimic action, and a natural mimic; hence, although he could only understand a word here and there, he obtained an accurate idea of the conversation between her father and the governor, and of her father's calm manner, and the gestures and intonations of apparent friendship but veiled menace. By putting her ears to a keyhole and hiding behind a curtain, she expressed the possibility of there being a spy in the very houschold, who would listen to the unguarded talk of her father and report it to the governor. Jack determined that he would watch every movement of the domestics, and especially observe if he could detect any sign of an understanding between one of them and the governor.

It was some four or five days after the count had returned that Count Smerskoff rode up to the door. Orders had already been given that if he arrived he should be shown to the count's private study. The midshipmen saw him riding up, and, according to the plan they had agreed upon, one stood near the entrance to observe whether any sign of recognition passed between him and any of the servants gathered upon the steps to receive him, the other took his place in the hall. The interview was not a long one.

"I am come, Count Preskoff," the governor said, "to renew my request for the hand of your daughter. I trust that upon consideration you will have thought it better to overlook the objections you preferred to my suit."

"Upon the contrary," the count said calmly, "I have thought the matter over in every light, and am more convinced even than before that such a marriage would not conduce to the happiness of my daughter. She herself is wholly repugnant to it, and even were it otherwise, I should myself most strongly object."

"On what grounds, count?" the officer said angrily. "Noble as your family is, my own is fully equal to it."

"That I am perfectly willing to allow, sir, and will frankly own that my objection is a purely personal one. The incidents of your past career are notorious. You have killed two men in duels, which, in both cases, you forced upon them. You have been involved in gambling transactions of such a description that it needed all the influence of your family to save you from public disgrace. To such a man it is impossible that I could intrust my daughter."

Count Smerskoff rose to his feet, bursting with passion.

"Since you know my reputation, count, it would have been wiser to abstain from insulting me. You shall hear from me before night."

"It is useless your sending your second to me," the count said calmly, "for I absolutely refuse to meet you. I shall publish my refusal, and state that the grounds upon which I base it are that you are a notorious ruffian; but that if you can find any man of honor to take up your quarrel, I shall be prepared to meet him."

"I will force you to it," the soldier said, burning with passion. "I will publicly insult you. I will strike you," and he drew a step nearer.

"You will do so at your peril," the count said, drawing a pistol from his pocket. "I know your method, sir, and am prepared for it. If you lay a finger upon me, if you insult me in public, I will shoot you dead where you stand, and take the consequences."

"You shall repent this," Count Smerskoff exclaimed. "There are lives worse than death, and you shall have cause to remember your words of to-day," and turning round he strode from the room.

Jack was still lounging in the hall as he passed out. One of the servants had also remained there, and when the governor was seen striding down the staircase, the man hastened to open the door. Jack saw the officer pause for a moment, "At eight to-night at the cross roads," he said, and passed out, and flinging himself upon his horse, rode off. Among the Russian words learned by the midshipmen were all words connected with roads. They had been specially desirous of asking questions which might enable them to find their way across country, and every word which would be likely to be included in a direction as to route had been learned. This was the more easy, as on their march there had been but few objects of interest to attract their attention. The expressions therefore "the road to the right," "the road to the left," "the turning by the wood or stream," "the cross roads," and other similar expressions had been learned by heart. Jack's quick ears, consequently, gathered the purport of the brief order.

"I have found the spy," he said triumphantly, when he joined his comrade outside. "Come for a stroll, Dick. I don't want to be seen talking here."

When well away from the house, Jack repeated the words he had overheard, and they determined that they would be present at the interview between the governor and his spy. They had a long discussion whether it would be better to invite the count himself to be present; but they agreed at last that it would be better not to do so, as he might break in upon the interview, and possibly only bring matters to a climax at once, which they agreed had better be avoided, as even if the men fought then and there, the fact of the governor being killed by the count would only precipitate the danger which already threatened. Still they agreed that it was absolutely necessary that the conversation should be thoroughly understood, and the few words which they would glean here and there might be insufficient to put them in possession of the full details of the plot.

They therefore resolved to take the coachman into their confidence. They knew that he was warmly attached to the count, and that he could be relied upon in an emergency. As they had full permission to take the horses or carriage whenever they pleased, they now went to the stable and told the coachman that they should like to go for a drive in the sledge, as the weather showed signs of breaking, and the snow would probably shortly disappear.

The horses were at once put to, and, in a few minutes they were whirling over the snow. They directed the coachman to drive into the forest where they had had the encounter with the wolves, and when well in its shelter they stopped the sledge and alighted, and requested the coachman to do the same. Much surprised, the unrolled the sheepskin wrappings from his legs and got down from his seat.

"Alexis, you love the count, your master, do you not?"

"Yes, young lord," the Russian said earnestly, though much surprised at the question. "His fathers have been the masters of mine for many generations. My good lord is always kind and considerate to his serfs. I drove his father before him. I drove him when he was a boy. He has never said a harsh word to me. I would give my life for him willingly. Why do the young lords ask?"

"Your master has enemies, Alexis. There are many who think that he is too kind to his serfs. They have poisoned the ear of the Czar against him. They have told him that your master is a dangerous man. They have turned the face of the Czar from him."

The Russian nodded. It was no secret that the count was banished from the capital.

"The chief of his enemies," Jack went on, "is the governor, Count Smerskoff. He wishes to marry the Countess Katinka, and because the count refuses he will try to injure him and to obtain his exile to Siberia."

"I will kill him," the coachman said. "I will slay him in the middle of his soldiers. They may kill me, but what of that, it is for my master."

"No, Alexis, not now," Jack said, laying his hand upon the arm of the angry Russian. "Perhaps later, but we will see. But I have found out that Paul, the hall servant, is acting as his spy. I heard the governor order him to meet him at the cross roads at eight o'clock to-night. I suppose he means where the road crosses that to town, about half-way along. We mean to be there, but you know we don't understand Russian well enough to hear all that is said. We want you to be there with us, too, to hear what they mean to do."

"I will be there," the Russian said; "and if the young lords think it well, I will kill them both."

"No, Alexis," Jack said; "that would never do. It might get about that the governor had been killed by order of the count, and this would do more harm than if he were alive. Will you be in the stables at seven o'clock? We will join you there. There are plenty of bushes at the cross-roads, and we shall be able to hide there without difficulty."

The coachman assented, and taking their seats, they again drove on. It must not be supposed that the conversation was conducted as simply and easily as has been narrated, for it needed all the efforts of the boys to make the Russian understand them, and they had to go over and over again many of the sentences, using their scanty vocabulary in every way, to convey their meaning to their hearer. The rest of the afternoon passed slowly. The count himself was tranquil and even cheerful, although his face wore an air of stern determination. The countess looked anxious and careworn. The eyes of the three girls were swollen with crying, and the lads afterwards learned that Katinka had gone down on her knees to her father, to implore him to allow her to sacrifice herself for the common good by marrying Count Smerskoff. This, however, the count had absolutely refused to do, and had even insisted upon her promising him that, should he be exiled and his estates confiscated, she would not afterwards purchase his release by consenting to marry her suitor. Respecting the grief and anxiety into which the family were plunged, the midshipmen kept apart from them all the afternoon, only joining them at the evening meal at six o'clock. As they withdrew, saying, in answer to the count's invitation that they should stop with them, that they were first going for a little walk, Jack whispered in Olga's ear, "Keep up your courage. All may not be lost yet."

The coachman was waiting for them in the stable, and they started at once in an opposite direction to that at which the meeting was to take place, in case Paul might by any possibility observe their departure. Taking a long *dètour*, they reached the cross-roads, and lay down under cover of the brushwood. It was nearly half an hour later before they heard footsteps approaching along the road from the chateau. On reaching the junction of the roads, the man stopped, and from their place of concealment they could dimly see his figure.

The boys had taken the precaution of abstracting a brace of pistols and two swords from the count's armory. The coachman they knew would have his knife. This they had done at Jack's suggestion that it was possible that their presence might be betrayed by a cough or other accidental noise, in which case they knew they would have to fight for their lives. A few minutes later they heard the tramp of a horse's hoof. It approached quickly, and the rider halted by the standing figure.

"Is that you, Paul?"

"It is, my lord," the serf said, bowing.

"You are alone?"

"No one had approached the place since I came here a quarter of an hour ago."

"It is time for action," the horseman said. "To-morrow you will come boldly at twelve o'clock to my house, and demand to see me on important business. You will be shown to my room, where two officers who I wish to have as witnesses will be present. You will then state to me that you wish to make a denunciation of your master, Count Preskoff. I shall ask what you have to say, and tell you that you are of course aware of the serious consequences to yourself should such statements be proved untrue. You will say that you are aware of that, but that you are compelled by your love for the Czar, our father, to speak. You will then say that you have heard the count using insulting words of the Czar, in speaking of him to his wife, on many occasions, and that since his return, on one occasion, you put your ear to the keyhole and heard him telling her of a great plot for a general rising of the serfs, and an overthrow of the government; that he said he had prepared the serfs of his estates in the north for the rising; that those of his estates here would all follow him; that many other nobles had joined in the plot, and that on a day which had not yet been agreed upon a rising would take place in twenty places simultaneously; and that the revolt once begun he was sure that the serfs, weary of the war and its heavy impositions, would everywhere join the movement. I shall cross-question you closely, but you will stick to your story. Make it as simple and straightforward as you can; say you cannot answer for the exact words, but that you will answer that this was the general sense of the conversation you overheard. Now, are you sure you thoroughly understand?"

"I quite understand, my lord," the man said humbly, "and for this your Excellency has promised me?"

"Five hundred roubles and your freedom."

"But when am I to be paid?" the man said doubtfully.

"Do you doubt my word, slave?" the horseman said angrily.

"By no means, your Excellency. But things might happen, and after I had told my story and it had been taken down before witnesses, your Excellency's memory might fail. I should prefer the money before I told my story."

The horseman was silent a moment.

"You are an insolent dog to doubt me," he said in an angry tone; "but you shall have the money; when you call to-morrow the sergeant of the guard will have instructions to hand you a letter which will contain notes for five hundred roubles."

"I thought," the man said, "your Excellency said gold. Five hundred roubles in notes are not worth two hundred in gold, and you see I shall have much to do to earn the money, for I may be sent to St. Petersburg and cross-questioned. I may even be confronted with my master; and after it is over and I am freed, I must, in any case, leave this part of the country, for my life will not be safe for a day here."

"Very well," the count said, "you shall have a thousand roubles in paper; but beware! if you fail me or break down in cross-examination, you shall end your life in the mines of Siberia."

So saying, without another word he turned and rode back, while the serf strode off towards the chateau. During this conversation, which the boys imperfectly understood, they had difficulty in restraining the count's faithful retainer, who, furious at hearing the details of the plot against his master, would have leaped up to attack the speakers, had not the boys kept their restraining hands on his shoulder, and whispered in his ear, "Be quiet, for the count's sake."

Jack Archer

Waiting long enough to be sure that the two men had passed not only out of sight but of the sound of their voices, the lads suffered their companion to rise, and to indulge his feelings in an explosion of deep oaths. Then, when he was a little calm, they obtained from him a repetition of the leading facts of the conversation.

The boys consulted among themselves, and agreed that it was necessary to acquaint the count with all the facts that they had discovered, and to leave him to act as seemed best according to his judgment.

They entered the house alone, telling the coachman to call in half an hour, and to say that the count had given orders that he was to see him to take instructions for the horses in the morning. Then they joined the family in the drawing-room. There all proceeded as usual.

Katinka, at her father's request, played on the piano, and a stranger would not have dreamed of the danger which menaced the household. When the half-hour had nearly expired, Jack said to the count,—

"I have told Alexis to call upon you for orders for to-morrow. Would you mind receiving him in your study? I have a very particular reason for asking it."

"But I have no orders to give Alexis," the count said, surprised.

"No, sir, but he has something he particularly wishes to say to you—something really important."

"Very well," the court replied, smiling; "you seem to be very mysterious, but of course I will do as you wish. Is he coming soon?"

"In two or three minutes, sir, I expect him."

"Then," the count remarked, "I suppose I had better go at once, and learn what all this mystery is about. He isn't coming, I hope, to break to me the news that one of my favorite horses is dead." So saying, with a smile, he left the room. No sooner had he gone than the girls overwhelmed the midshipmen with questions, but they told them that they must not be inquisitive, that their father would, no doubt, tell them the secret in due time.

"If you will allow me, countess," Dick said, "I will leave this door a little open, so that we may hear when Alexis goes in." The door was placed ajar, and a few minutes later the footsteps of two men were heard coming along the corridor. Paul opened the door. "Is his Excellency here?" he asked. "Alexis wishes to see him."

"He is in his study," the countess answered.

The study door was heard to close, and when the sound of Paul's feet returning along the corridor ceased Dick said, "You will excuse us, countess, we are going to join the conference."

"It is too bad," Katinka exclaimed, "to keep us in the dark in this way. Mind, if the secret is not something very important and delightful, you will be in disgrace, and we shall banish you from this room altogether."

The lads made a laughing reply, and then, promising they would soon be back, they went to the study. Alexis was standing silent before his master, having explained that he would rather not speak until the young English lords appeared. Jack began the narrative, and said that fearing Count Smerskoff, whom they knew to be his enemy, might have suborned one of the servants to act as his spy they had watched him closely, and had heard him make an appointment with Paul to meet him that evening at the cross-roads; that they had taken Alexis into their confidence, and had with him been concealed spectators of the interview; that they themselves had been able to gather only the general drift of the conversation, but that Alexis would give him a full report of it.

The count's face had at first expressed only surprise at Jack's narration, but the expression changed into one of fierce anger as he proceeded. Without a word he motioned to Alexis to continue, and the latter detailed word for word the conversation which he had overheard. When he had concluded, he added, "Your Excellency must pardon me for not having killed your enemies upon the spot, but the young English lords had told me that it was necessary to lie quiet, whatever I heard, and besides, the governor might have ridden off before I could reach him."

The count stood for a minute silent when the narration ceased. "You did well, Alexis," he said in a stern voice. "It is for me to judge and sentence. I had thought that I, at least, was safe from treachery among those around me. It seems I was wrong, and the traitor shall learn that the kind master can be the severe lord, who holds the life and death of his serfs in his hand." He was silent, and remained two or three minutes in deep thought. "Go to the stable, Alexis. You will be joined there soon by Ivan and Alexander. They will have their instructions. After that Paul will come out; seize him and bind him when he enters the stable. Now go. You have done well. Tell Paul, as you go out, that I wish to see the steward."

A minute or two later the steward, a white-headed old man, who had from childhood been in the service of the family, entered. "Demetri," he said, "will you tell Ivan and Alexander to go out into the stable? They will find Alexis waiting for them. Order them, when Paul joins them there, to aid Alexis in seizing him instantly. Give them your instructions quietly, and without attracting notice. Above all do not let Paul see you speaking to them. When you have seen them out, find Paul, and order him to go to the stable and tell Alexis that I wish to speak to him; when he has gone, join me here."

Chapter XV
A STRUGGLE FOR LIFE

COUNT PRESKOFF'S old steward received his orders with scarce a look of surprise, singular though they must have seemed to him. A Russian is accustomed to unquestioning obedience to the orders of his superior, and although never before had Count Preskoff issued such strange and unaccountable commands to the steward, the thought never occurred to the latter of questioning them for a moment.

When he had left the room, the Count turned to the midshipmen, and his brow relaxed. "I cannot tell you," he said, "under what obligation you have placed me and my family. Little did we think that any little kindness we might show to you, strangers and prisoners here, would be returned by a service of a hundredfold greater value. The danger which hangs over us may for the time be averted by your discovery. I know my enemy too well to suppose that it is more than postponed, but every delay is so much gained. I have news to-day that the Czar is alarmingly ill. Should Heaven take him, it would be the dawn of a better era for Russia. His son is a man of very different mould. He has fallen into disgrace with his father for his liberal ideas, and he is known to think, as I do, that serfdom is the curse of the empire."

"But surely," Dick Hawtry said, "if we draw out a document signed by us and Alexis, saying that we overheard the plot to obtain false evidence against you, the emperor would not believe other false accusations which your enemies might invent?"

"You little know Russia," the count said. "I believe that Nicholas, tyrannical and absolute as he is, yet wishes to be just, and that were such a document placed in his hands, it would open his eyes to the truth. But my enemies would take care that it never reached him. They are so powerful that few would dare to brave their hostility by presenting it. Nor, indeed, surrounded as Nicholas is by creatures whose great object is to prevent him from learning the true wishes of his people, would it be easy to obtain an opportunity for laying such a document before him. Even were the attempt made, and that successfully, such doubts would be thrown upon it, that he might well be deceived. It would be said that the evidence of Alexis, a serf devoted to his master, was valueless, and that you, as strangers, very imperfectly acquainted with the language, might well have misunderstood the conversation. Count Smerskoff would swear that he was only repeating statements which Paul had previously made to him, and that he only promised money because Paul insisted that, as a first condition of his informing against me, he should receive funds to enable him to leave this part of the country, where his life would assuredly be unsafe. I will thankfully take such a document from you, my friends, for it may be useful, but I must not trust too much to it. Now come with me," he continued, as the steward reappeared. "You have seen how a Russian noble can be kind to his serfs; you will now see how he punishes traitors."

Followed by the steward and the two midshipmen, the count proceeded to the stables. Here, by the light of the lantern, they saw Paul standing, bound

G. A. Henty

against the manger. His features were ghastly pale and contracted with fear. His conscience told him that his treachery had been discovered. Alexis and the two servants were standing by, in the attitude of stolid indifference habitual to the Russian peasant.

"Demetri, you, Ivan, and Alexander will be the court to try this man whom I accuse of being a traitor, who has plotted against my life and liberty, who would have sent me to the gallows or Siberia, and seen my wife and children turned beggared and disgraced on the world. You will form the court, and decide whether he is innocent or guilty. If the latter, I will pass sentence. Alexis and these English gentlemen are the witnesses against him."

The midshipmen first, and then Alexis related the conversation they had overheard.

"You have heard the evidence," the count said, turning to Demetri. "What is your opinion? is this man innocent or guilty?"

"He is guilty," the old man said, "of the basest treachery towards the best and kindest master in Russia, and he deserves to die."

"And so say we," said the other two together, looking with loathing horror at the prisoner; for in Russia for a serf to conspire against his master was a crime deemed almost equal in atrocity to parricide.

"You hear, Paul," his master said, sternly looking at him; "you have been found guilty, and must die. Alexis, you restrained yourself for my sake from taking the life of this wretch when you heard him plotting against me; you will now act as executioner."

"Right willingly," the man replied, taking down a huge axe which hung by the wall.

The wretched prisoner, who had hitherto maintained an absolute silence, now burst into an agony of cries, prayers for mercy, and curses. Seeing in the unmoved countenances of his judges that nothing would avail, and that Alexis was approaching him; he screamed out a demand for a priest before he died.

"That is reasonable," the count said. "Go into the house, Demetri, and ask Papa Ivanovitch to come hither"—for in the family of every Russian noble a priest resides, as a matter of course.

Presently the priest arrived with the steward.

"Papa Ivanovitch," the count said, "you are, I know, devoted to the family in which your father and grandfather were priests before you. You can, therefore, be trusted with our secret, a secret which will never go beyond those present. You are here to shrive a man about to die."

Then the count related the incidents of the discovery of the treachery of the prisoner, and the priest, who shared with the serfs their veneration and affection for their lord, could scarcely overcome his repugnance and horror of the prisoner so far as to approach and listen to him.

For five minutes all present withdrew from the stable, leaving the priest and the prisoner alone together. Then the door opened and the priest came out.

"It is finished," he said. "May God pardon the sinner!" and he moved away rapidly towards the house.

Alexis spoke a word to his fellow-servants, and these lifted a heavy log from the wood-pile in the courtyard, and carried it into the stable. Then they seized Paul, and in spite of his screams and struggles laid him with his head across the log. Alexis raised the heavy axe in the air; it flashed in the light of the lantern; there was a dull, heavy thud, and the head of the traitor rolled on the ground.

Jack Archer

"Now," the count said, unmoved, "put a horse into a cart, take picks and shovels, and carry the body of this traitor out to the forest and bury it there. Dig a hole deeply, that the wolves may not bring it to light. Demetri will give each of you to-morrow fifty roubles for your share in this night's work, and beware that you never let a syllable concerning it pass your lips, even when you are together and alone. Alexis, on you I bestow your freedom, if you care to have it, and also, as a gift to yourself and your heirs after you, the little farm that was vacant by the death of Nouvakeff last week."

So saying, followed by the two midshipmen who had been awed, but not disapproving spectators of the tragedy, he returned to the house, and led the way back to his study.

"You do not disapprove," he asked gravely, "of what I have done? It is not, I know, in accordance with your English ideas, nor even in Russia may a noble take a serf's life, according to law, though hundreds are killed in fits of hasty passion, or by slow ill-treatment, and no inquiry is ever made. Still, this was a case of life against life. My safety and happiness and that of my dear wife and daughters were concerned, and were the lives of fifty serfs at stake, I should not hesitate."

Although the boys felt that the matter, if brought before an English court of justice, might not be favorably considered, their sympathies were so thoroughly with the count, that they did not hesitate to say that they thought he could not have acted otherwise than he had done, and that the life of the traitor was most justly forfeited.

"I shall now have a respite for a short time," the count said. "Count Smerskoff will of course be perturbed and annoyed at the non-appearance of his spy, and will after a time quietly set inquiries on foot. But I will tell Demetri to give it to be understood that Paul has asked for leave of absence for a few days to go to a distance to visit a friend who is ill. He was always a silent and unsociable fellow, and the others will not wonder at his having started without mentioning his intention to any of them."

"What are we to say to the ladies, sir?" Jack asked. "We must invent some reason for our mysterious absence."

"Yes," the count agreed. "I would not burden them with such a secret as this on any account."

"I have an idea, sir," Jack said after a pause. "You know that beautiful pair of ponies which were brought here yesterday for sale? The ladies were in raptures over them, but you said that the price was preposterous, and that the owner wanted as much for them as you had given for your best pair of carriage horses. Now, sir, if you were to order Alexis to go over at daybreak to the town to purchase them, and have them at the door in a pony-carriage by breakfast-time, this would seem to explain the whole mystery of the coachman's coming to see you, and our private conference."

"It is a capital plan," the count assented; "admirable, and I will carry it out at once. It is true I refused to buy them, for we have all contributed to the extent of our means to enable the emperor to carry on the war, and I am really short of money. But of course the purchase of the ponies is not a matter of importance, one way or the other."

Upon the party returning to the drawing-room, they were assailed with questions; but the count told his daughters that their curiosity must remain unsatisfied until after breakfast on the morrow; and with this assurance they were obliged to be satisfied, although Olga pouted and told Jack that he had entirely forfeited her confidence. Fortunately it was now late, and the lads were not called upon long to maintain an appearance of gayety and ease which they were very far from feeling.

When they retired to their rooms, they had a long talk together. Both agreed that, according to English law, the whole proceeding was unjustifiable; but their final conclusion was that things in Russia were altogether different to what they were in England, and that, above all things, it was a case in which "it served him right."

Nevertheless it was long before they got to sleep, and for weeks the scene in the stable was constantly before their eyes, and the screams and entreaties of the dying man rang in their ears.

The next morning the sight of the ponies delighted the girls, and in their pleasure at the purchase they accepted at once the solution of the mystery, and never thought of questioning whether the long conference between their father and the midshipmen on the preceding evening was fully accounted for by the gift of the ponies.

Five days elapsed, and then one morning a sergeant rode up with an official letter for the count. The latter opened it and read an order from the governor for him to transfer the English prisoners in his charge to the bearer of the letter, who would conduct them to the quarters assigned to them. Most reluctantly the count ascended the stairs and informed the boys of the order which he had received.

"It is simply done to annoy me," he said. "No doubt he has heard that you ride about the estate with me and are treated as members of the family, and he thinks, and rightly, that it will be a serious annoyance to me if you are transferred elsewhere. However, I can do no less than obey the order, and I can only hope that you will spend most of your time here. Alexis shall bring the carriage over every morning for you, wherever you may be quartered."

The girls were as indignant and aggrieved as even the midshipmen could wish to see them, but there was no help for it. A quarter of an hour later a carriage was at the door, a portmanteau well filled with clothes placed behind, and with the sergeant trotting alongside, the boys left the chateau where they had been so hospitably entertained, promising to come over without fail the next morning.

They were conducted to the governor's house, and taken not to the large room where he conducted his public business, and where they had before seen him, but to a smaller room, fitted up as a private study on the second floor. The governor, who looked, Jack thought, even more savage and ill-tempered than usual, was seated at a writing-table. He signed to the sergeant who accompanied them to retire, and pointed to two chairs. "So," he said, "I am told that you are able to converse fairly in Russian, although you have chosen to sit silent whenever I have been present, as if you did not understand a word of what was being said. This is a bad sign, and gives weight to the report which has been brought to me, that you are meditating an escape."

"It is a lie, sir," Dick said firmly, "whoever told it you. As to our learning Russian, we have, as you see, picked up a little of the language, but I'm not aware of any rule or law by which gentlemen, whether prisoners or otherwise, are obliged to converse, unless it pleases them to do so. You never showed any signs of being even aware of our presence in the room, and there was therefore no occasion for us to address you."

Jack Archer

"I do not intend to bandy words with you," the governor replied savagely. "I repeat that I am informed you meditate attempting an escape, and as this is a breach of honor, and a grave offence upon the part of officers on parole, I shall at once revoke your privilege, and you will be confined in the same prison with common soldiers."

"In the first place," Jack said, "as my friend has told you, the report of our thinking of escaping is a lie. If we had wanted to escape, at any rate from this place, we could have done it at any time since we have been here. In the second place, I deny that we are prisoners on parole. We did not give you our promise, because you did not ask for it. You said to Dr. Bertmann, in our hearing, that our parole was no matter, one way or the other, as it would be impossible for us to escape. The doctor can of course be found, and will, I am sure, bear out what I say."

"Silence, sir!" shouted the governor. "I say that you were prisoners on parole, and that I have discovered you intended to break that parole. You will be committed to prison, and treated as men who have forfeited all right to be considered as officers and gentlemen."

The boys sat silent, looking with contempt at the angry Russian. The latter believed that he had now cowed them. He sat for a few minutes silent, in order to allow the prospect of imprisonment and disgrace to produce its full effect. Then he continued in a milder voice, "I do not wish to be severe upon such very young officers, and will therefore point out a way by which you may avoid the imprisonment and disgrace which your conduct has merited, and be enabled still to enjoy your freedom as before."

"What is it?" Dick asked briefly.

"It is this," the governor said. "I have here before me," and he touched some documents lying on the table, "a report which I am about to forward to the Czar respecting Count Preskoff. The report is not altogether favorable, for the count is a man of what are called advanced opinions. He has curious ideas as to the treatment of serfs, and has, no doubt, in your hearing expressed himself favorable to their emancipation."

The boys were silent.

"He has, I doubt not, done so, for he is rash and open of speech. I have here before me an information sworn to that effect, and if you will place your names as witnesses to it, I will not only pardon the indiscretion of which you have been guilty, but will do all in my power to make your stay pleasant."

The boys were speechless with indignation at the infamy of the proposal, and doubted not that the document contained far weightier charges than those specified by the governor.

"Who has signed that document?" Jack asked.

"I do not know that the name can matter to you," the governor said, "but it is one of the servants of the count, one Paul Petrofski."

"Then," Dick said, starting to his feet, "it is a forgery. Paul Petrofski never signed that document."

"What do you mean?" the governor exclaimed, leaping to his feet also, and laying his hand on his sword, while his face grew white with passion. "Do you accuse me of forgery?"

"I repeat," Dick said, his indignation altogether mastering his prudence, "that it is a forgery. You have never seen Paul Petrofski since I heard you offer him one thousand roubles at the cross-roads that night to betray his master."

G. A. Henty

With a short cry which reminded Jack of the sharp snarl of the wolves in the night in the forest, the Russian drew his sword and rushed upon Dick. The latter threw up his arm to defend himself, but the blow fell, cutting his arm severely, and laying open a great gash on his cheek.

The Russian raised his arm to repeat the blow, when Jack sprang upon him from behind, seizing him round the waist, and pinning his arms to his side.

The count struggled furiously, but Jack was a strongly built English lad of nearly sixteen years old, and he not only retained his grasp, but lifted his struggling captive from his feet. "Open the window, Dick!" he shouted. "It's his life or ours now." Dick though nearly blinded with blood, sprang to the window and threw it up.

There was a short, desperate struggle, as the Russian shouting furiously for aid, strove with his feet to keep himself away from the window, but Dick struck these aside. With a mighty effort Jack pushed his captive forward, and in another moment he was thrown through the open window. A rush of heavy steps was heard on the stairs. In an instant Jack darted to the table, seized the documents upon it, and cast them into the fire in the stove, slammed the door, and was standing by the window with Dick, when an officer and several soldiers burst into the room.

"What is the matter?" the former exclaimed; "and where is the governor?"

"The matter is," Jack said, quietly turning round, "that the governor has drawn his sword, and, as you see, tried to kill my friend. In order to prevent his doing so, my friend and I have thrown the governor out of the window."

"Thrown the governor out of the window!" gasped the astonished officer.

"Yes," Jack said. "It was painful, but we had to do it. If you look out, I fancy you'll see him."

The officer ran to the window.

"Good heavens!" he exclaimed; "it is true. They are lifting him up already. He seems to me to be dead. You will have to answer for this," he said, turning to the lads.

"Of course we shall answer for it," Jack said. "He brought it on himself. His temper, as no doubt you are aware, was not always under strict control."

The officer could not help smiling. He had himself often experienced the effects of that want of control of his temper on the part of his superior, and was at heart by no means sorry at the prospect of a new governor.

"His Excellency's temper was hasty," he said. "However, gentlemen, that is no business of mine." Then, turning to the soldiers, he continued, "You will take these officers into custody, and remain here in charge of them until you have further orders." He then left them, to inquire into the state of the governor. The soldiers muttered remarks to each other, by no means indicative of sorrow, for the tyranny of the governor had made him hated by all below him. One of them at Jack's request at once went out and returned with a jug of cold water and a towel, with which Jack bathed Dick's wounds, which were bleeding severely, and the midshipman was scarcely able to stand from loss of blood. Jack vainly attempted to stop the bleeding. "We must have a surgeon," he said, turning to the soldiers, "or, as you see, my friend will bleed to death. No doubt there are plenty of them below. Will one of you go and ask one of them to come up here, telling him how urgent is the need?"

Jack Archer

After a consultation among themselves, one of the soldiers retired, and in a minute or two returned with a surgeon, in whom, to his great delight, Jack recognized Doctor Bertmann, who upon seeing Dick's state at once proceeded to attend to him. Cutting off his coat and shirt-sleeve, he examined his arm, from which the blood was flowing in a stream.

"One of the small arteries is cut," he said. "It is lucky that aid was at hand, or he would have assuredly bled to death." The severed artery was speedily found and tied up, and then the wound on the face was plastered and bandaged, and Dick, as he lay on the couch, for he was far too weak to stand, felt comparatively comfortable.

Chapter XVI
AN ESCAPE FROM PRISON

WHEN he had dressed Dick's wounds, Doctor Bertmann said he would go down and see the governor. He had already told the lads that he had received fatal injuries, and was unconscious, and that he might, or might not, recover his senses before he died. It was an hour before he returned, accompanied by the other officer. Both looked grave.

"I'm sorry to say, my young friend," the doctor said to Jack, for Dick had now gone off in a quiet doze, "that the affair has assumed a very serious aspect. The count is dead. He recovered consciousness before he died, and denounced you both as having made a sudden and altogether unprovoked attack upon him. He had, he affirmed, discovered that you were meditating a breach of your parole, and that he had informed you that the privileges extended to you would, therefore, be withdrawn. Then, he said, transported by rage, you sprang upon him. He drew his sword and attempted to defend himself, but the two of you, closing with him, hurled him through the window, in spite of his struggles."

The other officer had, while the doctor was speaking, been examining the writing-table.

"I do not see the papers he spoke of," he said to the doctor.

Then, turning to the sergeants of the guard, he asked if any papers upon the table had been touched. The sergeant replied that no one had gone near the table since he had entered the room.

"In that case," the officer said, "his mind cannot have been quite clear, although he seemed to speak sensibly enough. You heard him order me, doctor, to fold up a report and attesting statement directed to the Minister of the Interior, and to post them immediately? It is clear that there are no such documents here. I entered the room with the sergeant almost at the moment when the struggle ended, and as no one has touched the table since, it is clear that they cannot have been here. Perhaps I may find them on the table downstairs. It is now," he said, turning to Jack, "my duty to inform you that you are in custody for the deliberate murder of Count Smerskoff, as sworn to by him in his last moments."

"He was a liar when he was alive," Jack said, "and he died with a falsehood on his lips. However, sir, we are at your orders."

A stretcher was brought in, Dick was placed upon it, and under a guard the midshipmen were marched to the prison, the soldiers with difficulty keeping back the crowd who pressed forward to see the English prisoners who had murdered the governor.

Doctor Bertmann walked with Jack to the prison door. Upon the way he assured Jack that he entirely believed his version of the story, as he knew the governor to be a thoroughly bad man.

"Singularly enough," he said, "I had intended to see you to-day. I went back to Sebastopol on the very day after you arrived here, with a regiment marching down, and left again with a convoy of wounded after only two days' stay there. I got here last night, and I had intended coming out to call upon you

Jack Archer

at Count Preskoff's to-day. You would, no doubt, like me to see him at once, and inform him of what has taken place."

Jack said that he would be very much obliged, if he would do so.

"I will return this afternoon to see my patient," Doctor Bertmann said, as they parted, "and will then bring you news from the count, who will, no doubt, come to see you himself."

The cell to which the boys were conducted was a small one, and horribly dirty. Jack shrugged his shoulders, as he looked at it.

"It is not fit for a pig," he said to himself. "After all, Russia is not such a pleasant place as I thought it yesterday."

When they were left alone, Jack set to work to cheer up his companion, who was weak, and inclined to be despondent from the loss of blood which he had suffered.

"At any rate, old boy," Jack said, in reply to Dick's assertion of his conviction that they would be shot, "we shall have the satisfaction that we have procured the safety of our friends at the chateau. Now that their enemy is gone, the count will no doubt be let alone. It was dreadful to think what would have become of the countess and the three girls if their father had been sent to Siberia, and they turned out penniless. Besides, old fellow, we are a long way from being dead yet. After all, it is only the governor's word against ours, and you may be sure that the count will move heaven and earth to bring matters right."

It was dusk before the doctor returned.

"I have seen the count," he said, "and the ladies and he were greatly distressed at my news. It is plain to see that you are prime favorites. The young ladies were very Niobes. The count was most anxious to learn all particulars, but I could only tell him that you asserted the governor had attacked you first. He drove in at once, and made no doubt that he should be allowed to see you. In this, however, he was disappointed, and indeed you have had a most fortunate escape. The officer second in command here is a relative of the late governor. Fortunately he was absent this morning, and only returned this afternoon. Like the late count he is of a violent and passionate temper, and when he heard the news swore that had he been here, he would have instantly had you brought out and shot in the square. Indeed, it was with difficulty that the other officers dissuaded him from doing so upon his return. He has ordered that a court-martial shall assemble to-morrow, and that you shall be at once tried and executed."

"But surely," Jack said, "no court-martial of officers would find us guilty. The count's violent temper was notorious, and it is against all reason that two unarmed men should make an attack upon one armed with a sword, and within call of assistance. You yourself know, Doctor Bertmann, that the reason which he alleged for the attack is a false one, as we were not asked for our parole."

"I am, of course, aware of that," the doctor said, "and should attend to give evidence, but the case is a doubtful one. The officers of our line regiments are, for the most part, poor and friendless men. Promotion is almost entirely by favoritism, and it would need a very considerable amount of courage and independence to give a verdict in the teeth of their commanding officer. In the next place, for I have heard them talking it over among themselves, there is a sort of feeling that, for the honor of the Russian army, it is almost necessary that you should be found guilty, since it would throw

G. A. Henty

discredit upon the whole service were it published to the world that two unarmed young English officers had been attacked with a sword by a Russian officer of rank."

"Then things look rather badly for us," said Jack. "Well, it can't be helped, you know, and the count will, no doubt, write to our people at home, to tell them the truth of the case."

"Oh," said the doctor, "you must not misunderstand me. I only said that the new commandant had ordered that you should be tried by court-martial, but that is a very different thing from its being done. We must get you out of prison to-night."

"You speak very confidently," Jack said, laughing, "but how is it to be done?"

"Oh," answered the doctor, "there is no great difficulty on that score. It may be taken as certain that as a rule every Russian official, from the highest to the lowest, is accessible to a bribe, and that no prisoner with powerful friends outside need give up hope. This is a military prison. The soldiers at the gate are open to imbibe an unlimited amount of vodka, whoever may send it. The officer in command of them will be easily accessible to reasons which will induce him to shut his eyes to what is going on. Your warder here can of course be bought. The count is already at work, and as his means are ample, and, although under a cloud at present, his connections powerful, there is little fear that he will fail in succeeding. By the way I have news to tell you. Do you hear the bells tolling? The news has arrived that Nicholas is dead. Alexander, our new Czar, is known to be liberally disposed, and, were there time, the count would go to St. Petersburg, obtain an audience with him, and explain the whole circumstances, which, by the way, he has related to me. This, of course, is out of the question, and even were there time for him to go and return, it would not be possible for him to obtain an audience with the new emperor just at present."

"I wish it could have been so," Jack said. "Of course Dick and I will be glad enough to avail ourselves of the chances of escape, for it would be foolish to insist upon waiting to be tried by a tribunal certain beforehand to condemn us. Still, one doesn't like the thought of making one's escape, and so leaving it to be supposed that we were conscious of guilt."

"Oh," the doctor said, "you need not trouble yourself upon that score. The governor was hated by every one, and no one really doubts that he attacked you first. Upon the contrary, the population are inclined to look upon you as public benefactors. There will then be no feeling against you here, but even if there were, it would make but little difference. At present every one in Russia is talking and thinking of nothing but the death of the Czar, and of the changes which may be made by his son, and the details of a squabble in an obscure town will attract no attention whatever, and will not probably even obtain the honor of a paragraph in the Odessa papers. The first thing for us to do is to get your friend into a fit state to walk. How do you feel?" he asked, bending over Dick and feeling his pulse.

"Ever so much better," Dick said cheerfully, "since I have heard from you that there is a chance of escape. I have been fretting so at the thought that I have got Jack into such a wretched mess by my folly in telling the governor that I knew of his treachery. If it had been only myself, I shouldn't have cared."

Jack Archer

"Why, my dear Dick," Jack said cheerfully, "I never dreamt of blaming you, and if you hadn't spoken out, I have no doubt I should have done so. No, no, old fellow, whatever comes of it, don't you blame yourself."

"Can you stand, do you think?" the doctor asked.

"Oh, I think so," Dick said; and rising, he managed to totter across the cell.

"That is all right," the doctor said. "In a quarter of an hour you shall have a good dinner sent in from a restaurant. I have arranged for that. It is of course contrary to rule, but a few roubles have settled it. There will be supper, too, at eleven o'clock; there will also be a couple of bottles of first-rate Burgundy from the count's cellar. You are to eat two good meals, and drink a third of a bottle at each of them. Your wounds are not in themselves serious, and the only thing that ails you is loss of blood. We must risk a little accession of fever for the sake of giving you strength. When you have had your supper, you had best both get to sleep, if you can, for an hour or two. Whatever arrangements we make will be for about two o'clock in the morning. And now good-bye for the present; keep up your spirits, and remember that even should any unexpected accident upset our plans for to-night, we will carry them out to-morrow night, as the court-martial will not take place till the afternoon, and there will be at least twenty-four, probably forty-eight hours, between the sentence and its execution."

So saying, the doctor took his departure, leaving the lads far more cheerful and confident than they had been when he entered. He seemed indeed to regard the success of the attempt which would be made for their evasion as secured. The meal, which consisted of some strong and nourishing soup, and a dish of well-cooked meat, shortly arrived, and Dick, after partaking of it, and drinking his prescribed allowance of Burgundy, announced that he felt a man again, and ready for a tussle with the commandant. After his meal he dozed quietly, for some hours, until aroused by the arrival of supper which consisted again of soup with some poached eggs served on vegetables.

Jack had not tried to sleep, but had enjoyed a pipe which the doctor had, with tobacco, handed to him, his own having been confiscated upon his entrance into the prison. After supper, however, he threw himself upon the straw and slept soundly, until awakened by a hand being placed on his shoulder. He leaped to his feet, and saw the warder beside him. The man carried a lantern. The candle with which the boys had been furnished by the doctor's arrangement had burned out. Jack aroused his comrade, and the two followed the warder, who led the way along the corridor and down the stairs into the courtyard of the prison.

The man did not walk with any particular caution, and the lads judged from his movements that he had no fear whatever of interruption. The door of the guard-room stood open, and by the light of the fire which blazed within, they could see the soldiers lying about in a drunken sleep. At the gate itself the sentry on duty was sitting on the ground with his back against a wall, and his musket beside him, in a heavy drunken sleep.

The warder unlocked the door, the key being already in the lock; the three issued out; the gate was closed and locked on the outside, and the key thrust under the gate. The warder then led the way through the streets, until he reached a small house near the outskirts. The door opened as their footsteps approached, and Count Preskoff came out.

G. A. Henty

"My dear boys," he exclaimed embracing them as if he had been their father, "how much you have suffered for the sake of me and mine! Here," he continued, turning to the warder, "is the reward I promised you. Go straight on to the chateau. You will find my coachman with a light carriage ready for starting. He will drive you twenty-five miles on your way, and you will then only have fifteen to walk before morning to the house of the woodman, your brother, where I hear you intend to remain hidden for the present. You can rely upon my protection after the affair has blown over. Now come in, lads, this is the house of a faithful serf of mine, who works here on his own account as an artisan, and you will be safe from interruption for the next hour or two."

Upon entering the cottage, the midshipmen were surprised to find the countess and her daughters, who greeted them no less warmly than the count had done.

"My husband has told me all that you have done for us," the countess said, "and how you first discovered the plot between the governor and that miserable traitor for our ruin. I have blamed him for hiding it from us at first, for surely a wife should know of the dangers to which her husband is exposed. Besides, I and my daughters would have remained ignorant of the obligation we owe you."

"And to think of the way you took us in with the ponies," Olga laughed. "Papa said that was your invention, Master Jack. That's another score against you."

"I hope," Dick said, "that you are running no risks on our account, countess. I fear that there may be suspicions that the count has been concerned in our escape."

"The deputy-commandant may suspect," the count said, "but he can prove nothing. All in the chateau are, I believe, faithful, but even were they not, none know of our absence, as we did not leave until all were asleep, and shall return before daylight. Alexis will himself drive the warder to his destination. He has the best pair of horses, and will do the fifty miles in under four hours so that he will be back before any one is stirring. The others concerned will hold their tongues for their own sakes. The soldiers will not admit that they have been drunk, but will declare that no one has passed the gate. The lieutenant in charge will hang up the key on its hook in the guard-room, and will declare that every time he made his rounds he found the men alert and vigilant. It will therefore be supposed that the warder has let you out by a rope or in some other way. No doubt there will be a vigilant hue-and-cry in the morning, and the commandant will search every house, will keep a sharp watch over the chateau, and will scour the country for miles round. But it will die away in time. I wrote yesterday afternoon to my friends in St. Petersburg, urging them to obtain the appointment of some friend to this post. The party of reform will be in the ascendency in the counsels of the emperor, and I have every hope that I shall shortly be restored to favor at court, a matter, by the way, which I care for very much more for the sake of my daughters than for myself. The countess and I are well content with our life in the country, but the girls naturally look forward to the gayeties of life at the capital. Beside which," he added, laughing, "I must be looking for husbands for them, and I fear that I should not find satisfactory suitors in this neighborhood."

Jack could not help glancing at Olga, for, with a midshipman's usual inflammatory tendency, he was convinced that he was hopelessly in love with that damsel. Olga colored, and then turned away, from which Jack could gain no indication favorable or otherwise for his hopes.

The count now explained the plans that had been adopted for their escape. "It would," he said, "seem the natural course to aid you, as we have done the warder, by driving you far into the country. But the descriptions of you are sure to be sent to every place within fifty miles. I know no one to whom I could safely entrust you, and the doctor says that it is impossible that our friend Dick should walk for any distance for the next two or three days. The doctor has fortunately received orders to-day to start at daybreak this morning with a convoy going back to Sebastopol. No doubt the new commandant had heard that he was prepared to give evidence at the court-martial contradicting the governor's statement that you were prisoners on parole, and therefore wished to get him out of the way. There are several of my carts which have been requisitioned for the service, in the convoy. I have here peasants' dresses for you. These you will put on, and when the carts come along from the chateau half an hour before daybreak it is arranged that you will take the places of two of the drivers, who will at once return home. There will be no loading to do, as the carts will be laden with flour for the army before they leave to-night, so you will only have to go along with the others, and take your places in the convoy. After starting the doctor will come along the line, and seeing Dick limping, will order him to take his place in one of the carts under his immediate charge, with medicines and bedding for the hospitals. One driver more or less in a team of some hundreds of wagons all following each other along a straight road will not be noticed. So you will journey south for a week or so, until Dick has thoroughly recovered his strength. You had then, we think, better make to the west by the Odessa road. The doctor will take two uniforms, there are plenty obtainable in the hospital, for you to put on. You must of course run the risk of questioning and detection by the way, but this cannot be avoided, and at least you will be beyond the range of search from here, and will be travelling by quite a different road from that which you would naturally take proceeding hence. And now tell us all about your affair with the governor. We have only so far heard his version of the affair, which of course we knew to be false; but why he should have attacked you in the way he did, we cannot quite understand."

Dick gave an account of the struggle and the causes which led to it, owning himself greatly to blame for his imprudence in acquainting the governor with his knowledge of his secret. He also gave full credit to Jack for his promptness, not only in seizing the governor and so saving a repetition of the blow, which would probably have been fatal, but also in destroying the report and forged evidence of Paul before interruption. The lads gained great credit with all for their gallantry, and Katinka said, laughing, "It is wrong to say so, I suppose, now he is dead, but I should like to have seen the count struggling as Jack carried him along, like a little ant with a great beetle." They all laughed.

"Oh, come now," Jack said; "there was not so much difference as all that. He was not over six feet, and I suppose I am only about five inches less, and I'm sure I was not much smaller round the shoulders than he was."

"And now about your route," the count said. "You must not lose time. Do you both quite agree with me that it would be next to impossible for you to pass through the lines of our army and to gain your own?"

G. A. Henty

"Quite impossible," Dick agreed. "Jack and I have talked it over again and again, and are of opinion that it could not be done even in Russian uniforms. We should be liable to be questioned by every officer who met us as to the reason of our being absent from our regiment, and should be certain to be found out. We thought that it might be possible to get hold of a fishing-boat, and sail down to join the fleet. There would be of course the risk of being blown off the shore or becalmed, and it would be difficult to lay in a stock of provisions."

"Besides," the count said, "there is no blockade at Odessa, and our small war-steamers cruise up and down the coast, so that you would be liable to capture. No, I am sure your best way will be to go by land through Poland. There are still large bodies of troops to the southwest, facing the Turks, and it would be better for you to keep north of these into Poland. You can go as wounded soldiers on furlough returning home; and, being taken for Poles, your broken Russian will appear natural. I will give you a letter which the countess has written to the intendant of her estates in Poland, and he will do everything in his power."

"I would rather not carry a letter," Dick said, "for it would compromise you if we were taken. It would be better, if I might suggest, for the countess to write to him direct, saying that when two persons arrive and give some pass-word, say, for instance, the names of your three daughters, we shall not forget them, he is to give us any help we may require."

This was agreed upon, and the party chatted until the count said that it was time for them to dress. Going into another room, the boys clad themselves in two peasant costumes, with the inseparable sheepskin coat which the Russian peasant clings to until the full heat of summer sets in, and which is, especially during a journey, invaluable. The count then insisted upon their taking a bundle of rouble notes to the value of 200 l., and upon their urging that they could have no possible need of so much money, he pointed out that there was no saying what emergencies might occur during their journey, and that after passing the frontier they would require a complete outfit, and would have to pay the expenses of their journey, either to England or the east, whichever they might decide upon. They rejoined the party in the front room just as a rumble of carts was heard approaching. There was a hasty parting. Father, mother, and daughters kissed the midshipmen affectionately. Jack squeezed Olga's hand at parting, and in another minute they were standing in front of the door.

"Yours will be the last two carts," the count said.

When these arrived opposite the house the count stepped forward and said a word to the drivers, who instantly fell behind, while the boys took up their places by the oxen and moved along with the procession of carts.

Chapter XVII
A JOURNEY IN DISGUISE

THE start was accomplished. Many hundreds of carts were assembled in the great square. A mounted officer and a small guard of soldiers had formed across the road which they were to follow, and as soon as daylight had fairly appeared he gave the word, and the carts began to file off along the southern road, an account being taken of each cart, as it passed out, by an officer on duty, to see that the number which had been requisitioned were all present. No question was asked of the boys.

As the driver of the first of those belonging to the count reported twelve carts, each laden with thirty sacks of flour supplied by Count Preskoff, the officer, seeing the number was correct, allowed them to pass without further question. Dick found himself still extremely weak, and could not have proceeded many hundred yards, if he had not taken a seat on the cart behind his oxen.

After two hours' travelling there was a halt for a quarter of an hour, and the doctor, passing along, spoke to Dick, and then walked with him back along the line to the hospital carts which were in the rear. Here Dick took his place among some bales of blankets, and another was thrown over him, in such a way that his presence there would not be suspected by any one riding past the cart. Upon the train proceeding Jack took charge of the two carts. This was an easy task, the oxen proceeding steadily along without deviating from the line, and requiring no attention whatever beyond an occasional shout and a blow of the stick when they loitered and left a gap in the line.

Alongside the drivers walked in groups of three or four, talking together, and thus the fact that one of the wagons was without its driver passed unnoticed. Alexis had told the count's serfs who accompanied the carts that their master had arranged at the last moment for hired men to take the places of two of their number, one of whom had a wife sick at home, and the other was engaged to be married shortly. He had also told them that it was their master's wish that they should enter into no conversation with the strangers, as these were from a northern province, and scarcely understood the southern dialect.

Accustomed to obey every command of their master without hesitation, the serfs expressed no wonder even among themselves at an order which must have appeared somewhat strange to them. It was the count's pleasure, and that was sufficient for them. At the end of the day, Dick rejoined his comrade, and assisted him to feed the oxen, who required no further attention except the removal of the yoke, when they lay down upon the ground and slept in their places. Dick brought him a supply of cold meat and white bread, and a bottle of wine; and the lads, choosing a place apart from the others, enjoyed their meal heartily, and then, climbing up on to the top of their flour sacks, wrapped themselves in their sheepskins and were soon sound asleep.

That evening a soldier brought a message to the officer in charge of the escort, telling him that the two English prisoners had by the aid of their warder effected their escape, bidding him search the convoy, and keep a sharp lookout

G. A. Henty

along the road and ordering him to give information to all village and military authorities, and instruct them to send messages to all places near, warning the authorities there not only to keep a sharp lookout, but again to forward on the news; so that in a short time it would be known in every village in the province.

In the morning, before starting, the officer in charge of the escort rode along the line, examining every wagon carefully, asking the names of the drivers, and referring to a paper with which he had been furnished by the owners of the carts, at starting, giving the names of the drivers. The head man of the party from Count Preskoff's responded at once for the twelve men under him; and satisfied that the fugitives were not in the convoy, the officer gave orders to proceed.

This time Dick was able to walk two or three miles before dropping back to the hospital wagon. The next day he went still farther, and by the end of a week announced himself to be as strong as ever, and the doctor allowed that he could now be trusted to travel.

On this night they had halted at a point where a road, running east and west, crossed the great road to the Crimea. Before starting, the boys had a long chat with their friend the doctor, who furnished them with military passes which he had procured from an officer. These testified that Ivan Petrofski and Alexis Meranof, of the 5th Polish Regiment, were proceeding home on sick-furlough.

The signature of the colonel was no doubt fictitious, but this mattered but little. Jack inquired whether their absence in the morning would not be likely to be remarked; but the doctor said that the head of the party had been informed by Demetri that the two strangers would only accompany them for a few days' march, and had only been hired to satisfy the authorities that the right number of men had been furnished, for the want of hands on the estate was now so great owing to the heavy drain of conscripts to fill up the losses caused by the war, that the count had been glad to retain the services of the two who had been left behind. There was therefore to be no remark concerning the disappearance of the new hands, but the others were to take charge of their carts, and if possible the authorities were to be kept unacquainted with the fact that their number was incomplete.

The peasants' dresses were now exchanged for the uniforms of Russian soldiers. Dick's head was wrapped in bandages, and his arm placed in a sling. Jack's leg was also enveloped in bandages, the trousers being slit up to the hip, and the sides loosely tied together by a piece of string, and the doctor gave him a pair of crutches, the same as those used in regimental hospitals.

"Now you will do," he said, surveying them by the light of a lantern. "Many of the soldiers who have joined since the outbreak of the war are mere boys, so your age will not be against you, only pray for a time give up all idea as to the necessity of washing. The dirtier your hands and faces, the better, especially if the dirt will hide your clear healthy color, which is very unlike the sallow complexions almost universal among our peasantry. And now, good-bye. I move about too much to hope to receive any letter from you, but as you have of course arranged with Count Preskoff to send him word when you have safely crossed the frontier, I shall hear of you from him."

With many deep and hearty thanks for the kindness he had shown them, the boys parted from him, and, setting their faces to the west, took the road to

Jack Archer

Odessa. Jack carried his crutches on his shoulders, as also the long strap which, when he used them, was to pass over his neck, and down under his foot, keeping it off the ground.

They had made many miles before morning, and as they had retained their sheepskin cloaks, which had been served out to many of the troops, they were able to get a comfortable sleep under shelter of a protecting wall. Five days' walking took them to Odessa. This town was not upon the direct road, but they still clung to the hope of getting away by sea.

On the journey they had met several bodies of troops and many convoys of provisions and stores. Whenever they observed the former to be approaching, they left the road, and sheltered themselves behind bushes or inequalities of the ground at a distance from the road, as they knew they would be liable to be questioned as to the state of things at the front. They did not, however, go out of their way for convoys, as they passed these with short salutations in reply to the greetings or pitying remarks from the drivers. Their Russian was good enough to pass muster when confined to short sentences of a formal kind. Their hearts beat when, on passing over a rise, they saw the blue water stretching out far before them, and they again debated the possibility of seizing a boat. But the sight of two gun-boats steaming slowly along the shore convinced them that the attempt would be an extremely dangerous one.

Odessa is not a fortress, and the boys consequently entered it unquestioned. The town was crowded with wounded and sick soldiers, and their appearance attracted no attention whatever. In the principal streets the lads saw many names of English firms over offices, and the majority of the shops appeared to be kept by Frenchmen and Germans. They walked down to the wharves and saw how great must have been the trade carried on before the war. Now all traffic and business was at an end.

The great foreign merchants interested in the corn trade had all left, and many of the shops were closed.

The harbor was deserted, save that a score or two of brigs employed in the coasting-trade, in the Black Sea lay moored by the wharves with hatches battened down and deserted decks. A little farther out lay at anchor two or three frigates and some gun-boats. Looking seaward, not a single sail broke the line of the horizon.

Returning into the town, they went up some small streets, entered a small eating-house, and asked for food, for the stock with which they had started four days before had been exhausted the previous evening. The landlord served them, and as they were eating he entered into conversation with them.

"I suppose you have leave out of hospital for the day?"

"No," Dick said, "my comrade and I have got leave to go home to Poland till our wounds are cured."

"Oh," the landlord said. "You are Poles. I thought you did not look quite like our men; but you speak Russian well for Poles. There is a regiment of your countrymen in the town now, and some of them come in sometimes for a glass of brandy. They like it better than vodka; curious, isn't it? Your true Russian thinks that there's nothing better than vodka."

Rather disturbed at the intelligence that there was a Polish regiment in the town, the boys hastened through their meal, and determined to lay in a stock of bread and meat sufficient for some days' consumption, and to leave Odessa at once. Just as they had finished, however, the door opened, and a sergeant and two soldiers entered.

"Ah, my friend," the landlord said to the former. "I am glad to see you. Are you come as usual for a glass of brandy? Real French stuff it is, I promise you, though for my part I like vodka. Here are two of your compatriots wounded; they have furlough to return home. Lucky fellows, say I. There are thousands at Sebastopol would be glad to change places with them, even at the cost of their wounds."

The sergeant strode to the table at which the lads were sitting, and, drawing a chair up, held out his hands to them. "Good-day, comrades," he said in Polish. "So are you on your way home? Lucky fellows! I would give my stripes to be in your place, if only for a fortnight."

Dick for a moment was stupefied, but Jack recalled to mind three sentences which the countess had taught him and which might, she said, prove of use to them, did they happen to come across any insurgent bands in Poland; for vague reports were current, in spite of the efforts of the authorities to repress them, that the Poles were seizing the opportunity of their oppressors being engaged in war, again to take up arms. The sentences were pass-words of a secret association of which the countess's father had been a member, and which were widely whispered among patriotic Poles. "The dawn will soon be at hand. We must get up in the morning. Poland will yet be free." The sergeant stared at them in astonishment, and answering in a low tone in some words which were, the boys guessed, the countersign to the pass, sat down by them. "But you are not Poles?" he said in a low voice in Russian. "Your language is strange. I could scarce understand you."

"No," Jack said, in similar tones, "we are not Poles, nor Russians. We are English, and England has always been the friend of Poland."

"That is so," the sergeant said heartily. "Landlord," he said, raising his voice, "a glass of vodka for each of my friends. I fear that my money will not run to brandy. And now," he said, when the landlord had returned to his place, "what are you doing here? Can I help you in any way?"

"We are English officers who have escaped, and are making our way to Poland. We expect to find friends there. Do you know the intendant of the Countess Preskoff at—?"

"Do I know him?" the soldier repeated. "Why, I belong to the next village. I have seen him hundreds of times. And the countess, do you know the countess?"

"Certainly we do," Jack said. "We have been living for six weeks in her chateau, it is she who has written to the intendant to aid us."

"You will be welcome everywhere for her sake. She is a kind mistress, and greatly beloved. It is a pity that she married a Russian, though they say he is a good fellow. Tell me, can I do anything for you? Do you want for money?"

"No, indeed," Jack replied. "The countess has taken care of that."

"Look here," the sergeant said. "I will give you a note to my brother, who is a horse-dealer at Warsaw. It may be useful to you. He knows every one, and if, as they say, there is trouble in Poland, he is sure to be in the thick of it, and at any rate he will be able to give you advice which may be useful, and addresses of safe people in different towns to whom you can go. Landlord, give me some paper and pen and ink. My comrades here know friends of mine at home, and will carry a letter for me."

Jack Archer

"Please be careful," Dick said, as the soldier began to write. "It is possible we may be searched on the way; so do not say anything that a Russian official might not read."

"Trust me," the sergeant answered, laughing. "We Poles have been learning to conceal our feelings for generations. Trust me to write a letter which my brother will understand at once, but which will seem the most innocent thing in the world to any Russian official who may read it."

In a few minutes the letter was finished, and the three left the place together, the sergeant telling his comrades that he would return shortly for them. He then accompanied the midshipmen, and did their shopping for them, and, bidding him a hearty adieu, they were soon on their way out of Odessa, Jack swinging along upon his crutches at a fair pace. Once fairly away from the town, he took his foot from the strap, shouldered his crutches and again they trudged along upon their journey.

They found their walking powers improve day by day as they went on, and were soon able to make thirty-five miles a day without inconvenience. Travelling in this way, without any interruption or incident save an occasional demand for a view of their passport by some Russian official, they journeyed across the south of Russia, and ten days after leaving Odessa they entered Poland.

Here they foresaw that their difficulties would be far greater than before, and that their characters as Polish soldiers on their way home could no longer be sustained. They took, therefore, the first opportunity of purchasing two suits similar to those worn by Polish peasants, and, entering a wood, dressed themselves in their new attire, and, rolling their dirt-stained uniforms into a bundle, thrust them into a clump of underwood. Into this Jack also joyfully tossed his crutches and strap. Dick had long been able to dispense with his sling, but the wound on his face was scarcely healed, and was still angry-looking and irritable.

They now trudged steadily along, avoiding all conversation as much as possible, and making their purchases only in a quiet villages. They met many bodies of troops moving about the roads, and although they could understand nothing of the language, and were wholly ignorant of what was going on, they judged from the manner in which these troops marched, by the advance guard thrown out in front, the strong detachments which accompanied the baggage, and the general air of vigilance which marked them, that the country was in a troubled state.

Once convinced of this, they took care to conceal themselves whenever they saw troops approaching, as they feared that questions might be addressed to them which they might find it difficult to answer. There was the less difficulty in their doing this as the country was for the most part thickly wooded, the roads sometimes running for miles through forests. Upon one occasion, when, just as it was dusk, they had gone in among the trees, having seen a Russian column moving along the road, they were astonished at being suddenly seized, gagged, and carried off through the wood. So suddenly had this been done, that they had time neither to cry nor struggle.

After being carried some distance, they were thrown down on the ground, and the men who had carried them hurried away. Just as they did so there was a sudden outburst of musketry, mingled with loud yells and shouts; then, after a moment's pause, came the rattle of a rolling musketry fire. The first, Jack judged to be the fire of insurgents upon the column; the second, that of the troops. For a while the din of battle went on. Sharp ringing volleys, heavy irregular firing, the fierce, wild shouts of the insurgents, and occasionally the hoarse hurrah of Russian soldiery.

Presently the sounds grew fainter, and the lads judged by the direction that the Russian column was falling back in retreat. Ere long the sounds of firing ceased altogether, and in scattered knots of three and four, men came through the wood to the wide open space in which the midshipmen were lying bound. No attention was paid to them for some time, until a large body of men were collected. Then the lads were suddenly raised and carried to a large fire which was now-blazing in the centre of the clearing. Here the gags were taken from their mouths, and the cords unbound, and they saw confronting them a young man evidently by his dress and bearing a person of rank and authority, and, as they judged by the attitude of those standing round, the leader of the insurgent band.

"Where do you come from, and what are you doing here?" he asked in Polish.

The boys shook their heads in token of their ignorance of the language.

"I thought so," he said angrily in Russian. "You are spies, Russian spies. I thought as much when the news came to me that two peasants had entered a village shop to buy goods, but had been unable to ask for them except by pointing to them, and had given a rouble note and allowed the woman who served them to take her own change. You are detected, sirs, and may prepare for the death you deserve. Hang them at once," he said in Polish, to those standing near. "But first search them thoroughly, and see if they are the bearers of any documents."

The lads in vain endeavored to explain, but their voices were drowned in the execrations of the angry peasants, fresh from the excitement of the battle, and in many cases bleeding from bullet and bayonet wounds, for the Polish peasants always rush to close quarters. Concealed in Dick's waistband was found a heavy roll of Russian notes, and the yell which greeted its appearance showed that it was considered confirmatory of the guilt of the prisoners.

Upon Jack was found only the letter which the sergeant had given him to his brother, the horse-dealer. This was taken to the leader, and he opened and read it by the light of a blazing brand which one of his followers held beside him. "Stop!" he shouted, after reading the first line or two, to the men who were already hurrying the lads towards the nearest tree. "Wait till I have read this through." He read it to the end, and then beginning afresh again, went carefully through it. "Bring the prisoners here," he said. "Young men," he went on, when the lads were again placed before him, "there may be some mistake here. This letter purports to be from a sergeant of the 12th Polish regiment to his brother, Horni Varlofski. Now Varlofski is well known to many of us. I do not know whether he has a brother a sergeant. Does any one here know?"

Two or three of the men raised their voices to say that they knew that Varlofski the horse-dealer had a brother who was drafted into the army as a punishment for having struck a Russian sergeant in a brawl.

"This must be the man, then," the leader said. "The letter is written carefully, apparently with a view to avoid any suspicion, should it be opened and read by any but him for whom it is intended; but in fact it contains assurances couched in language which I understand, that the bearers are enemies of Russia and friends of Poland, and that every confidence may be placed in them. Now, sirs, will you explain to me how you, who speak no Polish come to be in the middle of the forest, dressed as Polish, peasants, and the bearers of a letter such as this?"

"We are English officers," Dick began, "who were taken prisoners at Sebastopol, and have since escaped."

He then proceeded to explain the circumstances of their residence at Count Preskoff's, of their recommendation to the intendant of the countess's estates in Poland, of their acquaintance with the insurgent pass-words, and their meeting with the sergeant at Odessa. When they had concluded, the young leader held out his hand to them.

"Gentlemen," he said, "I ask your pardon for the roughness with which you have been treated, and shall never forgive myself for having without sufficient inquiry condemned you to death. It will be a lesson to me never to judge by appearances in future. I knew the countess well before her marriage. Her estates are but a few miles distant from my own, and I last saw her some three years since, when she was there with her husband and daughters. By the way," he said carelessly, "what are their names?"

Dick instantly repeated them.

"Right," the Pole answered. "Pardon me this last test, but one cannot be too particular when the lives of hundreds depend upon a mistake not being made. I am satisfied now. Welcome, heartily welcome to our camp."

Chapter XVIII
THE POLISH INSURGENTS

A FEW words from the leader explained to his followers that the new-comers were friends. Their money was instantly restored to them, and those who a few minutes before were so eager to hurry them to execution were profuse in their apologies and demonstrations of respect. The Poles regarded England as a friendly power, and were eagerly watching the war in the Crimea, hoping that the strength of Russia would be so exhausted there that she would be obliged to weaken her hold on Poland. So far, however, great as were the number of troops that Russia had poured down to meet the Allies, she had in no way weakened her hold upon Poland. Indeed even larger numbers of troops than usual were massed in that country. The insurrection at present going on was intended rather as a proof to Europe that Poland yet lived, ground down though she was under the heel of Russian tyranny, than as a movement from which success could be reasonably hoped for.

The lads were now able to look round at the wild group which filled the clearing. The greater portion were peasants, although the dress and bearing of several proclaimed that they belonged to a superior class. Some of the peasants were armed with guns, but these were quite in the minority, the greater portion carrying scythe blades fastened to long handles. These, although clumsy to look at, were terrible weapons in a close onslaught, and the Russian soldiers could seldom be kept firm by their officers when, in spite of their fire, the Polish peasantry rushed among them. The Poles were in high spirits. Their own loss had been small, and they had inflicted great slaughter upon the head of the Russian column, and had gained a considerable number of arms. A party which had attacked the rear of the column at the same moment when the main body fell upon its head, had for a time obtained possession of a wagon with spare ammunition, and had succeeded in carrying off the greater part of it.

The leader of the party, having given orders to his men and seen that the wounded were carried away on stretchers roughly formed of boughs, either to their own villages, or when these were too distant, to a collection of wood-cutters' huts in the heart of the forest, returned and took a seat by the lads near the fire.

"We have not introduced ourselves yet," he said in Russian, laughing. "My name is Stanislaus Chernatony."

Dick named himself and his comrades.

"Tell me now," the Pole said, "how you got here, and what are your plans."

Dick in reply gave him a narrative of their adventures, and said that they were making their way to the Austrian frontier.

"It would be absolutely impossible," the Pole said, "for you to succeed in making your way in safety. Every town is full of Russian troops, who are forever scouring the roads. It would be out of the question for any one except a native to succeed in getting through, and even a Pole would find difficulty, so strictly is every one questioned. Of course their object is to prevent our bands from increasing, and to capture any of us who may be returning to our homes. We only manage to assemble by marching constantly in the woods by paths known only to villagers. You would find it, too, a matter of extreme difficulty to cross the frontier, even should you gain it, as there is a perfect cordon of troops posted along the frontier, to prevent any one from escaping. Once in Austria, you would be safe, but you could not cross into Prussia, even if you succeeded in passing the Russian troops stationed along that line; for Prussia, who is as harsh a master to the Poles under her rule as is Russia, acts as policeman for the latter, and turns all fugitives back who may cross the frontier. At present I fear I can give you no assistance; but there is a talk of a union of several of our bands further west, and in that case you might travel with us, and we might pass you on, and see that you had guides. For the present I can either lodge you in the village where our wounded are now taken, and where it is not likely that the Russians will find you, at any rate for the present; or if you like to join us, I need not say how glad we shall be to receive you as comrades. England has always been the friend of Poland and more than one of your countrymen has fought in the Polish ranks. As England is at war at present with Russia, you will be doing as much service by fighting her here as in the Crimea. Here, too, you will have the satisfaction that you are fighting for an oppressed people struggling for freedom against tremendous odds."

The lads asked for twelve hours before giving a final answer, and then, having shared the Pole's rough meal, they chatted with him for a long time upon the progress and chances of the insurrection. The Polish leader told them that there were a score of bands like his own in the forests; but he admitted that he saw but little hope of final success unless Russia were completely crippled in the war with England and France.

"But," he said, "we in Poland do not rise only when we consider success possible. We take up arms when we are goaded to it. When some act of Russian tyranny more gross and brutal than usual goads us to desperation, we take up arms to kill and to die. You know not the awful persecution to which we Poles are exposed. Whole villages are destroyed, and the inhabitants banished to Siberia; our young men are taken and compelled to serve in the Russian army. Scores are shot down, after a mockery of a trial, on the pretence of discontent with Russian rule. Women, ay, and ladies, are publicly flogged. Priests are massacred, our churches closed, our very language proscribed. Death is a thousand times preferable to the living torture we undergo, and when we at last rise, it is vengeance and death that we seek rather than with any thought of finally freeing Poland from her oppressors. And now," he said, "you will excuse me if I suggest that we follow the example of my comrades, and turn off to sleep. We have marched fifty miles since yesterday evening, and shall be off before daybreak to-morrow."

For half an hour after the Polish leader had rolled himself in his cloak and gone off to sleep, the boys chatted together as to the course they should adopt, and finally resolved to throw in their fortunes with those of the Polish patriots. They saw that it would be impossible for them to make their way on to the frontier alone, and considered that their chance of life was no less if captured in action by the Russians than if found in a village with a number of wounded insurgents. The wrongs of Poland were in those days a subject which moved men's hearts in England, and the midshipmen rejoiced at the thought of striking a blow in so good a cause.

G. A. Henty

These were the reasons which, in talking the matter over, they assigned to each other, but in reality their love of adventure and excitement in no slight degree influenced them. To have taken part in a real Polish insurrection, to join in guerilla attacks and fierce onslaughts on Russian columns, to live a wild life in the woods, were things that appealed strongly to the imagination of the midshipmen; and in the morning they expressed to Stanislas Chernatony their willingness to join him, and fight against the Russians until an opportunity occurred for them to cross the frontier and rejoin the forces before the Sebastopol.

"Good," the Pole said. "I am heartily glad to have two English officers fighting under me. The warfare is of a kind very different to that to which you are accustomed, but I can guarantee that you shall see that we Poles, undisciplined, badly armed, and fighting a hopeless battle, can yet die as bravely as your own trained soldiers in the Crimea. We are now going back to the place we left the day before yesterday, and which we regard as our headquarters. We had news that the column we attacked was to set out, and as so far none of our bands had visited this neighborhood, we thought we might take them by surprise. We succeeded in doing them much damage, but our success was not as great as that which we gained in our last fight, when we succeeded in capturing two cannons. By the way," he said, "you as marine officers, are accustomed to artillery."

"Yes," Dick replied, "we are drilled, not only with heavy ship's guns, but with light field-pieces, of which every large vessel carries a few to be used in case of a landing."

"Capital!" the Pole exclaimed. "We have not a man who has any idea of artillery, and I will appoint you to the command of the guns. You shall each pick out as many men as you require, and train them as artillerymen. This will be an invaluable service to us."

Late at night they reached their halting-place. The guns had been hidden in a thicket, every man having marched with his leader to the attack of the column. The next morning thirty-six men were chosen, eighteen to each gun, in order that the places of those who might be killed could be filled at once, or, should some more pieces be taken, men would be available already trained to the work.

For four days drill went on without intermission. The lads found the Polish peasants very intelligent, although it was difficult for them to understand why each movement should be performed with mechanical regularity. At first, too, the boys' ignorance of Polish caused them great difficulty; but Stanislas wrote down for them the translation of the words of command, and the movements were taught by the boys themselves performing them, and insisting upon their motions being accurately imitated. They worked from morning till night, and by the end of the fourth day were satisfied that their men could serve the guns in a workmanlike and regular way.

The Poles themselves were delighted when they found how swiftly and smoothly the work could be done now that they had mastered it, and looked forward with anxiety to try the results upon the Russians. They had not long to wait. In a short time friends from the next garrison town brought the news that considerable bodies of fresh troops had arrived there, and that an attack was to be made on the following day by two heavy columns. Messengers were sent off at once, and during the night the insurgents were joined by three other bands, raising their numbers to nearly 1500 men. Stanislas told the lads that he intended to move before daybreak, so as to attack one of the columns as soon as it entered the forest, and while the other was too far away to arrive at the scene of action until all would be over.

"I propose," he said, "to fell some trees across the road, arranging them so that the guns can fire between them, while the trunks will afford the gunners some shelter. Half the men will be arranged among the trees on either side, so that while the guns sweep the column we shall attack it upon either flank. I will place a hundred of my best men at the barricade to defend the guns should the column press forward in spite of our efforts; but I believe that we shall have an easy victory. Our recent partial successes have considerably added to our stock of arms, and as this is the first time that we have brought cannon into play, we may rely upon their effect being considerable."

The lads begged that they might go forward with the party charged with felling the trees, in order that they might choose the spot, and themselves see to the construction of the defence. Stanislas chose one of his lieutenants who spoke Russian, and, giving him 200 men, ordered him to carry out the instructions of the lads. They set off an hour before daylight, and just as the dawn began, arrived at the spot where the struggle was to take place.

They selected a point where a rise of six feet afforded a view of the road far in advance, and placed the guns just so far behind the trees that while they would sweep the road, their muzzles only could be seen by an advancing foe. Two large trees felled and stripped of their boughs were placed across the road in front of the guns, being, when placed, just high enough for the gunners to look over them. A strong party were then set to work to cut sods, and with these an earthwork was thrown up across the road, four feet high. Embrasures were left for the guns, and these were made very narrow, as the fire would be directly in front. On either side trees were felled with their boughs outward, so as to form a chevaux-de-frise, extending at an angle on each side of the road for fifty yards in advance of the guns.

Fifty of the men were to remain in the road in the rear of the guns, in readiness to man the earthwork, should the Russians advance to take it by storm, while the rest were to lie down behind the chevaux-de-frise and to open fire upon both flanks of the advancing column. A few green boughs were scattered on the road in front of the battery, and the lads, going along the roads by which the Russians would advance, were pleased to see that at a distance the work was scarcely noticeable. Just as they had finished their preparations Stanislas with the main body arrived, and all were greatly pleased at the position which the boys had constructed. The guns and ammunition wagons had been dragged along by ropes to which hundreds of the peasants had harnessed themselves.

The Poles now took up the positions assigned to them for the attack. Stanislas and his principal officers held a consultation with the midshipmen, and it was agreed that the Russian column should be allowed to approach near to the guns before these opened fire, and that their doing so should be the signal for the general attack upon the column. Half an hour later a peasant who had been placed near the edge of the wood announced that the Russian column was in sight, that so far as he could judge from his observations made from a tree-top, it numbered about 2000 infantry, with a battery of artillery.

"That is just a fair match for us," Stanislaus said. "The 500 men extra do not count for much, and their superiority of arms will be counterbalanced by our advantages of surprise, and to the effect which cannon brought against them for the first time may exercise on the minds of the soldiers."

Presently along the straight road the black column of the enemy could be seen. They were advancing in a heavy mass, some forty men abreast, and were preceded at a distance of 300 yards by an advance guard of 200 men. When distant some 400 yards from them the midshipmen observed the advance guard halt, and guessed that an obstacle of some sort or other across the road had been made out. A mounted officer rode back from the advance guard to the main body, and was there joined by several other mounted men. After some conversation a movement was seen in the column. A mounted officer rode back, and as he did so the column divided, leaving a passage in the centre of the road.

There was a long pause, and then the lads could see the Russian guns coming through the line. They halted and formed across the road half-way between the main body and the advance guard, and, unlimbering, prepared to open fire upon the unknown obstacle in their front. The midshipmen had arranged with Stanislas that, as it would be difficult for the parties on the flank of the Russian column to distinguish between the sound of the enemy's guns and their own, a white handkerchief should be hoisted on a long pole when they themselves opened fire, and a chain of men were placed along back in the wood to repeat the signal down to the spot where the Poles were lying ready for attack.

The Russians opened fire over the heads of their advance guard, who lay down in the road. The shot for the most part either struck the slope or flew overhead, very few striking the upper part of the battery face, which was alone exposed to their fire. For five minutes the Russians continued to fire. Then, deceived by the absolute silence which reigned, and supposing the obstacle was an accidental one, or that the insurgents had retired, the guns were limbered up, the advance guard again moved forward, and the main column marched on close behind the guns.

The whole of the 200 men who had been placed behind the barricade were armed with muskets, and each hidden behind the leafy screen rested his piece on a branch, and prepared to pour his fire into the column as it advanced. It was not until the advance guard was within fifty yards of them that the lads, who had themselves trained the guns to sweep the road, gave the signal, and the silence was broken by the roar of the two guns loaded to the muzzle with grape-shot. The effect was tremendous. Two lanes were literally mown through the ranks of the Russian infantry, the shot which flew high doing terrible execution among the artillery behind them.

The echoes had not died away when a tremendous fire of musketry was opened by the Poles hidden behind the abattis. More than half of the advance guard fell under that terrible discharge, and the artillery crowded behind them fell into confusion.

The Russian officers strove by voice and example to gather the survivors of the advance guard together; but the consternation which the slaughter had caused was heightened by the sound of a tremendous yell far behind, followed by a steady roll of musketry, showing that the column was hotly engaged there also. The artillery attempted to unlimber and to bring their guns to bear again, but the confusion that prevailed in the crowded spot rendered this next to impossible, and long before it could be accomplished the iron hail again swept through the ranks, and two rattling volleys from their invisible foes behind the flanking abattis again flashed out. The advance guard were annihilated, the artillery in confusion, but the general commanding the main column pushed his men on through the frightened horses of the artillery, and, opening a heavy musketry fire on their unseen foes, pressed forward to the assault.

The conflict now became a desperate one. The midshipmen fired their guns alternately as fast as they could load, the Poles working as steadily and coolly as if they had been long-trained artillerymen. Several times the Russians advanced to within twenty yards of the defences, but each time, shattered by the fire of grape-shot and by the storm of bullets from the abattis, they recoiled. In vain they flung themselves upon the trees and tried to hew a way through them. In vain the officers called upon them to gather themselves together and carry the battery at a rush. Receiving no aid from their own artillery, which, mingled in the throng of infantry, were helpless, shaken by the shouts of the assailants, and by the battle raging in their rear which told them their retreat was menaced, the Russians lost heart and began to fall back. Then, retaining only fifty men as a guard to the battery, the midshipmen ordered the rest of the defenders of the abattis to move forward among the trees on the flanks of the Russians, keeping up a constant fire, until they joined the main body in their attack on the Russian rear.

In the battery now they could see little of what was going forward. The woods were full of dense smoke. The whole Russian column as it fell back was maintaining a wild fire at random into the bushes around them.

But though the lads could see nothing, the road in front afforded them a sure guide for their aim, and ceaselessly the guns kept up their fire into the retreating mass of Russians.

For half an hour the roar of guns continued unabated, and then, as it died away, the triumphant shouts of the Pole told them that the victory was won, and that the Russian column, defeated and shattered, had retired from the forest and gained the open country beyond. Then the defenders of the battery raised an answering cheer to their friends in the distance, and, exhausted with their exertions, threw themselves on the ground.

Of those working the guns but three had been wounded by rifle bullets which had passed through the embrasures.

Several of the riflemen had fallen shot through the head, as they fired over the top of the battery, while thirty or forty lay killed and wounded behind the abattis.

After a few minutes' rest the party advanced, and soon joined their friends, who saluted them with loud acclamations. The victory had been a complete one. The whole of the spare ammunition and stores had fallen into the hands of the victors, upon overpowering the rear-guard, had cut the traces and carried off the horses. The column had made a sturdy resistance at this point, and although the desperate onslaughts of the scythe-armed Poles had several times broken their ranks and carried slaughter among them, they had yet stood firm, and it was only the crushing of the head of the column, and its subsequent retreat, which had at last decided the day.

For some hundred yards in front of the guns the ground was covered with Russian dead. Most of the artillery horses had fallen, and but two of the guns had been carried off the field. The loss of the enemy in killed and wounded left upon the ground amounted to nearly 800, and the wounded were all killed as soon as discovered by the infuriated peasants.

Of the Poles some 250 had been put *hors-de-combat*. The delight of the insurgents was unbounded. It was by far the most important victory which they had won. They had now come into possession of sufficient muskets to arm the whole body, and an abundant supply of ammunition, and had in all a complete battery of artillery, with enough horses, taken from the wagons, to give two to each gun, and leave a sufficient number for the ammunition wagons. The two midshipmen received the warmest thanks of the Polish leader, who attributed his success entirely to the slaughter which the guns had wrought, and to the dispositions taken for their defence.

Chapter XIX
TO THE RESCUE

A CONSULTATION was held on the evening of the battle. As was the custom of the Polish peasants after a success, many wished to return for a while to their homes and families. Several plans were proposed among the group of officers, and the leader asked the young midshipmen for their opinion.

Dick said that in his ignorance of the circumstances and the geography of the country he could offer none; but Jack, on being appealed to, said,—

"It seems to me that you will never do any good if you confine yourselves to beating back a Russian column occasionally, and then dispersing until they again advance. My opinion is that it is absolutely necessary to follow up the victory we have gained, and to do something which will induce the whole country to believe that there is a prospect of success. We have gained a very fair victory to-day. I propose that while the men are all in high spirits, and the Russians proportionately depressed, we take the offensive and fall upon one of their garrisons. Hitherto, as you say, you have always contented yourselves with attacking the columns sent out against you, and the Russians will be altogether unprepared for an attack on them in their own quarters. If we fall suddenly at night upon Piaski, we ought to succeed in nearly annihilating them. There are about 1200 men of the column whom we have fought, and about 2000 in the other column which marched out against us this morning, but fell back when they heard of the defeat of their comrades. It is probable that pretty nearly the whole force in the town came out, so that altogether there cannot be above 2500 men. If we can fall upon them at night, we ought to be able to defeat them easily. At any rate before they rally we should inflict tremendous damage upon them."

Jack's proposition was received with acclamation, and it was decided that the attack should take place on the following night. The officers therefore went among the men, and appealed to them to remain for another forty-eight hours, in order that they might annihilate the garrison of Piaski.

The men assented, the more readily that abundant supplies of bread and spirits had been found in the captured wagons, the Russian commander having deemed it probable that the expedition might extend over a period of some days.

The next morning all were instructed in the use of the Russian muskets, many of the peasants being wholly unacquainted with the management of fire-arms. It was arranged that each peasant should, in addition to his gun, carry his scythe, his favorite weapon for close conflict.

When night came on all was ready for the march. The bands were to advance separately, each under orders of its own leader, and were to unite in the market-place as the clock struck one. There were three barracks, and a certain proportion were told off for the attack of each. Three of the guns were hidden in the forest. The other three, each drawn by four horses, accompanied the column, the duty assigned to them being to blow in the gates of the several barracks. Coarse grass was cut and swathed round the wheels, and the horses' feet were also muffled. The peasants were all clad in sandals, and there was therefore no fear of the noise of their advance being heard.

At nine o'clock the column set out for the town, which was nine miles distant, and upon nearing it separated, so as to enter as arranged in different directions. Each column was preceded at a distance of some hundred yards by four or five men, chosen for their activity, their duty being to seize and silence any watchmen they might meet in the streets.

The town seemed absolutely asleep when the band of Stanislas, with which for the time were the three cannon, entered it a few minutes before one.

Once the lads thought that they could hear a stifled cry, but if so it attracted no attention, for the streets were deserted, and not a single window opened as they passed. The other hands had already arrived in the market-place when that commanded by Stanislas reached it.

A few words were exchanged by the leaders, a gun told off to each column, and the bands started to their respective destinations. The contingent of Count Stanislas, to which Jack Archer was attached with his gun, was intended to attack the principal barrack. This was built in the form of a large quadrangle, and contained some seven or eight hundred infantry and a battery of artillery.

As the head of the column entered the street leading to the gate, a sentry on the outside challenged. No answer was made, and a moment later a gun was fired.

There was no longer any need for concealment, and with a wild cheer the column rushed forward. Some of the men threw themselves with axes upon the postern gate, which the sentry had entered and closed behind him.

The gun, which was close to the head of the column, was brought up and placed in position within a few feet of the gate, its muzzle directed towards the lock. The explosion tore a hole in the gate, but a massive bar still kept this in its place. Another discharge broke this also, and the Poles with exulting shouts surged in.

As they entered, a scattered fire opened upon them from the windows, but, without pausing, the band broke up into parties, each under its chief, and rushed at the entrances leading to the staircases.

Then ensued a desperate conflict. The Russians, taken wholly by surprise, appalled by the suddenness of the attack, and knowing the ferocity with which their assailants fought, in some cases offered but slight resistance, and leaped by scores from the windows at the back, preferring the risk of death or broken limbs to awaiting the rush of their enemies. Others defended themselves desperately, gathering on the top of the stairs, barring the doors, and resisting foot by foot until every man had been cut down.

The absence of their officers, who were quartered together in a different part of the barracks, proved fatal to the defenders; accustomed to act like machines, and to move only at the command of their officers, they were bewildered at finding themselves under such circumstances without head or direction, and in ten minutes after the entry had been effected all resistance had ceased, and the barracks remained in the hands of the victorious Poles.

The instant that his own part of the work was done, Jack Archer, with a band of fifty men who had been told off to act under his orders, proceeded to the stables. The artillery horses were all brought out and harnessed to the guns and wagons, and by the time that the resistance had ceased these were ready to depart.

Jack Archer

The Poles, taking the muskets of the Russian soldiers, and lading themselves with blankets and such other articles as they fancied, swarmed out into the courtyard. In the store-rooms of the barracks were found large quantities of uniforms ready for issue to the troops, and a number of these Count Stanislas ordered to be brought out and stowed in an empty wagon.

Three minutes later the barrack was set on fire in a dozen places. Then the newly-captured artillery started at a trot for the forest, while the Poles moved away to render any assistance which might be necessary to the other columns.

The division to which Dick Hawtry was attached had experienced a success as complete as that which attended the principal column, and the flames were already rising in the air as the latter issued into the town.

The other barrack was, however, successfully defending itself. It was supposed that some watchman must have conveyed the news of the advance of the insurgents, for the instant the column appeared within sight of the barracks a musketry fire was opened upon it by the guard at the gate, and two or three minutes later every window bearing upon it was thrown up, and the Russian infantry opened a heavy fire. The gunners in vain attempted to bring up their piece close to the gate. The horses had been shot down, but scores of willing hands pushed forward the gun; but so heavy was the destruction which the Russian bullets wrought among them that these also were brought to a standstill, and when Count Stanislas arrived he found that a furious musketry encounter was raging between the Poles, now scattered all round the barrack, and the Russians pouring from the upper windows. After a hasty consultation with the other leaders, it was agreed that as the victory had been complete so far, two out of the three barracks carried and burnt, 1500 Russians killed, and a battery of artillery taken, it would be a pity to risk a final repulse by an attack upon a building which, now that the garrison were prepared for resistance, could only be carried with a great loss of life.

The horns were accordingly sounded, and the assailants drawn off, and the column marched through the town, now illuminated by the flames of the two burning barracks. It was but half an hour since the attack had begun, but the appearance of the town had changed as if by magic. Every house was lit up, every window open, crowds of people thronged the streets, while the windows were filled with women and children. All were delirious with delight, and cheered, shouted, and waved their handkerchiefs as the patriot band marched along. Not a few of the younger men, bidding a hasty adieu to their friends, joined the ranks of their countrymen, and, seizing one of the captured muskets, prepared to take a part in the strife which had been so well begun.

Upon gaining the forest a halt was ordered. Great fires were lit, and the companies mustered, when it was found that some eighty of those present had received wounds, and that forty had fallen. All the wounded unable to walk had been carried off, as to leave them where they fell would be to expose them to certain death when found by the Russians. A plentiful supply of spirits had been found in the stores, and several barrels brought off. An ample allowance was now served out, and after an hour's carouse in honor of the victory the band, fatigued by their exertions, went off to sleep.

In the morning the guns—now amounting to two complete batteries—were taken some miles farther into the forest. The greater part of the band insisted upon returning to their homes for a few days, and their leader, finding himself powerless to resist the determination gave them leave to do so. All agreed to return at the end of ten days. Some 400 men remained, and from these the count requested the midshipmen to choose a sufficient number to constitute two batteries, each eighty strong, and to drill them as far as possible in the interval. He himself started to visit his estates, which lay about eighty miles from their present position. Here he hoped to raise a further contingent of men, and all who went home were bidden to bring back fresh recruits, and to spread everywhere the news of the victory.

Six days elapsed, and the band in the forest had already been increased by many hundreds of new-comers, whom the news of the successes which had been gained had induced to take up arms, and the time of the various leaders was fully occupied in giving some notion of drill and of the use of the musket to the new levies.

On the evening of the sixth day a peasant arrived with intelligence which spread dismay in the encampment. Count Stanislas had been captured by the Russians, having been surprised by a body of Russian cavalry, who, doubtless by means of a spy, had obtained news of his return home. He had been conveyed to Lublin, where he would doubtless be at once tried and executed.

A council of the leaders was hastily summoned.

Lublin was a large town garrisoned by some 5000 Russian troops, and even had the whole of the insurgent bands been collected, they would not have been strong enough to attempt a repetition of their late successful surprise, especially, as after that occurrence, the Russian troops would be everywhere on the alert.

All agreed that the loss of their most successful leader would be a death-blow to the revolt in that part of the country. The personal popularity of the young leader was immense, and the prestige which he had won by his several successes had excited the greatest confidence among his followers. So important was his life considered that the midshipmen urged that at all costs his rescue should be attempted, and although the enterprise appeared a desperate one, their proposal was finally agreed to.

A few men were at once despatched to Lublin to find out what was going on, and when and where the execution would take place, while 500 chosen men prepared to march through the forests to a point within a few miles of the town, where the spies were to rejoin them.

Just as they were starting the idea struck Dick that the Russian uniforms might be utilized, and, much to their disgust, half the party were ordered to dress themselves in the hated garb. The transformation was soon effected, and the band set out on their march.

Upon the third evening they arrived at the indicated spot, where several of the spies were already awaiting them. These informed them that the trial would take place on the following day, and that it was generally supposed that the count would be executed the next morning as there could be no doubt what the finding of the court would be.

Next day the midshipmen, accompanied by several of the leaders, all in peasants' dress, visited the town to learn its general features, and make themselves acquainted with the approaches to the great square, where it was considered probable the execution would take place. They found the whole population moody and depressed. The news of the successes of the patriot bands had already spread far and wide, and had excited high hopes in every

Jack Archer

Polish breast. The fact, then, that the most successful leader was in the hands of their enemies had spread universal grief and consternation. After learning all the particulars they desired, the party rejoined their friends in the forest. The greatest difficulty existed from the fact that it would be impossible for the rescuing party to carry either muskets or their long scythes. Some twenty revolvers had fallen into their hands in the two fights, and with these the officers had all armed themselves. A certain portion of the men cut long sticks, like ox-goads, made to fit the bayonets; others fitted short handles to their scythes, while others carried short heavy sticks, to which again bayonets were fitted. A hundred of those dressed as soldiers were to carry their muskets, and, under the orders of one of their leaders, to march boldly down the street, so timing their arrival as to reach the square just at the time at which the execution was to take place, while the rest were to mix with the crowd.

Late at night the news was brought to them that proclamations had been posted through the town, saying that the execution would take place at eight in the morning in the grand square. Orders had been issued, it was learnt, that 1000 troops should be present, and the others were ordered to be in readiness in their barracks, in case any sign of popular feeling should be manifested. As it was evident, therefore, that no soldiers in uniform would be loitering in the street, it was determined that the 250 men so dressed should march together to the square with their arms.

In the morning the insurgents, in twos and threes, started for the town, and joined the town's-people assembling in the great square. Across the square, within thirty or forty paces of one side, was formed up a strong battalion of Russian infantry, the rest of the square being occupied by the town's-people, all of whom had attired themselves in mourning. In the centre of the square, behind the soldiers, a scaffold had been erected, as by the sentence of the court-martial the count was to die by hanging.

The midshipmen and their friends made their way through the crowd to the front, the latter giving way upon a whisper being circulated that an attempt was to be made to rescue the prisoner, and the 250 insurgents were soon gathered in a close body in front of the soldiers standing before the scaffold. Each man had his scythe or bayonet hidden under his long coat, the leaders grasping their pistols. The men had been ordered to refrain from any expression of excitement, and to assume, as far as possible, a look of quiet grief. Behind the infantry were a number of mounted officers, among whom General Borodoff, the governor of the town and district, was pointed out to the midshipmen, and near the general, under a strong guard, the prisoner was standing. All the insurgents, with the exception of those forming the first line, quietly fitted their scythes and bayonets to the handles and waited the signal.

Presently there was a movement behind the troops, who were drawn up six deep. Then a man was seen mounting the scaffold followed by the priest, behind whom came the prisoner between two warders. Just at this moment there was a stir in the crowd at the end of the square, and over the heads of the people a line of glittering bayonets could be seen coming down the street. The general looked in that direction with surprise, and immediately gave orders to a mounted officer beside him, who, passing through the line of soldiers, tried to make his way through the crowd. This, however, either from its denseness or an unwillingness to move from the place it had gained, made way for him but slowly, in spite of his angry shouts to the people to clear a way.

Chapter XX
IN A LION'S DEN

UPON one side of the lane which the fugitives had entered ran a high wall. Upon the other was a very large mansion. Its lower windows were five feet from the ground. As the lads ran they saw an open window. Without a moment's hesitation they placed their hands on the sill, threw themselves into it, and flung down the window. There was a scream as they entered, followed by an exclamation in English. The boys looked round, and saw a young lady who had started back in terror to a corner of the room.

"Are you English?" Jack exclaimed in astonishment. "We are English officers escaping from a Russian prison. In heaven's name do not betray us!"

As he spoke the Russian cavalry came along the lane at full gallop.

"I am English," the young lady said, as she recovered from her astonishment, "I am governess to the younger daughters of the governor. You are now in his palace. But what has taken place? I heard the firing and went to the window to listen."

"We have been aiding in the rescue of a Polish leader who was to have been executed this morning," Dick said. "We succeeded in that, but were attacked and cut up afterwards, and had to scatter. I fear that they will suspect we must have entered this place, for they were close behind us, and there was no other escape possible. Can you conceal us? It seems almost like a miracle finding an English lady here."

"A great many of the Russian nobility have English tutors or governesses, and although some went back to England at the beginning of the war, the greater number have remained quietly at their work. I fear that the whole palace will be searched if it is suspected that you have taken refuge here. How imprudent of you to have mixed yourselves up in this rebellion!"

"We could hardly help ourselves," Jack said, "but it is too late to discuss that now. Will you look out of the window and see if the lane is empty? If so, we had best make off without delay."

The young lady went to the window.

"No," she replied at once, "there is a soldier on horseback a few yards to the right."

"Don't open the window, then," Jack said. "They have evidently put a line of patrols along the lane. We must not get you into trouble," he continued, turning towards her. "If you will show us the way, we will go at once and give ourselves up."

"Oh, no," the lady exclaimed. "That must not be. But where can I hide you?" and she stood for a minute or two thinking. "I think the safest place of all," she said at last, "the only place where you would have a chance of escaping, if a search is made, is in the general's own writing-room. It is very bare of furniture, but there are heavy curtains to the windows. No one would think of searching that room, and the chances are that no one will go near the windows."

The lads agreed that the plan was a good one, and the young lady hurried away to see if the room, which was not far from her own, was still empty. She returned in a minute, and beckoned to them to follow her. They soon arrived at a room which was simply furnished with a few chairs and an armchair placed at a table. Across the two windows hung heavy curtains, and behind these the midshipmen took their places, the curtains extending far enough beyond the windows for them to stand between them and the walls; so that any one going to the windows would not necessarily see them. Then leaving them with many injunctions to remain quiet, and with a promise to return at the end of the day and release them, she left, being, she said, due with her pupils at nine o'clock.

For half an hour the boys conversed in low tones with each other as to their chances of escape. Then footsteps were heard, and the governor entered, followed by several officers. He took his seat at the table.

"If," he said to one of them, "your report, that you were so short a distance behind these men that it was impossible they could have reached the end of the lane before you entered it, be correct, it is clear they must have taken refuge here. You did quite right to place a cordon all round the palace. Write an order at once for the chief of police to send down twenty men to search the house thoroughly from top to bottom. Let them visit every room, not excepting even the apartments of my wife and daughters. You say that they were most conspicuous in the attack upon your cavalry, and I myself observed two very young men leading the attack upon the infantry. Well, sir," turning to another officer, "what is your report of the losses?"

"Two hundred and three of the cavalry have been killed, sir. There are only ten wounded. One hundred and sixty-three infantry killed, and 204 wounded. We have found the bodies of 133 armed men, who were killed either in the square or in the pursuit, and 97 bodies, apparently those of town's-people in the square."

"Put them all down as insurgents," the general said. "They are traitors and rebels, the whole brood. Let strong bodies of infantry patrol the streets. Order all shops to be shut and the inhabitants to keep within doors, and let a body of troops be placed at the disposal of the chief of police for a search from house to house. Some of these scoundrels may be hidden in the town."

All day, officers, the bearers of reports, or who came to receive orders, entered and left the room, among them the chief of police, who reported that he had searched the palace from top to bottom, without the omission of a single room, and had failed altogether to find any traces of the fugitives.

"If they entered, they must be somewhere," said the general. "Let a close cordon be kept around the house all night, with orders to shoot down any one they may see leaving it. To-morrow you will repeat your search of the house. If they are here, they must be found."

The hours seemed intolerably long to the lads, standing upright and motionless against the wall. No one approached their hiding-place. At four o'clock the general gave orders that his horse and escort should be at the door, and a few minutes afterwards he went out, and the room was left deserted. The midshipmen were now able to stand in easier positions, but they did not venture to leave their hiding-places, in case any one should suddenly return. The hours passed slowly on, and it was nine o'clock before the door opened. It closed again, and a voice asked in low tones whether they were still there.

The lads joyfully replied that they were.

"Follow me, then," she said, "as quietly as you can. There is no one about."

G. A. Henty

They were soon in the room where they had first entered. The curtains were drawn, and candles burning on the table.

"You are safe here," the lady said. "I have just dined with my charges, and my duties are over for the day. No one is likely to disturb us here. This is my private sitting-room. My bedroom is next door. If any one is heard coming, you must hide there. I will go in at once and change my dress for a dressing-gown, and I can then lock the door; so that if any one comes, there will be time for you to go in there, and when I open it, and say I am preparing for bed, it will account for the door being locked."

She did as she had said, and then produced from a cupboard a box of biscuits and a decanter of wine, which she placed before them.

"You must be starving," she said. "I am sorry that I have nothing more to offer you, but it was impossible for me to get any food. I have been thinking all day," she went on, as the boys fell to at the biscuits, "how you are to be smuggled out; I can only think of one plan, and that is a fearfully dangerous one. But I do not know that it is more so than your continued stay here. The palace is to be searched to-morrow afternoon again, even more strictly than to-day, and that was strict enough. They turned every room topsy-turvy, opened every closet, and not only looked under the beds, but pulled the beds to pieces, to assure themselves that nobody was hidden within them. I hear that the general says that he is so convinced that you are here somewhere, that he will keep the soldiers round the house, and search it every day till you are found, if it is a month hence. Consequently, great as is the risk of the plan I have thought of, it is scarcely as great as that of remaining here."

The midshipmen expressed their willingness to try any plan, however desperate, rather than remain day after day standing in the governor's room, with the risk of betrayal by a cough or other involuntary movement.

"This is my plan, then. The governor's eldest daughters are women as old as myself. They are tall and stout, and as far as figure goes I think you might pass in their places. They go out for a drive every morning. I have this afternoon slipped into their rooms and have borrowed two of their dresses, mantles and bonnets. Fortunately they usually wear veils. They do not generally go to dress until the carriage is at the door, and I propose that you shall boldly walk down and take their places. Of course, the risk is dreadful, but I really see no other chance for your escape. What do you say?"

The midshipmen at once agreed to make the attempt, and were soon dressed in the clothes which their friend had brought them. Walking about the room, she gave them lessons in carriage and manner, imitated herself the air with which the general's daughters bowed to the officers as they saluted them as they passed, and even gave them instructions in the tone of voice in which they should order the driver to take the way to the public promenade. At length she pronounced that they ought to pass muster at a casual inspection, and then, bidding them good-night, she retired to her own room, while the lads were soon asleep, the one on the couch, the other on the hearthrug.

At seven o'clock their friend, who had told them that her name was Agnes Sinclair, came into the room dressed, unlocked the door, and then led them into her bedroom, as she said that at half-past seven the servants would come to do up the sitting-room, light the fire, and prepare breakfast.

"I am my own mistress," she said, "till nine o'clock, and as the servants do not go into my bedroom till I have gone to my pupils, you will be quite

127

safe. You must have some more biscuits for breakfast, for I am a very small eater, and it would not do were it noticed that a greater quantity of food than usual had disappeared."

The boys were now again dressed in the clothes prepared for them, and this time put on gloves which Miss Sinclair had also brought, and into which it needed all the boys' efforts to pass their hands. Fortunately the bonnets of the time completely enveloped the head, concealing the back half, and coming well forward over the face, and when the veils were dropped Miss Sinclair said that unless she had known the truth, she should not have suspected the deception.

When the servant knocked at the door, and said that breakfast was ready, the governess left them, and presently returned, bringing them the biscuits.

"Now," she said, "in a quarter of an hour the carriage will be at the door. It always comes punctually at nine. From the window of the opposite room I can see when it arrives. Now, you quite understand? You walk straight along this passage. At the end is a wider one to the right, which will take you into the great hall. Here there will be several servants, and perhaps some officers standing about. All will bow as you pass through them. You are to bow slightly as I have shown you. If any of the officers come up to speak, as is possible, though not likely, for none of high enough rank to do so are likely to be there so early, answer only in a word or two in the voice you practised last night. Two servants will show you into the carriage. As you take your seats, you will say to the coachman, 'To the promenade.' After that you must do as you judge best. There is one drawback, I forgot to tell you, an escort of two soldiers always rides fifty or sixty yards behind the carriage."

"So that we once get through the town," Jack said, "we shan't care much for the two soldiers, for we still have our revolvers. Now you promise, Miss Sinclair, that when you come to England you will let our people know. We have given you the addresses. They will want to thank you for our escape if we get away, and for your kindness even if the worst comes to the worst. I do hope that there is no possibility of a suspicion falling upon you about the missing dresses."

"Oh, no," Miss Sinclair said, "I'm sure no one saw me go to their rooms, and it will be supposed that you were hidden somewhere there, and have taken them yourselves. I shall make the things you have taken off into a bundle, slip into a room close to theirs, and throw them under a bed. If it were known that you are English, it is possible that some suspicion might fall upon me. As it is, there is no reason why I more than any one else should have been concerned in the matter. Now, it is just nine o'clock. I will go across into the other room, and look out. Fortunately it is unoccupied."

Three minutes later she returned.

"It is at the door," she said. "Wait two or three minutes. I will go straight now, hide your clothes, and take my place with my pupils as usual. I am always punctual to the minute."

With another word or two of thanks the boys said good-bye to her, and Miss Sinclair at once went on her way with a final warning, "Be sure and be leisurely in your movements. Do not show the least haste. Peep out before you start, so as to be sure there's no one in this passage, as otherwise you might be seen coming from this room."

The boys waited another minute or two, and then, seeing that the passage was clear, moved along it, walking slowly and stiffly as they had been directed, with short steps and gliding movement. Both had their pistols in their pockets ready to hand, as they were resolved to be killed rather than taken. Fortunately there was no one in the next passage into which they turned, and they reached the grand hall unnoticed. Here were a number of servants and officers, who bowed deeply on perceiving, as they supposed, the daughters of the governor. Two servants threw open the grand door, and an official preceded them to the carriage. The boys bowed slightly and passed on. No one accosted them, and they took their seats in the carriage with the deliberation and dignity which had been impressed upon them. The official spread a bear-skin rug over their knees, and demanded which way they would go.

Jack replied, "To the promenade." The carriage—which was an open one—proceeded on its way at a rapid pace, and the boys' hopes rose higher and higher. They had not gone far when they heard a horse's hoofs behind them, and, turning round, saw an officer galloping rapidly.

"Keep steady, Jack," Dick whispered.

When the officer reached the side of the carriage he reined in his horse, and took off his cap. "Ladies," he said, "his excellency the governor saw you drive away, and ordered me to ride after you, and tell you that he did not know you were going out, and that he considered it more prudent for you to remain at home for a day or two until the excitement of the late events has cooled down."

"Thank you," Dick said in his best Russian, and speaking in a feigned voice. "Will you tell my father that we will return in a few minutes? Drive on," he said to the coachman.

The officer sat for a minute looking after them, for something in the accent with which Dick spoke seemed strange to him, but being fortunately unacquainted with the ladies of the general's family, he suspected nothing wrong. It was evident to the boys, however, that the coachman was struck with the sound of the voice, as he rapidly spoke to the man sitting next him, and the latter once or twice endeavored privately to glance back.

They had now reached the promenade, which, owing to the governor's order that all inhabitants should keep their houses, was entirely deserted, except by a few Russian officers walking or riding. These all saluted as the general's carriage passed them. On reaching the end of the drive the coachman was about to turn, when the lads jumped to their feet, and commanded him to stop. The coachman looked round astonished, but at the sight of two pistols pointed at their heads, he and his fellow-servant, with a cry of alarm and astonishment, leaped from the box. Jack in an instant scrambled over and seized the reins. The soldiers had halted upon seeing the carriage stop, and remained stupefied with astonishment as they saw the two servants leap off, and one of the ladies climb into their seat. Nor did they move until the servants, running up hastily, explained what had happened. Then, putting the spurs into their horses, they galloped forward. Dick, who was looking back, saw at the same moment several horsemen at full gallop appear at the other end of the promenade.

"The general has found out the trick, Jack," he said. "Keep them going steadily and steer straight. I can answer for those fellows behind. They can't be sure yet what's up."

As the soldiers approached, Dick leaned his pistol on the back of the

Jack Archer

carriage and took a steady aim, and when they were within twenty yards, fired, aiming at the head of one of the horses. In an instant there was a crash, and the horse and rider were on the ground. The other soldier at once reined up his horse, bewildered at what had happened, and not knowing even now that the carriage was not occupied by the general's daughters.

"That's right, Jack," Dick said. "We have got nearly half a mile start of the others, and the forest is, Miss Sinclair said, scarce three miles away. Let them go it, but be sure you steer straight."

The horses were now tearing along at a furious gallop. Presently another long, straight bit of road enabled them to see their pursuers again. The horsemen had been increased in number by the officers who had been riding in the promenade, and were now some twenty in number. Of these, at least half whose helmets glistening in the sun showed Dick that they were soldiers, had already fallen in the rear, the others had gained upon them considerably. They were now, however, fully half way to the forest.

"That's right, Jack, keep them going," Dick said, as Jack flogged the animals to their highest speed. "We shall have plenty of time to get away into the wood before they come up, only for goodness' sake keep us straight."

When they reached the forest their pursuers were still some hundreds of yards in the rear. Checking the horses where the underwood was thickest, the midshipmen leaped out, gave a parting lash to the horses, which started them again at full speed, and then dashed into the thicket.

Any one who had seen them would have been astounded and amused at the spectacle of two fashionably-dressed ladies dashing recklessly through the thick brushwood. After a quarter of an hour's run they paused breathless. Jack dashed his bonnet to the ground.

"For goodness' sake, Dick!" he said, shaking off his mantle, "unhook the back of my dress, and let me get rid of the thing. I used to laugh at my sisters for not running as fast as I could. Now I wonder how on earth they manage to run at all."

Their borrowed finery was soon got rid of, and in their shirts and trousers the boys proceeded. Presently they came suddenly upon four peasants seated on the ground, who upon seeing them leaped to their feet and greeted them with signs of vehement joy, making signs to them to follow them, and presently led them to a spot where the remains of the insurgent band were gathered. A shout greeted them as soon as they were recognized, and Count Stanislas, running forward, threw his arms round their necks and embraced them, while the other leaders crowded round.

"It is indeed happiness to see you again," the count said. "We feared you had fallen into the hands of the Russians. I sent spies last night into the town, but they brought back word that the streets were absolutely deserted, and they dared not enter. I resolved to wait for a day or two until we could hear with certainty what had befallen you. Now tell us all that has happened."

The midshipmen recounted their adventures, saying that they had remained concealed in the very writing-room of the governor, and giving full details of their escape dressed as his daughters; saving only the part which Miss Sinclair had played, for they thought that in case any of the band fell into the hands of the enemy, they might under the influence of the torture, which the Russians freely administered to their captives, reveal all that they had heard. They then inquired what were the count's intentions.

G. A. Henty

"I shall move farther west," he said, "and after gathering my old band together, move to join some others, who I hear have been doing good work in that direction. We shall not be far from the frontier; and, much as I shall regret to lose you, I will, if you wish it, lead a party to the frontier, and cut a way through the cordon of troops there for you."

The boys gladly accepted the offer. They had had more than enough of insurrectionary warfare, and longed to be back again with their comrades at Sebastopol.

Three days' marching took the band back to the forest, where some 1500 men were assembled, awaiting anxiously the return of the party.

A day was given for rest, and then horses were harnessed to the two batteries of artillery, and moving by little-frequented roads through the forest, the small army marched west.

For ten days the march continued, for the roads were heavy and the horses unable to accomplish such marches as those of which the peasants were capable. At last they effected a junction with the band which they had come to join, whose numbers amounted to nearly 4000 men. Their arrival, and especially the advent of the artillery, was greeted with enthusiasm, and it was at once proposed to take the offensive. Count Stanislas said, however, that his horses were completely knocked up with the fatigue they had undergone, and that a rest of two or three days was necessary in order to recruit.

"Now," he said to the midshipmen, "I will redeem my promise. The frontier is only fifty miles distant. I will send on a man at once to ascertain some point at which there are boats on this side of the river. I will march at daylight with 150 picked men, and no fear but with a sudden attack we shall break through the patrols."

The plan was carried out. The boys, inured to marching, made the fifty miles journey before nightfall. They were met by the spy, who stated that the boats had almost all been removed, but that a number were gathered at a village which was occupied by 200 Russian infantry.

The midshipmen proposed that they should steal through and endeavor to get one of the boats, but their friend would not hear of their running such a risk, and after taking some hours of rest the party proceeded on their march. It was an hour before daybreak when they entered the village. Just as they reached it a sentry fired his musket, and with a rush the Poles charged forward. It had been arranged that the count and the midshipmen with five men should run straight through the village down to the water-side, and that the rest of the force were to commence a furious attack upon the houses inhabited by the troops, who, believing that they were assailed by superior forces, would be some time before they took the offensive.

Chapter XXI
BACK AT THE FRONT

AROUSED by the sound of the sentry's musket, the Russian soldiers rushed to their windows and doors and opened a scattering fire, which was heavily responded to by the Poles. The midshipmen with their party ran hastily down the village. There were two sentries over the boats, but these, alarmed by the din in the village and the sight of the approaching figures, fired their muskets and fled. Dick uttered a low exclamation.

"What is the matter, Dick? are you hit?"

"Yes," Dick said. "My arm is broken. Never mind, let us push on."

They leaped into a boat. Jack seized the sculls, the rope which fastened them to the shore was cut, and with a last shout of farewell to the count, they pulled off into the stream. For a few minutes the sound of battle continued, and then suddenly died away, as Count Stanislas, his object accomplished, drew off his men.

A few minutes' rowing brought the boat to the opposite bank. Here they found Austrian sentries, who accosted them in German. As, however, the Austrian Government offered no obstacle to Polish fugitives entering the frontier, the lads were conducted to the officer of the troops at the little village which faced that on the Russian bank. Here they were questioned, first in Polish and then in German, but upon the boys repeating the word "English," the officer, who spoke a little French, addressed them in that language, and Dick explained that they were English naval officers taken prisoners at Sebastopol, and making their escape through Poland. He then asked if there was a surgeon who could dress his wound, but was told that none was procurable nearer than a town fifteen miles away. A country cart was speedily procured and filled with straw, and upon this Dick lay down, while Jack took his seat by the peasant who was to drive the cart.

It was eleven o'clock in the day when they entered the town, and the peasant drew up, in accordance with the instructions he had received, at the best hotel, the landlord of which was in no slight degree surprised at such an arrival, and was disposed to refuse them admittance. Jack, however, produced a bundle of Russian notes, at which sight the landlord's hesitation vanished at once, and in half an hour a surgeon stood by Dick's bedside dressing his wound. It was a severe one, the bone being broken between the elbow and shoulder.

The next day Dick was in a state of high fever, due more to the hardship and exposure through which he bad passed than to the wound, and for a week lay between life and death. Then he began to mend, but the doctor said that it would be long before he could use his arm again, and that rest and quiet were absolutely necessary to restore him.

A week later, therefore, the midshipmen left the town, Dick having determined that he would travel home by easy stages, while Jack, of course, would journey direct to join his ship.

He had written immediately upon his arrival to acquaint his family, and that of Dick, that both were alive and had escaped from Russia. The tailors had been set to work, and the midshipmen presented a respectable appearance. Dick was still so weak that he could scarcely stand, and Jack tried hard to persuade him to stay for another week. But Dick was pining to be home, and would not hear of delay. A day's travel in a diligence brought them to a railway station, and twelve hours later they arrived at Vienna.

Here they stopped for a day in luxurious quarters, and then Jack, after seeing his friend into the train on his way home, started to travel over the Semmering pass down to Trieste, where he knew he should find no difficulty in obtaining a steamer to Constantinople.

After forty-eight hours' diligence travelling, Jack reached the pretty seaport on the northern shore of the Adriatic. He found to his satisfaction that one of the Austrian Lloyd's steamers would sail for Constantinople on the following morning. He spent the evening in buying a great stock of such articles as he had most found the want of in camp, and had accumulated quite a respectable stock of baggage by the time he went on board ship. After six days' steaming, during which they were never out of sight of land, they cast anchor opposite Constantinople.

Jack did not report himself to the naval authorities here, as he thought it quite possible that the "Falcon" had been recalled or sent on other service, and he hoped that in that case he would, upon reaching the front, be appointed to some other ship.

There was no difficulty in obtaining a passage to Balaklava, for two or three transports, or merchantmen laden with stores, were going up every day. He paused, however, for three days, as it was absolutely necessary for him to obtain a fit-out of fresh uniforms before rejoining, and at Galata he found European tailors perfectly capable of turning out such articles.

Jack felt uncommonly pleased as he surveyed himself in a glass in his new equipment; for it was now eight months since he had landed in the Crimea, and the dilapidation of his garments had from that time been rapid. The difficulties of toilet had, too, been great, and white shirts were things absolutely unknown; so that Jack had never felt really presentable from the time when he landed.

The day he had obtained his outfit he took a passage in a ship laden with stores, and sailed for the Crimea. He had already learned that the "Falcon" was still there, and when the vessel entered the harbor he was delighted at seeing her lying as one of the guard-ships there. An hour later, one of the ship's boats conveyed him and his baggage to the side of the "Falcon." The first person he saw on reaching the deck was Mr. Hethcote. The officer stared when Jack saluted and reported himself in the usual words, "Come aboard, sir," and fell back a pace in astonishment.

"What, Jack! Jack Archer!" he exclaimed. "My dear boy, is it really you?"

"It's me, sure enough, sir," Jack said, and the next moment Mr. Hethcote was shaking his hand as if he would have wrung it off.

"Why, my dear Jack," he exclaimed, "the men all reported that both you and poor Hawtry were killed. They said they saw him shot, and, looking back, saw you killed over his body. It was never doubted a moment, and your names appeared in the list of the killed."

"Well, sir, we are alive nevertheless, and Dick is by this time at home with his people. He would have come on and joined with me at once, sir, only he got his arm broken, and was laid up with fever after some fighting we had among the Polish insurgents."

"Among what!" Mr. Hethcote exclaimed, astonished. "But never mind that now; I am glad indeed to hear that Hawtry also is alive, but you must tell me all about it presently. There are your other friends waiting to speak to you."

By this time the news of Jack's return had spread through the ship. The midshipmen had all run on deck, and the men crowded the waist, or, regardless of discipline, stood on the bulwarks. Jack had been a general favorite. The gallantry which he and his comrade had displayed on the night of the storm had greatly endeared them to the crew, and the men had bitterly regretted that they had not stood with him over Hawtry's body; but, indeed, it was not until they had passed on, and it was too late to return, that they had noticed his absence.

As Jack turned from Mr. Hethcote, his messmates crowded round him, and the men broke into a hearty cheer, again and again repeated. Jack, gratified and touched by this hearty welcome, could scarce reply to the questions which his comrades poured upon him, and was speedily dragged below to the midshipmen's berth, where he gave a very brief outline of what had happened since he saw them, a story which filled them with astonishment and some little envy.

"I will tell you all about it fully, later on," Jack said, "but it would take me till night to give you the full yarn now. But first you must tell me what has happened here. You know I have heard nothing, and only know that Sebastopol is not yet taken."

The recital was a long one, and Jack was fain to admit that the hardships which he had gone through were as nothing to those which had been borne by our soldiers in the Crimea during the six months he had been away from them. The trials and discomforts of the great storm had been but a sample of what was to be undergone. After Inkerman, it had been plain to the generals in command that all idea of taking Sebastopol must be abandoned until the spring, and that at the utmost they could do no more than hold their position before it. This had been rendered still more difficult by the storm, in which enormous quantities of stores, warm clothing, and other necessaries had been lost.

It was now too late to think of making a road from Balaklava to the front, a work which, had the authorities in the first place dreamt that the army would have to pass the winter on the plateau, was of all others the most necessary. The consequence of this omission was that the sufferings of the troops were terrible.

While Balaklava harbor was crowded with ships full of huts, clothing, and fuel, the men at the front were dying in hundreds from wet, cold, and insufficient food. Between them and abundance extended an almost impassable quagmire, in which horses and bullocks sank and died in thousands, although laden only with weights which a donkey in ordinary times could carry. Had the strength of the regiments in front been sufficient, the soldiers might have been marched down, when off duty, to Balaklava, to carry up the necessaries they required. But so reduced were they by over-work and fatigue, that those fit for duty had often to spend five nights out of seven in the trenches, and were physically too exhausted and worn-out to go down to

G. A. Henty

Balaklava for necessaries, even of the most urgent kind. Many of the regiments were almost annihilated. Large numbers of fresh troops had come out, and drafts for those already there, but the new-comers, mostly raw lads, broke down under the strain almost as fast as they arrived, and in spite of the number sent out, the total available strength did not increase. One regiment could only muster nine men fit for duty. Many were reduced to the strength of a company. The few survivors of one regiment were sent down to Scutari until fresh drafts should arrive and the regiment could be reorganized, and yet this regiment had not been engaged in any of the battles. Scarce a general of those who had commanded divisions and brigades at the Alma now remained, and the regimental officers had suffered proportionally. The regiments which had won the Alma still remained before Sebastopol, but their constituents had almost entirely changed, and the proportion of those who had first landed in the Crimea that still remained there when Jack returned was small indeed.

The sufferings of the French, although great, had not been nearly so severe as our own. Their camps were much nearer to their port, the organization of their services was far better and more complete, and as in the first place the siege work had been equally divided between them, the numbers at that time being nearly the same, the work of our men had become increasingly hard as their numbers diminished, while that of the French grew lighter, for their strength had been trebled by reinforcements from home. Thus, while our men were often five nights out of the seven on duty in the cold and wet, the French had five nights out of seven in bed. This gave them far greater time to forage for fuel, which was principally obtained by digging up the roots of the vines and brushwood—every twig above the surface having long since been cleared away—to dig deep holes under their tents, to dry their clothes and to make life comfortable.

At last the strength of the English diminished to such a point that they were at length incapable of holding the long line of trenches, and they were obliged to ask the French to relieve them, which they did by taking over the right of our attack, a measure which placed them opposite to the two Russian positions of the Mamelon and Malakoff batteries, which proved to be the keys of Sebastopol.

As spring came on matters brightened fast. English contractors sent out large bodies of navvies, and began to lay down a railway from Balaklava to the front, reinforcements poured in, and the health of the troops began to improve. Troops of transport animals from every country on the Mediterranean were landed. A village of shops, set up by enterprising settlers, was started two miles out of Balaklava. Huts sprang up in all directions, and all sorts of comforts purchased by the subscriptions of the English people when they heard of the sufferings of their soldiers, were landed and distributed.

The work of getting up siege guns and storing ammunition for a re-opening of the bombardment in earnest, went on merrily, and the arrival of 15,000 Turkish troops, and of nearly 20,000 Sardinians, who pitched their camps on the plain, rendered the allies secure from an attack in that direction, and enabled them to concentrate all their efforts on the siege.

So far the success had lain wholly with the Russians. For every earthwork and battery raised and armed by the allies, the Russians threw up two, and whereas when our armies arrived before it on 25th September,

Jack Archer

Sebastopol was little more than an open town, which could have been carried by the first assault, it was now a fortified place, bristling with batteries in every direction, of immense strength, and constructed upon the most scientific principles. Many of their works, especially the Mamelon, Malakoff, and Tower batteries, were fortresses in themselves, with refuges dug deeply in the earth, where the garrison slept, secure from the heaviest fire of our guns, and surrounded by works on every side.

In the trenches it was the Russians who were always the aggressors. Sortie after sortie was made throughout the winter, and in these the Russians often obtained possession for a time of portions of our trenches or those of the French. Along in front of their works the ground was studded with rifle-pits, sometimes so close to our works that it was impossible for a man to show his head above them, and the artillerymen were frequently unable to work their guns, owing to the storm of bullets which the Russians sent through the embrasures whenever a sign of movement was discerned. In the desperate fights in darkness in the trenches we lost more men than in either of the pitched battles of the campaign; and it was only the dogged courage of our soldiers and the devotion of the officers which enabled us to maintain our footing in the trenches before the city which we were supposed to be besieging.

Throughout the winter the fleet had lain inactive, although why they should have done so none knew, when they had it in their power, by attacking the Russian forts in the Sea of Azof, to destroy the granaries upon which the besieged depended for their supplies.

The midshipmen, however, were able to tell Jack that they had not been altogether idle, as the fleet had at last, on the 22d of May, been set in motion, and they had but two days before returned from their expedition. All the light vessels of the English and French fleets had taken part in it. The fort of Yenikale which commanded the entrance of the Bay of Kertch had been captured, the batteries silenced, and the town occupied, and in four days after the squadron had entered the straits of Kertch they had destroyed 245 Russian vessels employed in carrying provisions to the Russian army in the Crimea. Besides this, enormous magazines of corn and flour were destroyed at Berdiansk, Genitchi and Kertch, and at the latter place immense quantities of military and naval stores also fell into our hands. Had this expedition taken place in October instead of May, it is probable that the Russians would have been unable to maintain their hold of Sebastopol.

A portion of the fleet had remained in possession of the Sea of Azof, and thenceforth the Russians had to depend upon land carriage. This, however, mattered comparatively little, as the country was now firm and dry, and all the roads from Russia to the Crimea were available.

All their comrades had taken share in the work in the batteries and Jack learned to his surprise that Captain Stuart had been transferred to a larger ship, and that Mr. Hethcote had got his promotion, and now commanded the "Falcon," Jack, in the first excitement of meeting him, not having noticed the changes in uniform which marked his advance.

After two hours' conversation with his friends, Jack received a message that Captain Hethcote invited him to dine in his cabin, and here a quarter of an hour later he found not only the captain, but the first and second lieutenants.

After dinner was over, Jack was requested to give a full narrative of his adventures, which greatly astonished his auditors, and was not concluded until late in the evening. The lieutenants then retired, and Jack was left alone with the captain, who signified that he wished to speak further with him.

"Well, Jack," he said, when they were alone, "I did not think when I offered my uncle to get you a midshipman's berth, that I was going to put you in the way of passing through such a wonderful series of adventures. They have been sadly cut up at home at the news of your death. I hope that you wrote to them as soon as you had a chance."

"I wrote on the very day I crossed the frontier, sir," Jack said. "Besides I wrote twice from Russia, but I don't suppose they ever got the letters."

"And so you speak Russian fluently now, Jack?"

"I speak it quite well enough to get on with, sir," Jack said. "You see, I was speaking nothing else for five months. I expect my grammar is very shaky, as I picked it all up entirely by ear, and no doubt I make awful mistakes, but I can get on fast enough."

"I shall report your return to-morrow to the Admiral," Captain Hethcote said. "It is not improbable that he will at once attach you to the battery in front again. The bombardment is to re-open next week, and the generals expect to carry the town by assault; though, between ourselves, I have no belief that our batteries will be able to silence the enemy's guns sufficiently to make an assault upon such a tremendous position possible. However, as they expect to do it, it is probable that they will like having an officer who can speak Russian at the front, as interpreters would, of course, be useful. I suppose you would rather stay on board for a bit."

"Yes, sir; I have had such a lot of knocking about since I left Breslau, that I should certainly have liked a month's quiet; but of course, I am ready to do as ordered, and, indeed, as the fun seems about to begin at last, I should like to be in it."

The next morning the captain sent his report to the Admiral, and received in reply a message that the Admiral would be glad if Captain Hethcote would dine with him that day, and would bring Mr. Archer with him.

Admiral Lyons was very kind to the young midshipman, and insisted upon his giving him an account in full of all his adventures. He confirmed Captain Hethcote's opinion as to Jack's movements, by saying, as he bade him good-bye, that in the morning he would receive a written order to go up to the front and to report himself to the officer in command of the naval brigade there.

The next morning, being that of the 5th June, Jack received his order, and an hour later he started for the front, with two sailors to carry his baggage. He was astonished at the change which had been wrought at Balaklava. A perfect town of wooden huts had sprung up. The principal portion of these was devoted to the general hospital, the others were crammed with stores. The greater part of the old Tartar village had been completely cleared away, the streets and roads were levelled, and in good order.

Such troops as were about had received new uniforms, and looked clean and tidy. Everywhere gangs of laborers were at work, and the whole place wore a bright and cheerful aspect. Just outside the town an engine with a number of laden wagons was upon the point of starting. The sun was blazing fiercely down, and at the suggestion of one of the sailors, who, though ready enough for a spree on shore, were viewing with some apprehension the

Jack Archer

prospect of the long trudge along the dusty road to Sebastopol, Jack asked the officer in charge of the train for permission to ride up. This was at once granted, and Jack, his trunk and the sailors, were soon perched on the top of a truck-load of barrels of salt pork.

Jack could scarcely believe that the place was the same which he had last seen, just when winter was setting in. A large village had grown up near the mouth of the valley, wooden huts for the numerous gangs of navvies and laborers stood by the side of the railway. Officers trotted past on ponies, numbers of soldiers, English, French, Turkish, and Sardinian, trudged along the road on their way to or from Balaklava. The wide plain across which our cavalry had charged was bright with flowers, and dotted with the tents of the Turks and Sardinians. Nature wore a holiday aspect. Every one seemed cheerful and in high spirits, and it needed the dull boom of the guns around Sebastopol to recall the fact that the work upon which they were engaged was one of grim earnest.

Upon arriving at the camp, Jack found that its aspect was not less changed than that of the surrounding country. Many of the regiments were already in huts. The roads and the streets between the tents were scrupulously clean and neat, and before many of the officers' tents, clumps of flowers brought up from the plain had been planted. The railway was not yet completed quite to the front, and the last two miles had to be traversed on foot.

Upon presenting his written orders to the officer in command of the naval brigade, Jack was at once told off to a tent with two other midshipmen, and was told that he would not, for the present, be placed upon regular duty, but that he would be employed as aide-de-camp to the commander, and as interpreter, should his services in that way be required.

Chapter XXII
THE REPULSE AT THE REDAN

THE first impulse of Jack, after having stowed his traps in the tent and introduced himself to his new mess-mates, was to make his way to the lines of the 33d. Here he found that Harry had been sent home sick in January, but that he had sailed from England again with a draft, and was expected to arrive in the course of a few days. Jack found but few of the officers still there whom he had before known. Several, however, were expected shortly back either from England or from the hospitals at Scutari.

Greatly relieved to find that his brother was alive and well, Jack returned to the naval camp, where he speedily made himself at home. When he first mentioned to his messmates, two lads about his own age, that he had been a prisoner in Russia, the statement was received with incredulity, and when, at their request, he proceeded to tell some of his adventures, they regarded him with admiration as the most stupendous liar they had ever met. It was long indeed before his statements were in any way believed, and it was only when, upon the occasion of one day dining with the officer in command of the brigade, Jack, at his request, related in the presence of several officers his adventures in Russia, that his statements were really accepted as facts; for it was agreed that whatever yarns a fellow might invent to astonish his comrades, he would not venture upon relating them as facts to a post-captain. This, however, was later on.

On the morning after his arrival all was expectation, for it was known that the bombardment was about to recommence. At half-past two o'clock the roar of 157 guns and mortars in the British batteries, and over 800 in those of the French, broke the silence, answered a minute or two later by that of the Russian guns along their whole line of batteries. The day was hot and almost without a breeze, and the smoke from so vast a number of guns hung heavily on the hill-side, and nothing could be seen as to the effect which the cannonade was producing. It was not until next morning that the effect of the fire was visible. The faces of the Russian batteries were pitted and scarred, but no injury of importance had been inflicted upon them. All day the fire continued with unabated fury on the side of the allies, the Russians replying intermittently. Presently the news circulated through the camp that an assault would be made at six o'clock, and all officers and men of duty thronged the brow of the plateau, looking down upon the town.

At half-past six a body of French troops were observed to leave their trenches, and, in skirmishing order, to make their way towards the Mamelon. The guns of the Russian fort roared out, but already the assailants were too close for these to have much effect. Soon a great shout from the spectators on the hill proclaimed that the Zouaves, who always led the French attacks, had gained the parapet. Then, from within, a host of figures surged up against the sky, and a curious conflict raged on the very summit of the work. Soon, however, the increasing mass of the French, as they streamed up, enabled them to maintain the footing they had gained, and pouring down into the fort, they drove the Russians from it, the French pouring out in their rear. Twice fresh bodies of Russian reserves, coming up, attempted to roll back the French attack; but these, exultant with success, pressed forward, and, in spite of the fire which the guns of the Round Tower fort poured upon them, drove their enemies down the hill. It was growing dark now, and it could with difficulty be seen how the fight was going. Fresh masses of French troops poured from their advance trenches into the Mamelon, and there was no question that that point was decidedly gained.

Still however, the battle raged around it. The Zouaves, flushed with success, attempted to carry the Round Tower with a rush, and swept up to the abattis surrounding it. The Russians brought up fresh supports, and the whole hill-side was alive with the flicker of musketry. The Russian guns of all the batteries bearing upon the scene of action opened it, while those of our right attack, which were close to the French, opened their fire to aid our allies. Had the Zouaves been supported, it is probable that they would have carried the Round Tower with their rush, but this was not in the plan of operations, and, after fighting heroically for some time, they fell back to the Mamelon.

The fight on the British side had been less exciting. With a sudden rush our men had leaped on the advance trenches and driven the Russians from their position in the quarries. Then, rapidly turning the gabions of the trenches, they prepared to hold the ground they had taken. They were not to maintain their conquest unmolested, for soon the Russians poured down masses of troops to retake it. All night long the flash of fire flickered round the position, and six times the Russian officers led up their troops to the attack.

Our assaulting force was over 1000 men, and out of these 365 men and thirty-five officers were killed or wounded. Had a stronger body been detailed, there is no doubt that the Redan, which was near the quarries, could have been taken, for it was almost empty of troops, and our men, in the impetuosity of their first assault, arrived close to it. Great discontent was felt that measures should not have been taken to follow up the success, and both our allies and our own troops felt that a great opportunity had been missed, owing to the want of forethought of their generals.

The next day there was an armistice, from one till six, to collect and bury the dead, and the officers and men of the contending parties moved over the ground which had been the scene of conflict, chatting freely together, exchanging cigars and other little articles. Jack, who had gone down with his commanding officer, created no slight astonishment among the Russians by conversing with them in their own language. In answer to their questions, he told them that he had been a prisoner among them, and begged them to forward a note which he had that morning written to Count Preskoff at Berislav, acquainting him that he had made his escape across the Russian frontier, and had rejoined the army, for he thought it probable that the letter which he had given to Count Stanislaus to post, after he left him, might never have come to hand.

At six o'clock the guns again re-opened; the Russians having made good use of their time in arming fresh batteries to counteract the effect of the works we had carried. We had indeed hard work in maintaining our hold of the quarries, which were commanded by several batteries, whose position placed them outside the range of our guns. Our loss was very heavy, as also was that of the French in the Mamelon, which was made a centre for the Russian fire.

On the nights of the 16th and 17th some of the British and French ships stood in close to Sebastopol, and kept up a heavy fire upon the town. On the 16th it was decided by Marshal Pelissier and Lord Raglan that the assault should take place on the morning of the 18th of June, and every arrangement was made for the attack. The British force told off for the work consisted of detachments of the light, second, and third divisions, and was divided into three columns. Sir John Campbell had charge of the left, Colonel Shadforth of the right, and Colonel Lacy Yea of the centre column. General Barnard was directed to take his brigade of the third division down to a ravine near the quarries, while General Eyre moved his brigade of the same division still farther along. His orders were that in case of the assault on the Redan being successful, he should attack the works on its right.

On the French left, three columns, each 6000 strong, under General De Salles, were to attack three of the Russian bastions; while on their right, three columns of equal force were to attack the Russian positions: General D'Autemarre assailing the Gervais battery and the right flank of the Malakoff, General Brunet to fall upon the left flank of the Malakoff and the little Redan from the Mamelon, while General Mayrau was to carry the Russian battery near the careening creek.

Thus the French were to assault in six columns, numbering in all 36,000 men, with reserves of 25,000. Our assaulting columns contained only 1200 men, while 10,000 were in reserve. The attack was to commence at day-break, but by some mistake the column of General Mayrau attacked before the signal was given. In a few minutes they were repulsed with great loss, their general being mortally wounded. Four thousand of the Imperial Guard were sent to their assistance, and three rockets being fired as a signal, the assault was made all along the line. The Russians, however, had been prepared for what was coming by the assault on their left. Their reserves were brought up, the Redan was crowded with troops, the guns were loaded with grape, and as the little English columns leaped from their trenches and rushed to the assault, they were received with tremendous fire.

The inevitable result of sending 1000 men to attack a tremendously strong position, held by ten times their own strength, and across a ground swept by half a dozen batteries, followed. The handful of British struggled nobly forward, broken up into groups by the irregularity of the ground and by the gaps made by the enemy's fire.

Parties of brave men struggled up to the very abattis of the Redan, and there, unsupported and powerless, were shot down. Nothing could exceed the bravery which our soldiers manifested. But their bravery was in vain. The three officers in command of the columns, Sir John Campbell, Colonel Shadforth, and Colonel Yea, were all killed. In vain the officers strove to lead their men to an attack. There were indeed scarce any to lead, and the Russians, in mockery of the foolishness of such an attack, stood upon their parapets and asked our men why they did not come in. At last, the remnants of the shattered columns were called off. Upon the left, the brigade under General Eyre carried the cemetery by a sudden attack. But so hot a fire was opened upon him that it was with difficulty the position could be held.

This, however, was the sole success of the day. Both, the French columns were repulsed with heavy loss from the Malakoff, and although Gervais battery was carried, it could not be maintained.

The naval brigade furnished four parties of sixty men to carry scaling-ladders and wool-bags. Two of these parties were held in reserve, and did not advance. Captain Peel was in command, and was wounded, as was Mr. Wood, a midshipman of H.M.S. "Queen," who acted as his aide-de-camp. The three officers of one detachment were all wounded, and of the other one was killed, and one wounded.

Jack had in the morning regretted that he was not in orders for the service, but when at night the loss which those who bad taken part in it had suffered was known, he could not but congratulate himself that he had not been detailed for the duty. The total British loss was twenty-two officers and 247 men killed, seventy-eight officers and 1207 men wounded. The French lost thirty-nine officers killed, and ninety-three wounded, 1600 men killed or taken prisoners and about the same number wounded; so that our losses were enormously greater than those of the French in proportion to our numbers. The Russians admitted a loss of 5800 killed and wounded.

Jack was with many others a spectator of this scene from Cathcart Hill; but it must not be imagined that even a vague idea of what was passing could be gleaned by the lookers-on. The Redan, which was the point of view immediately opposite, was fully a mile away. In a few minutes from the commencement of the fight the air was thick with smoke, and the din of battle along so extended a front was so continuous and overpowering that it was impossible to judge by the sound of firing how the fight was going on at any particular point.

Upon the night before there was a general sanguine feeling as to the success of the attack, and many a laughing invitation was given to future dinners in the hotels of Sebastopol. Great, then, was the disappointment when, an hour after its opening, the tremendous roll of musketry gradually died away, while the fire of the allied batteries angrily opened, telling the tale that all along the line the allies had been defeated, save only for the slight success at the cemetery.

Eagerly were the wounded questioned, as, carried on stretchers, or slowly and painfully making their way upon foot, they ascended the hill. In most of them regret at their defeat or anger at the incompetence of those who had rendered defeat certain, predominated over the pain of the wounds.

"Be jabers," said a little Irishman, "but it was cruel work entirely. There was myself and six others and the captain made our way up to a lot of high stakes stuck in the ground before the place. We looked round, and divil another soul was there near. We couldn't climb over the stakes, and if we had got over 'em there was a deep ditch beyond, and no way of getting in or out. And what would have been the good if we had, when there were about 50,000 Russians inside a-shouting and yelling at the top of their voices, and a-firing away tons of ammunition? We stopped there five minutes, it may be, waiting to see if any one else was coming, and then when four of us was killed and the captain wounded, I thought it time to be laving; so I lifted him up and carried him in, and got an ugly baste of a Russian bullet into my shoulder as I did so. Ye may call it fightin', but it's just murder I call it meself."

Something like this was the tale told by scores of wounded men, and it is little wonder that, sore with defeat and disappointment, and heart-sick at the loss which had been suffered, the feelings of the army found vent in deep grumblings at the generals who had sent out a handful of men to assault a fortress.

G. A. Henty

The next day there was another truce to allow of the burial of the dead and the collection of the wounded who lay thickly on the ground between the rival trenches. It did not take place, however, till four in the afternoon, by which time the wounded had been lying for thirty hours without water or aid, the greater portion of the time exposed to the heat of a burning sun.

Ten days later Lord Raglan died. He was a brave soldier, an honorable man, a most courteous and perfect English gentleman, but he was most certainly not a great general. He was succeeded by General Simpson, who appears to have been chosen solely because he had, as a lad, served in the Peninsula; the authorities seeming to forget that for the work upon which the army was engaged, no school of war could compare with that of the Crimea itself, and that generals who had received their training there were incomparably fitter for the task than any others could be.

Two days after the repulse at the Redan, Jack was delighted by the entry of his brother into his tent. Harry had of course left England before the receipt of Jack's letter written when he had crossed the frontier, and was overwhelmed with delight at the news which he had received ten minutes before, on arriving at the camp, that his brother was alive, and was again with the naval brigade close by. Jack's tent-mates were fortunately absent, and the brothers were therefore able to enjoy the delight of their meeting alone, and, when the first rapture was over, to sit down for a long talk. Jack was eager to learn what had happened at home, of which he had heard nothing for six months, and which Harry had so lately left. He was delighted to hear that all were well; that his elder sister was engaged to be married; and that although the shock of the news of his death had greatly affected his mother she had regained her strength, and would, Harry was sure, be as bright and cheerful as ever when she heard of his safety. Not till he had received answers to every question about home would Jack satisfy his brother's curiosity as to his own adventures, and then he astonished him indeed with an account of what he had gone through.

"Well, Jack, you are a lucky fellow!" Harry said, when he had finished. "To think of your having gone through all those adventures and living to tell of them. Why, it will be something to talk about all your life."

"And you, Harry, are you quite recovered?"

"I am as well as ever," Harry said. "It was a case of typhus and frost-bite mixed. I lost two of my toes, and they were afraid that I should be lame in consequence. However, I can march well enough for all practical purposes, though I do limp a little. As to the typhus, it left me very weak; but I soon picked up when the wind from England was blowing in my face. Only to think that all the time I was grieving for you as dead and buried by the Russians among the hills over there that you were larking about with those jolly Russian girls."

"Oh, yes, that's all very well," Jack said. "But you must remember that all that pretty nearly led to my being hung or shot, and it was a hot time among those Poles, too, I can tell you."

The next few days passed quietly. On the 12th of July Jack rode out with his commanding officer, who, with many others, accompanied the reconnaissance made by the Turks and French, on a foraging and reconnoitring party, towards Baidar, but they did not come in contact with the Russians.

Both parties still worked steadily at their trenches. The French were fortunate in having soft ground before them, and were rapidly pushing their advances up towards the Malakoff. This position, which could without difficulty have been seized by the allies at the commencement was in reality the key of the Russian position. Its guns completely commanded the Redan, and its position would render that post untenable, while the whole of the south side of Sebastopol would lay at our mercy. In front of the English the ground was hard and stony, and it was next to impossible to advance our trenches towards the Redan, and the greater portion of the earth indeed had to be carried in sacks on men's backs from points in the rear.

The working parties were also exposed to a cross-fire, and large numbers of men were killed every day.

On the 31st a tremendous storm broke upon the camp, but the soldiers were now accustomed to such occurrences, the tents were well secured, and but little damage was suffered. Save for a few sorties by the Russians, the next fortnight passed quietly.

The cavalry were now pushed some distance inland, and the officers made up parties to ride through the pretty valleys and visit the villas and country houses scattered along the shores.

Chapter XXIII
THE BATTLE OF THE TCHERNAYA

ON the evening of the 15th of August several Tartars brought in news that the Russians were preparing for an attack; but so often had similar rumors been received that little attention was paid to their statements. It was known indeed that they had received very large reinforcements, and the troops had been several times called under arms to resist their repeated attacks. These, however, had all passed off quietly, and when the troops retired to rest none thought that a great battle was going to take place on the morrow.

The Tchernaya, after leaving the valley of Baidar, flows between a number of low swells of ground, and formed the front of the allied armies on the plains. On the extreme right the Turks were stationed. Next them came the Sardinians, whose position extended from a stream flowing into the Tchernaya at right angles to an eminence known as Mount Hasfort. In front, and divided from it by an aqueduct which, too, ran parallel to the river, was another hillock accessible from the first by a stone bridge at which the Sardinians had a breastwork. Their outposts extended some distance on the other side of the Tchernaya. The French occupied a series of hillocks to the left of the Sardinians, guarding the road leading from Balaklava to McKenzie's farm. The river and aqueduct both flowed along their front. The road crossed the former by a bridge known as the Traktia Bridge, the latter by a stone bridge. In front of the Traktia Bridge was a breastwork.

At dawn a strong body of Russians were seen upon the heights opposite to those occupied by the Sardinians, and thence, being on ground higher than that upon our side of the river, they commanded both the Sardinian and French positions. The bridge was held by a company of infantry and a company of Bersaglieri, and General Della Marmora at once despatched another company of Bersaglieri to enable the advance to hold their post until the army got under arms. They mounted the opposite plateau, but this was so swept by the Russian guns, that they were forced at once to retire to the bridge.

Soon the artillery opened along the whole line on both sides. The French outposts had also been driven in, and before the troops were fairly under arms, the Russians had crossed the bridge, and were charging forward. The aqueduct, which was nine or ten feet wide and several feet deep, now formed the front of the French defence. It ran along on the face of the hill, with a very steep slope facing the Russians.

In spite of the fire of the French artillery in front, and of the Sardinian artillery which swept them in flank, the Russian soldiers pressed most gallantly forward, crossed the aqueduct, and tried to storm the height. The Sardinian fire, however, was too severe, and after ten minutes the Russians fell back. It met another column advancing at the double, and uniting, they again rushed forward. While they forded the river, two guns crossed by the bridge and another by a ford, and opened upon the French. The infantry, rushing breast deep through the water, began to scale the heights. But the French met them boldly, and after a fierce fight drove them down and across the bridge. On their left another column had attacked the French right, and in spite of the Sardinian guns which ploughed long lanes in their ranks, crossed the aqueduct and scaled the heights. But as they reached the plateau so terrible a storm of grape and musket-balls swept upon them, that the head of the column melted away as it surmounted the crest. Fresh men took the place of those that fell, but when the French infantry, with a mighty cheer, rushed upon them, the Russians broke and ran. So great was the crowd that they could not pass the river in time, and 200 prisoners were taken, while the French and Sardinian artillery swept the remains of the column, as it retreated, with a terrible cross fire.

At the bridge, however, the Russians made one more effort. The reserves were brought up, and they again crossed the river and aqueduct. The French, however, were now thoroughly prepared, and the attack was, like the preceding one, beaten back with terrible slaughter. The Russians fell back along their whole line, covered by the fire of their artillery, while five regiments of cavalry took post to oppose that of the allies, should they attempt to harass the retreat.

The loss of the French was nine officers killed and fifty-three wounded, 172 men killed and 1163 wounded. The Sardinians had two officers killed and eight wounded; sixty-two men killed, and 135 wounded. The Russian loss was twenty-seven officers killed, and eighty-five wounded; 3329 men killed, 4785 wounded. Never were the advantages of position more clearly shown, for the Russians lost fifteen times as many killed as the allies, four times as many wounded, although they had all the advantages of a surprise on their side. The English had only a battery of heavy guns under Captain Mowbray engaged. These did good service.

Jack Archer saw but little of this battle. It commenced at daybreak and lasted little over an hour, and when Jack, with hundreds of other officers and soldiers, reached points from which a view of the plain could be commanded, a thick cloud of smoke was drifting across it, through which nothing could be seen until the heavy masses of Russians were observed making their way back covered by their cavalry, and the dying away of the cannonade told that the battle was over.

Life in camp was very cheery now. The troops were in splendid health and high spirits. Races were got up in each division, for almost all officers possessed ponies of some kind or other, and great amusement was caused by these events. Some of the lately-arrived regiments had brought their regimental bands with them, and these added to the liveliness of the camps. A good supply of eatables and wine could be obtained from the sutlers, and dinner-parties were constantly taking place. Altogether life in camp was very enjoyable.

The French, who during the winter had fared much better than ourselves, were now in a very inferior condition. The full publicity which had been given to the sufferings of our troops had so roused the British public, that not only had they insisted that Government should take all measures for the comfort of the soldiers, but very large sums had been collected, and ships laden with comforts and luxuries of all kinds despatched to the seat of war. Consequently our troops were now in every respect well fed and comfortable. Upon the other hand, the details of the sufferings of the French troops had been carefully concealed from the French people. Consequently nothing was done for them, and their food was the same now as it had been at Varna in the previous year.

G. A. Henty

They were consequently exposed to the attacks of the same illness, and while the British army was enjoying perfect health, the French hospitals were crowded, and many thousands died of cholera and fever.

After the Tchernaya, as there was no probability of a renewal of the bombardment for a short time, Jack asked leave to spend a few days on board ship, as his services as interpreter were not likely to be required. This was readily granted. Here he had perfect rest. Captain Hethcote did not put him in a watch, and every day, with some of his messmates, he rowed out of the harbor, and coasted along at the foot of the lofty cliffs, sometimes fishing, sometimes taking a bath in the cool waters. This week's rest and change did Jack a great deal of good, for he had been feeling the effects of the long strain of excitement. He had had several slight touches of fever, and the naval doctor had begun to speak of the probability of sending him down to the hospital-ship at Constantinople. The week's rest, however, completely set him up, and he was delighted with the receipt of a budget of letters from home, written upon the receipt of his letter announcing his safety.

None but those who have gone through a long and tedious campaign, or who may be living a struggling life in some young colony, can know how great is the delight afforded by letters from home. For a time the readers forget their surroundings, and all the toil and struggle of their existence, and are again in thought among the dear ones at home. Retiring to some quiet place apart from their comrades, they read through their letters again and again, and it is not till every little item is got by heart, that the letters are folded up and put away, to be re-read over and over again until the next batch arrive.

Jack, of course, had heard much of his family from his brother, but the long letters of his father and mother, the large, scrawling handwriting of his little brothers and sisters, brought them before him far more vividly than any account could have done. Enclosed in his father's letter was one with a Russian postmark, and this Jack found was from Count Preskoff. It had been written six weeks after he had left them, and had, curiously enough, arrived in England on the very day after his own letter had reached home. The count wrote expressing their anxiety regarding him, and their earnest hopes that he had effected his escape. He said that his wife and daughters diligently read every paper they could get from end to end, but having seen no notice of the capture of two young Englishmen in disguise, they entertained strong hopes that their friends had effected their escape. The count said he was sure that Jack would be glad to hear that things in Russia looked brighter; that it was rumored that the Emperor Alexander intended on the occasion of his coronation to proclaim a general emancipation of the serfs, and that other measures of reform would follow. The party of progress were strong in the councils of the new monarch. The decree for his own banishment from court had been cancelled, and he was on the point of starting for St. Petersburg with his wife and daughters. A personal friend of his own had been appointed commandant of Berislav, and the late deputy commandant had been sent to join his regiment in the Crimea. The countess and his daughters were well, and Olga was studying English. He said that when the war was over he intended with his family to make a tour through the capitals of Europe, and hoped that they should see Jack in England. This was very welcome news, and Jack returned to the naval camp at the front in high glee.

One morning a lieutenant named Myers, asked Jack if he would like to

Jack Archer

accompany him on a reconnaissance, which he heard that a party of the Sardinian cavalry were going to push some little distance up the Baida Valley. Jack said that he would like it very much if he could borrow a pony. Mr. Myers said that he could manage this for him, and at once went and obtained the loan of a pony from another officer who was just going down into the battery. A quarter of an hour afterwards, having taken the precaution to put some biscuits and cold meat into their haversacks, and to fill their flasks with rum and water, they started and rode across the plain to the Sardinian camp.

The lieutenant had obtained the news of the proposed reconnaissance from an officer with whom he was acquainted on the Sardinian staff. The news, however, had been kept secret, as upon previous occasions so many officers off duty had accompanied these reconnaissances as to constitute an inconvenience. On the present occasion the secret had been so well kept that only some four or five pleasure-seekers had assembled when the column, consisting of 400 cavalry, started.

Jack, accustomed only to the flat plains of southern and western Russia, was delighted with the beauty of the valley through which they now rode. It was beautifully wooded, and here and there Tartar villages nestled among the trees. These had long since been deserted by the inhabitants, and had been looted by successive parties of friends and foes, of everything portable.

Presently they turned out of the valley they had first passed through and followed a road over a slope into another valley, similar to the first. For an hour they rode on, and then some distance ahead of the column they heard the report of a shot.

"The Cossacks have got sight of us," Mr. Myers said. "We shall soon learn if the Russians have any troops in the neighborhood."

Presently a scattered fire was opened from the walls of a country house, standing embowered in trees on an eminence near what appeared to be the mouth of the valley. The officer in command of the party dismounted one of the squadrons, and sent the men up in skirmishing order against the house. Two other squadrons trotted down the valley, and the rest remained in reserve. A sharp musketry conflict went on for a short time around the chateau. Then the Sardinians made a rush, and their shouts of triumph and the cessation of musketry proclaimed their victory.

At the same moment a soldier rode back from the cavalry that had gone up the valley, to say that a strong body of the enemy's horse were approaching across the plain. The order was given for a general advance, and the cavalry trotted down the valley to join the party in advance.

"Now, Mr. Archer," Lieutenant Myers said, "the best thing for us to do will be to ride forward to that house up there. See, the attacking party are coming back to their horses. We ought to have a good view over the plain, and shall see the fight between the Sardinians and the enemy. Besides, we may pick up some loot."

They soon reached the house, and, tying up their horses, entered. It was a fine chateau, handsomely furnished, but short as was the time that the Sardinians had held possession, they had already tumbled everything into confusion in their search for plunder. Tables and couches had been upset, closets and chiffoniers burst open with the butt-ends of the swords or with the discharge of a pistol into the lock. Looking-glasses had been smashed, valuable vases lay in fragments on the floor, bottles of wine whose necks had

G. A. Henty

been hastily knocked off stood on the table. In the courtyard were signs of strife. Three or four Cossacks and two Sardinian horsemen lay dead.

"We will go out to the terrace in front of the house," Mr. Myers said. "From that we ought to have a view over the country."

Owing, however, to the trees which grew around, they were obliged to advance 100 yards or so from the house before they could see the plain. Then some half-mile out they saw the blue mass of Sardinian cavalry advancing by squadrons. Still farther two bodies of Russian horse, each nearly equal in strength to the Italians, were seen. There was a movement among the Sardinian horse. They formed into two bodies and dashed at the Russians. There was a cloud of dust, swords could be seen flashing in the sun, a confused mèlée for a minute or two, and then the Russians broke and rode across the plain, pursued by the Sardinians.

"A very pretty charge," Mr. Myers said. "Now we'll go in and look at the house. It will be fully half an hour before they return again."

They went in and wandered from room to room. The place had evidently been tenanted until quite lately. Articles of woman's work lay upon the table. A canary bird was singing in his cage. A fire burnt in the kitchen, and a meal was evidently in course of preparation when the first alarm had been given. The officers wandered from room to room, and collected a number of little trifles to take home as remembrances, small pictures of the Greek saints, such as are found in every Russian house, a little bronze statuette, two or three small but handsomely bound books, a couple of curious old plates; and Jack took possession, as a present for his elder sister, of a small work-box beautifully fitted up. Having made two bundles of their plunder, they prepared to go out again to see if the Sardinians were returning, when Jack, looking out of the window, uttered an exclamation of surprise and alarm. One of the thick fogs which are so common in the Black Sea, and on the surrounding coasts, had suddenly rolled down upon them, and it was difficult to see five yards from the window. Jack's exclamation was echoed by Mr. Myers.

"This is a nice business!" the latter exclaimed. "We had better find our ponies and make our way down into the valley at once. Seeing how thick the fog has come on, the Sardinians may not return here at all."

So saying, they hurried to the spot where they had tied up their ponies, and, leading them by the reins, descended into the valley.

"The fog is getting thicker and thicker," Mr. Myers said. "I cannot see three yards before me. We must listen for them as they pass, and then join them, although it's by no means impossible that we may be received with a shot."

Half an hour passed, and they grew more and more anxious. Another half-hour, and still no sound was heard.

"I do not think they can possibly have passed without our seeing them, Mr. Archer. The valley is a quarter of a mile wide, but we should be sure to hear the trampling of the horses and the jingling of the sabres."

"Yes, sir, I'm sure they have not passed since we got here. But they may possibly have seen the fog coming on and have ridden rapidly back, and passed before we came down, or they may have gone round by the mouth of the valley parallel to this, which we left to cross into this one."

"That is just what I have been thinking." Mr. Myers said. "What do you think we had better do? It is quite impossible that we can find our way back through such a fog as this."

Jack Archer

"Quite impossible, sir," Jack said. "If we were to move from where we are, we should lose all idea of our bearings in three minutes, and should be as likely to go into the plain as up the valley."

"It's a most awkward position," Mr. Myers said anxiously. "Now, Mr. Archer, you have had some sort of experience of this kind before. Tell me frankly what you think is the best thing to be done."

"I have been thinking it over, sir, for the last half hour," Jack said, "and it appears to me that the best thing to do would be for me to find my way up to the house again. I can't well miss that, as we came straight down hill. I will bring back two of those Cossacks' cloaks and lances. Then we had better move about till we come on a clump of trees, and make ourselves as comfortable there as we can. These fogs last, as you know, sometimes for two or three days. When it gets clear, whether it is to-day or to-morrow, we will look out and see whether there are any of the enemy about. Of course, as they know the way, they can come back in the fog. If we see any of them, we must put on the Cossack's cloaks, take their lances, and boldly ride off. They are always galloping about in pairs all over the country; so that we shall attract no attention."

"But if they catch us," the lieutenant said, "we shall be liable to be shot as spies."

"I suppose we shall, sir," Jack answered; "but I would rather run the risk of being shot as a spy than the certainty of being caught as a naval officer, and imprisoned till the war is over."

"Well, Mr Archer, I certainly can suggest nothing better," the lieutenant said. "Will you go up, then, and, get the cloaks you speak of?"

Leaving his pony with the lieutenant, Jack made his way up the hill. Fortunately, in their descent they had followed a small track worn by persons going to and from the chateau from the valley, and he had, therefore, but little difficulty in finding the house. He paused when he reached the courtyard, for he heard voices in the chateau. Listening attentively, he discovered that they were Russians, no doubt some of the party who had been driven thence by the Sardinians, and who had, upon the retirement of the latter, ridden straight back from the plain. Fortunately, the fog was so thick that there was no probability whatever of his movements being discovered, and he therefore proceeded to strip off two of the long coats, reaching almost down to the heels, which form the distinctive Cossack dress, from the dead men. He took possession also of their caps, their bandoliers for cartridges, worn over one shoulder, and of their carbines and lances, and then retraced his steps down the hill to his companion. Leading their ponies, they wandered aimlessly through the fog for a considerable time before they came to some trees.

"If you will hold my horse, sir," Jack said, "I will just look round, and see if this is a small wood. I shall lose you before I have gone a yard, so when you hear me whistle, please whistle back, but not loud, for there may be enemies close by for aught I know. I thought I heard voices just now."

Searching about, Jack found that the clump of trees extended for some little distance. Returning to the lieutenant, they entered the wood, and moved a little way among the trees, so as to be out of sight if the fog lifted suddenly. Then they loosened the saddle-girths, gathered some sticks and lit a fire, and using the Cossack coats for rugs, began to discuss the meal they had brought with them.

G. A. Henty

"If the Russians really advance again, and get between us and Balaklava, I do not see how on earth we are to pass through them," Mr. Myers said.

"No, sir, I don't think we could," Jack answered. "I should propose that we make a wide sweep round so as to come down upon the shore some distance away. As you know, boats from the ships often land at some of the deserted places along there in search of loot; so that we ought to be able to be taken off. If, when we are riding, we come upon any Russian troops suddenly, so that we cannot move away in any other direction without exciting suspicion, you must put a good face on it. My Russian is good enough to pass muster as a Cossack. All we have to do is to avoid any of these fellows, for they would detect at once that I did not belong to them."

"Well, Mr. Archer, you take things very coolly, and I hope you will get us out of the scrape we have got into. If I had been by myself, I should have ridden up and surrendered to the first Russians I saw."

"That would have been the best way, sir, had it not been for those poor beggars having been killed up above there; for in our naval dress we could not have hoped to have escaped. As it is, if we have any luck, we shall soon be back at Balaklava again."

Chapter XXIV
A FORTUNATE STORM

THE fog seemed to get thicker and thicker as the day went on. At nightfall, when it became evident that no move could be made before morning, they gave a biscuit to each of their ponies, cut some grass and laid it before them, and then, wrapping themselves in the Cossack cloaks to keep off the damp fog, were soon asleep. At day-break the fog was still thick, but as the sun rose it gradually dispersed it, and they were shortly able to see up the valley. They found that in their wandering in the mist they must have moved partly in a circle, for they were still little more than a quarter of a mile from the point where they had left it to ascend to the chateau. Round this they could see many soldiers moving about. Looking up the valley, they perceived lines of horses, picqueted by a village but a few hundred yards away.

"Those were the voices I thought I heard, no doubt, when we first came here," Jack said. "It's lucky we found these trees, for if we had wandered about a little longer, we might have stumbled into the middle of them. Now, sir, we had better finish the biscuits we put aside for breakfast, and be off. It is quite evident the direct way to the camp is close to us."

Saddling up their horses, and putting on the Cossack black sheepskin caps and long coats, and taking the lances and carbines, the latter of which were carried across the saddle before them, they mounted their ponies and rode off, quitting the wood at such a point that it formed a screen between them and the cavalry in the distance, until they had gone well down the valley. They were unnoticed, or at any rate, unchallenged by the party at the chateau, and, issuing from the valley, rode out into the open country.

Far out in the plain they saw several Russians moving about, and judged that these were occupied in searching those who had fallen in the cavalry fight of the preceding day. They did not approach them, but turning to the right, trotted briskly along, skirting the foot of the hills. They passed through two or three Tartar villages whose inhabitants scarcely glanced at them, so accustomed were they to the sight of small parties of Cossacks riding hither and thither.

In one, which stood just at the mouth of the valley which they had determined to enter, as a road running up it seemed to indicate that it led to some place, perhaps upon the sea-shore, they found several Russian soldiers loitering about. Lieutenant Myers would have checked his pony, but Jack rode unhesitatingly forward. An officer came out of one of the cottages.

"Any news?" he asked.

"None," Jack said. "The enemy's horse came out yesterday, through the Baida valley, but we beat them back again."

"Where are you going?" the Russian asked.

"Down towards the sea," Jack answered, "to pick up stragglers who land to plunder. A whole sotina is coming down. They will be here presently," so saying, with a wave of his hand, he resumed his way up the valley, Lieutenant Myers having ridden on, lest any questions should be addressed to him. The road mounted steadily, and after some hours' riding they crossed a brow, and

G. A. Henty

found themselves at the head of a valley opening before them, and between the cliffs at its end they could see the sea.

They could scarcely restrain a shout of joy, and, quickening their speed, rode rapidly down the valley. Presently they perceived before them a small village lying on the sea-shore, to the left of which stood a large chateau, half hidden among trees.

"Do you think it's safe to ride in?" Mr. Myers asked.

"Most of these villages have been found deserted, sir," Jack said, "by our fellows when they landed. I'm afraid we are beyond the point to which they come, for I should think we must be twenty miles from Balaklava. However, there are not likely to be any troops here, and we needn't mind the Tartars."

They found, as they expected, that the village was wholly deserted, and, riding through it, they dismounted at the chateau. The doors were fastened, but, walking round it, they perceived no signs of life, and, breaking a window, they soon effected an entrance.

They found that the house, which was of great size and evidently belonged to a Russian magnate, was splendidly furnished, and that it had so far not been visited by any parties from the ships. Some fine pictures hung on the walls, choice pieces of statuary were scattered here and there, tables of malachite and other rare stones stood about, and Eastern carpets covered the floors.

"We are in clover now, sir," Jack said, "and if we could but charter a ship, we should be able to make a rich prize. But as our ponies can only carry us, I'm afraid that all these valuables are worthless to us."

"I'd give the whole lot of them," the lieutenant said, "for a good meal. At any rate, we are sure to find something for the ponies."

In the stables behind the house were great quantities of forage and the ponies soon had their fill.

The officers, taking some corn, of which also there was an abundance, hammered a quantity between two flat stones, and moistening the rough flour so obtained, with water, made two flat cakes, with which, baked over a wood fire, they satisfied their hunger. A consultation was held while they ate their meal, and it was agreed that as the place was evidently beyond the range of boats from Balaklava, they had better ride along the cliffs till they reached some village, where, as they would find from the state of the houses, parties were in the habit of coming.

After a couple of hours' stay to give the horses time to rest, they again saddled up and took the road along the coast. After riding two miles along the edge of the cliffs, they simultaneously checked their horses, as, upon mounting a slight rise, they saw before them the tents of a considerable party of Russian soldiers. As they had paused the moment their heads came above the level, they were themselves unobserved, and turning, they rode back to the chateau they had quitted, where, having made their ponies comfortable, they prepared to pass the night. There were plenty of luxurious beds, and they slept profoundly all night. In the morning they went down to the sea. Not a vestige of a boat was to be seen, and they began to question whether it would not be possible to make a small raft, and to paddle along the foot of the cliffs.

"We need not trouble about that now," Lieutenant Myers said, "for, unless I am mistaken, we're going to have a regular Black Sea gale in an hour or two. The wind is freshening fast, and the clouds banking up."

Jack Archer

The lieutenant was not mistaken. In an hour the wind was blowing in furious gusts, and the sea breaking heavily in the little bay.

Having nothing to do, they sat under the shelter of a rock, and watched the progress of the gale. The wind was blowing dead along the shore, and grew fiercer and fiercer. Three hours passed, and then Lieutenant Myers leaped to his feet.

"See," he said, "there is a boat coming round the point!"

It was so. Driving before the gale was a ship's boat, a rag of sail was set, and they could see figures on board.

"She is making in here!" the lieutenant exclaimed. "Let us run down and signal to them to beach her at that level spot just in front of the village. No doubt it is some ship's boat which came out to picnic at one of the villages near Balaklava, and they have been blown along the coast and have been unable to effect a landing."

The boat's head was now turned towards shore, the sail lowered, and the oars got out. So high was the sea already, that the spectators feared every moment she would be swamped, but she was well handled, and once in the little bay the water grew smoother, and she soon made her way to the spot where the officers were standing. The latter were astonished when the men leaped out instantly, and, without a word, rushed at them, and in a moment both were levelled to the ground by blows of stretchers. When they recovered from the shock and astonishment, they found the sailors grouped round them.

"Hallo!" Jack exclaimed in astonishment, "Mr. Simmonds, is that you? What on earth are you knocking us about like that for?"

"Why, Jack Archer!" exclaimed the officer addressed, "where on earth did you come from? and what are you masquerading as a Cossack for? We saw you here, and of course took you for an enemy. I thought you were up at the front."

"So we were," Jack replied, "but, as you see, we are here now. This is Lieutenant Myers, of the 'Tartar.'"

"I'm awfully sorry!" Mr. Simmonds said, holding out his hand, and helping them to their feet.

"It was not your fault," Mr. Myers answered. "We forgot all about our Cossack dresses. Of course you supposed that we were enemies. It is fortunate indeed for us that you came here. But I fear you must put to sea again. There is a Russian camp two miles off on the hill, and the boat is sure to have been seen."

"It will be awkward," Lieutenant Simmonds said, looking at the sky, "for it is blowing tremendously. I think, though, that it is breaking already. These Black Sea gales do not often last long. At any rate, it would be better to take our chance there than to see the inside of a Russian prison."

"If you send a man along the road to that crest," Lieutenant Myers suggested, "he will see them coming, and if we all keep close to the boat, we may get out of gunshot in time."

A sailor was accordingly despatched up the hill. The instant he reached the top he was seen to turn hastily, and to come running back at full speed.

"Now, lads," Mr. Simmonds said, "put your shoulders to her. Now, all together, get her into the water, and be ready to jump in and push off when Atkins arrives."

When the sailor was still a hundred yards away the head of a column of

G. A. Henty

Russian infantry appeared over the crest. When they saw the boat they gave a shout, and breaking, ran down the hill at full speed. Before they reached the village, however, Atkins had leaped into the boat, and with a cheer the men ran her out into the surf, and scrambled in.

"Out oars, lads, and row for your lives!" Mr. Simmonds said, and, with steady strokes the sailors drove their boat through the waves.

The Russians opened fire the instant they reached the beach, but the boat was already 150 yards away, and although the bullets fell thickly round, no one was hit.

"I think, Mr. Myers," Lieutenant Simmonds said, "we had better lay-to, before we get quite out of shelter of the bay. With steady rowing we can keep her there, and we shall be out of range of the Russians."

Mr. Myers assented, and for two hours the men, rowing their utmost, kept the boat stationary, partly sheltered by the cliffs at the mouth of the bay. The Russians continued to fire, but although the boat was not wholly beyond their range, and the bullets sometimes fell near, these were for the most part carried to leeward by the wind, and not a single casualty occurred.

"The wind is falling fast," Lieutenant Simmonds said. "We could show a rag of canvas outside now. We had best make a long leg out to sea, and then, when the wind goes down, we can make Balaklava."

For four or five hours the boat was buffeted in the tremendous seas, but gradually, as the wind went down, these abated, and after running twenty miles off the land, the boat's head was turned, and she began to beat back to Balaklava. It was eleven o'clock that night before they reached the "Falcon," officers and men completely worn out with their exertions.

Jack found to his satisfaction that no report of his being missing had been received by the captain, and next morning at daybreak he and Lieutenant Myers walked up to camp, regretting the loss of their ponies, which would, however, they were sure, be found by the Russians long ere they finished the stores of provender within their reach.

Upon reaching camp they found that their absence had not been noticed until the afternoon of the second day of their absence. They had been seen to ride away together, and when in the evening they were found to be absent, it was supposed that they had gone down to Balaklava and slept there. When upon the following day they were still missing, it was supposed that the admiral had retained them for duty on board ship. The storm, which had scattered everything, had put them out of the thoughts of the commanding officer, and it was only that morning that, no letter respecting them having been received, he was about to write to their respective captains to inquire the cause of their absence. This was now explained, and as they had been detained by circumstances altogether beyond their control, they escaped without a reprimand, and were indeed warmly congratulated upon the adventures they had passed through.

In the meantime the cannonade had been going on very heavily in front. The Russian outworks were showing signs of weakness after the tremendous pounding they were receiving. The French were pushing their trenches close up to the Malakoff, and upon both sides the soldiers were busy with pick and shovel. On the night of the 30th August a tremendous explosion took place, a Russian shell exploding in a French ammunition wagon, which blew up, killing and wounding 150 officers and men.

Jack Archer

On the following night the naval brigade astonished the camp by giving private theatricals. The bill was headed "Theatre Royal, Naval Brigade. On Friday evening, 31st August, will be performed, 'Deaf as a Post,' to be followed by 'The Silent Woman,' the whole to conclude with a laughable farce, entitled 'Slasher and Crasher.' Seats to be taken at seven o'clock. Performance to commence precisely at eight. God save the Queen. Rule Britannia." The scenes were furnished from H.M.S. "London." The actors were all sailors of the brigade, the ladies' parts being taken by young boatswains' mates. Two thousand spectators closely packed were present, and the performance was immensely enjoyed in spite of the fact that the shell from the Russian long-range guns occasionally burst in the neighborhood of the theatre.

The French had now pushed forward their trenches so far that from their front sap they could absolutely touch the abattis of the Malakoff. On the 3d the Russians made a sortie, and some heavy fighting took place in the trenches. The time was now at hand when the last bombardment was to commence. The French began it early on the morning of the 5th. They had now got no less than 627 guns in position, while the English had 202. The news that it was to commence was kept a profound secret, and few of the English officers knew what was about to take place. Our own trenches were comparatively empty, while those of the French were crowded with men who kept carefully out of sight of the enemy.

Suddenly three jets of earth and dust sprung into the air. The French had exploded three mines, and at the signal a stream of fire three miles in length ran from battery to battery, as the whole of their guns opened fire. The effect of this stupendous volley was terrible. The iron shower ploughed up the batteries and entrenchments of the Russians, and crashed among the houses far behind. In a moment the hillside was wreathed with smoke. With the greatest energy the French worked their guns, and the roar was continuous and terrible.

For a time the Russians seemed paralyzed by this tremendous fire; lying quietly in their sheltered subterranean caves, they had no thought of what was preparing for them, and the storm which burst upon them took them wholly by surprise. Soon, however, they recovered from their astonishment, and steadily opened fire in return. The English guns now joined their voices to the concert, and for two hours the storm of fire continued unabating on both sides.

After two hours and a half the din ceased, the French artillery-men waiting to allow their guns to cool. At ten o'clock the French again exploded some mines, and for two hours renewed their cannonade as hotly as ever. The Russians could be seen pouring troops across the bridge over the harbor from their camps on the north side, to resist the expected attack. From twelve to five the firing was slack. At that hour the French again began their cannonade as vigorously as before.

When darkness came on, and accurate firing at the enemy's batteries was no longer possible, the mortars and heavy guns opened fire on the place. The sky was streaked with lines of fire as the heavy shells described their curves, bursting with heavy explosions over the town. Presently a cheer rose from the spectators who thronged the crest of the bill, for flames were seen bursting out from one of the Russian frigates. Higher and higher they rose, although by their light the Russians could be perceived working vigorously to extinguish them. At last they were seen to be leaving the ship. Soon the flames caught the mast and rigging, and the pillar of fire lit up the whole town and surrounding country. Not a moment did our fire slacken, but no answering flash now shot out from the Russian lines of defence. All night the fire continued, to prevent the enemy from repairing damages.

The next morning the English played the principal part in the attack, our batteries commencing at daylight, and continuing their fire all day. The Russians could be seen to be extremely busy. Hitherto they had believed that the allies would never be able to take the town; but the tremendous fire which the allies had now opened, and the close approach of the French to the Malakoff, had clearly shaken their confidence at last.

Large quantities of stores were transported during the day to the north side, and on the heights there great numbers of men were seen to be laboring at fortifications. The Russian army in the field was observed to be moving towards Inkerman, and it was believed that it was about to repeat the experiment of the Tchernaya and to make a desperate effort to relieve the town by defeating the allied armies in the field.

All that night the bombardment continued without intermission, the troops in the trenches keeping up a heavy musketry fire upon the enemy's works, to prevent them from repairing damages in the dark.

The next day was a repetition of those which had gone before it. The Russians replied but seldom, and occasionally when the smoke blew aside, it could be seen that terrible damage was being inflicted on the Russian batteries. At dusk the cannonade ceased, the shell bombardment took place, and at eleven a tremendous explosion occurred in the town.

The Russians from time to time lit up the works with fire-balls and carcasses, evidently fearing a sudden night attack. During the day a great council of war was held; and as orders were sent to the surgeons to send all the patients in the hospital down to Balaklava, and to prepare for the reception of wounded, it was known that the attack would take place next day.

Although the Russian fire in reply to the bombardment had been comparatively slight, from the 3d to the 6th we had three officers and forty-three men killed; three officers and 189 men wounded.

During these days Jack had been on duty in the batteries, and the sailors had taken their full part in the work.

There was some disappointment that night in the naval camp when it was known by the issue of the divisional orders that the sailors were not to be engaged in the assault. Jack, however, aroused the indignation of his tent-mates by saying frankly that he was glad that they were not going to share in the attack.

"It is all very well," he said, "to fight when you have some chance of hitting back, but to rush across ground swept by a couple of hundred guns is no joke; and to be potted at by thousands of fellows in shelter behind trenches. One knows what it was last time. The French send 12,000 men to attack a battery, we try to carry an equally strong place with 1000. If I were ordered, of course I should go; but I tell you fairly, I don't care about being murdered, and I call it nothing short of murder to send 1000 men to attack such a position as that. We used to say that an Englishman could lick three Frenchmen, but we never did it in any battle I ever heard of. Our general seems to think that an Englishman can lick ten Russians, although he's in the open, and they're behind shelter, and covered by the fire of any number of pieces of artillery."

Jack Archer

"But we're certain to get in to-morrow, Jack."

"Are we?" Jack questioned; "so every one said last time. It's all very well for the French, who are already right under the guns of the Malakoff, and have only twenty yards to run. When they get in and drive the Russians out, there they are in a big circular fort, just as they were in the Mamelon, and can hold their own, no matter how many men the Russians bring up to retake it. We've 300 yards to run to get into the Redan, and when we get in where are we? Nowhere. Just in an open work where the Russians can bring their whole strength down upon us. I don't feel at all sure we're going to take the place to-morrow."

"Why, Archer, you're a regular croaker!" one of the others said. "We shall have a laugh at you to-morrow evening."

"I hope you will," Jack said; "but I have my doubts. I wish to-morrow was over, I can tell you. The light division are, as usual, to bear the brunt of it, and the 33d will do their share. Harry has had good luck so far, but it will be a hotter thing to-morrow than anything he has gone into yet, unless indeed the bombardment of the last three days has taken all heart out of the Russians. Well, let's turn in, for its bitterly cold to-night, and I for one don't feel disposed for talking."

Chapter XXV
THE CAPTURE OF SEBASTOPOL

THE morning of the 8th of September was bitterly cold, and a keen wind blowing from the town raised clouds of dust.

The storming parties were to be furnished by the light and second divisions. The first storming party of the light division was to consist of 160 men of the 97th regiment, who were to form in rear of a covering party of 100 men, furnished by the second battalion, Rifle brigade. They were to carry ladders for descending into the ditch of the Redan. Behind them were to come 200 men of the 97th and 300 of the 90th. The supports consisted of 750 men of the 19th and 88th regiments.

Therefore the assault was to be made by about 750 men, with an equal body in support, the remainder of the light division being in reserve.

The covering party of the second division consisted of 100 men of the 3d Buffs; the storming party, with ladders, of 160 of the 3d Buffs, supported by 260 of the 3d Buffs, 300 of the 41st, with 200 of the 62d, and 100 of the 41st. The rest of the second division were in reserve.

The first and Highland divisions were to be formed in the third parallel.

The orders were that the British attack was not to commence until the French had gained possession of the Malakoff. This they did with but slight loss. The storming columns were immensely strong, as 30,000 men were gathered in their trenches for the attack upon the Malakoff. This was effected almost instantaneously.

Upon the signal being given, they leaped in crowds from the advanced trench, climbed over the abattis, descended the ditch and swarmed up the rugged slope in hundreds.

The Russians, taken wholly by surprise, vainly fired their cannon, but ere the men could come out from their underground caves, the French were already leaping down upon them. It was a slaughter rather than a fight, and in an incredibly short time the Malakoff was completely in the possession of the French. In less than a minute from the time they leaped from the trenches their flag floated on the parapet.

The Russians, recovered from their first surprise, soon made tremendous attempts to regain their lost position, and five minutes after the French had entered, great masses of Russians moved forward to dispute its possession. For seven hours, from twelve to dusk, the Russians strove obstinately to recover the Malakoff, but the masses of men which the French poured in as soon as it was captured, enabled them to resist the assaults.

At length, when night came on, the Russian general, seeing that the tremendous slaughter which his troops were suffering availed nothing, withdrew them from the attack.

As the French flag appeared on the Malakoff, the English covering parties leaped from the trenches, and rushed forward. As they did so a storm of shot and shell swept upon them, and a great number of men and officers were killed as they crossed the 250 yards between the trenches and the Redan. This work was a salient, that is to say a work whose centre is advanced, the

Jack Archer

two sides meeting there at an angle. In case of the Redan it was a very obtuse angle, and the attacks should have been delivered far up the sides, as men entering at the angle itself would be exposed to the concentrated fire of the enemy behind the breastworks which ran across the broad base of the triangle. The projecting angle was, however, of course the point nearest to the English lines, and, exposed as they were to the sweeping fire of the enemy while crossing the open, both columns of assault naturally made for this point.

The Russian resistance was slight, and the stormers burst into the work. The abattis had been torn to pieces by the cannonade, and the men did not wait for the ladders, but leapt into the ditch and scrambled up on the other side.

The Russians within ran back, and opened a fire from their traverses and works in the rear. As the English troops entered, they halted to fire upon the enemy, instead of advancing upon them. The consequence was that the Russians, who were rapidly reinforced, were soon able to open a tremendous concentrated fire upon the mass of men in the angle, and these, pressed upon by their comrades who flocked in behind them, impeded by the numerous internal works, mixed up in confusion, all regimental order being lost, were unable either to advance or to use their arms with effect. In vain the officers strove by example and shouts to induce them to advance. The men had an idea that the place was mined, and that if they went forward they would be blown into the air. They remained stationary, holding their ground, but refusing to go forward.

Every minute the Russians brought up fresh reserves, and a terrific fire was concentrated upon the British. The officers, showing themselves in front, were soon shot down in numbers, and success, which had been in their hands at first, was now impossible.

For an hour and a half the slaughter continued, and then, as the Russian masses poured forward to attack them, the remnant who remained of the storming parties leaped from the parapet and made their way as best they could through the storm of bullet and shot, back to the trenches.

The fight had lasted an hour and three quarters, and in that time we had lost more men than at Inkerman. Our loss was 24 officers and 119 men killed; 134 officers, and 1897 men wounded. Had the regiments engaged been composed of the same materials as those who won the heights of the Alma, the result might have been different, although even in that case it is questionable whether the small force told off for the assault would have finally maintained itself against the masses which the Russians brought up against them. But composed as they were of young troops, many being lads sent off to the front a few weeks after being recruited, the success of such an attack, so managed, was well-nigh impossible from the first.

It was a gloomy evening in the British camps. We were defeated, while the French were victorious. The fact, too, that the attack had failed in some degree owing to the misconduct of the men added to the effect of the failure. It was said that the attack was to be renewed next morning, and that the Guards and Highland Brigade were to take part in it. Very gloomy was the talk over the tremendous loss which had taken place among the officers. From the manner in which these had exposed themselves to induce their men to follow them, their casualties had been nearly four times as large as they should have been in proportion to their numbers.

Jack Archer was in deep grief, for his brother had been severely wounded, and the doctors gave no strong hopes of his life. He had been shot in the hip, as he strove to get the men of his company together, and had been carried to the rear just before the Russian advance drove the last remnants of the assailants from the salient.

Jack had, with the permission of his commanding officer, gone to sit by his brother's bedside, and to give his services generally as a nurse to the wounded.

At eleven o'clock the hut was shaken by a tremendous explosion, followed a few minutes afterwards by another. Several of the wounded officers begged Jack to go to Cathcart's Hill, to see what was doing.

Jack willingly complied, and found numbers of officers and men hastening in the same direction. A lurid light hung over Sebastopol, and it was evident that something altogether unusual was taking place.

When he reached the spot from which he could obtain a view of Sebastopol, a wonderful sight met his eye. In a score of places the town was on fire. Explosion after explosion followed, and by their light, crowds of soldiers could be seen crossing the bridge. Hour after hour the grandeur of the scene increased, as fort after fort was blown up by the Russians. At four o'clock the whole camp was shaken by a tremendous explosion behind the Redan, and a little later the magazines of the Flagstaff and Garden batteries were blown up, and the whole of the Russian fleet, with the exception of the steamers, had disappeared under the water, scuttled by their late owners. At half-past five two of the great southern forts, the Quarantine and Alexander, were blown up, and soon flames began to ascend from Fort Nicholas.

The Russian steamers were all night busy towing boats laden with stores, from the south to the north side, and when their work was done, dense columns of smoke were seen rising from the decks. At seven o'clock in the morning the whole of the Russian troops were safely across the bridge, which was then dismembered and the boats which composed it taken over to the north side. By this time Sebastopol was, from end to end, a mass of flames, and by nightfall nothing save a heap of smoking ruins, surrounded by shattered batteries, remained of the city which had, for so many months, kept at bay the armies of England and France.

All through the night Jack Archer had travelled backwards and forwards between the crest of the hill and the hospital; for so great was the interest of the wounded in what was taking place that he could not resist their entreaties, especially as he could do nothing for his brother, who was lying in a quiet, half-dreamy state.

The delight of the English army at the fall of the south side of Sebastopol was greatly tempered by the knowledge that it was due to the capture of the Malakoff by the French. Their own share in the attack having terminated by a defeat, and the feeling which had been excited by the fact that the Guards and Highlanders, who had taken no part whatever in the trench-work during the winter, and who were in a high state of efficiency, should have been kept in reserve, while the boy battalions bore the whole brunt of the attack, found angry expression among the men.

All that day the allied armies remained quiescent. It was useless to attempt to occupy the burning town, and the troops might have been injured by the explosions which took place from time to time of stores of powder.

The Zouaves, however, and our own sailors made their way down in considerable numbers, and returned laden with loot from houses which had so far escaped the conflagration.

Happily the success of the French, and our own failure, did not create any feeling of unpleasantness between the troops of the two nations. As the remnants of the French regiments, engaged in the Malakoff, marched in the morning to their camps, the second division was drawn up on parade. As the leading regiment of Zouaves came along, the English regiment nearest to them burst into a hearty cheer, which was taken up by the other regiments as the French came along, and as they passed, the English presented arms to their brave allies and the officers on both sides saluted with their swords.

The next day the officers thronged down to see the ground where the fighting had taken place. Around the Malakoff the ground was heaped with dead. Not less had been the slaughter outside the work known as the Little Redan, where the French attack had been repulsed with prodigious loss.

The houses of the portion of the town nearest the batteries were found full of dead men who had crawled in when wounded in front. As a considerable number of the Russian steamers of war were still floating under the guns of their batteries on the north side, preparations were made at once to mount two heavy guns by the water-side; but the Russians, seeing that the last remains of their fleet would speedily be destroyed, took matters in their own hands, and on the night of the 11th the six steamers that remained were burnt by the Russians.

After the din which had raged so fiercely for the previous four days, and the dropping fire which had gone on for a year, the silence which reigned was strange and almost oppressive. There was nothing to be done. No turn in the trenches or batteries to be served, nothing to do but to rest and to prepare for the next winter, which was now almost upon them.

A week after the fall of Sebastopol the anniversary of the battle of Alma was celebrated. What great events had taken place since that time!

None of those who had rested that night on the vine-clad hill they had won, dreamed of what was before them, or that they were soon to take part in the greatest siege which the world has ever known. Small indeed was the proportion of those who had fought at the Alma now present with the army at Sebastopol. The fight of Inkerman, the mighty wear and tear in the trenches, the deadly repulses at the Redan, and above all, the hardships of that terrible winter, had swept away the noble armies which had landed in the Crimea, and scarcely one in ten of those who heard the first gun in the Alma was present at the fall of Sebastopol.

The naval camp was now broken up, the sailors returned on board ship, and the army prepared to go into winter quarters, that is to say, to dig deep holes under their tents, to erect sheltering walls, and in some instances to dig complete subterranean rooms.

A week after the assault Harry Archer was carried down to Balaklava and put on board ship. The surgeons had in vain endeavored to extract the bullet, and were unable to give any cheering reply to Jack's anxious inquiries.

His brother might live; but they owned that his chances were slight. It was a question of general health and constitution. If mortification did not set in the wound might heal, and he might recover and carry the bullet about with him all his life. Of course he had youth and health on his side, and Jack must hope for the best. The report was not reassuring, but they could say no more.

G. A. Henty

Weeks passed on, and the two armies lay watching each other from the heights they occupied. At last it was determined to utilize the magnificent fleet which had hitherto done so little. Accordingly an expedition was prepared, whose object was to destroy the forts at Kinburn and occupy that place, and so further reduce the sources from which the Russians drew their food.

The sight was an imposing one, as the allied squadrons in two long lines steamed north past the harbor of Sebastopol. The British contingent consisted of six line-of-battle ships, seventeen steam frigates and sloops, ten gun-boats, six mortar vessels, and nine transports.

On board the men-of-war were 8340 infantry, and 1350 marines. The transports carried the Royal Artillery, the medical commissariat and transport corps, stores of all kinds, and the reserve of ammunition. The French fleet was nearly equal in number to our own.

Steaming slowly, the great squadrons kept their course towards Odessa, and cast anchor three miles off the town. Odessa is one of the most stately cities of the sea; broad esplanades lined with trees, with a background of stately mansions; terrace after terrace of fine houses rising behind, with numbers of public buildings, barracks, palaces and churches; stretching away on the flanks, woods dotted with villas and country houses.

Odessa possessed forts and batteries capable of defending it against the attack of any small naval force; but these could have made no defence whatever against so tremendous an armament as that collected before it. With telescopes those on board were able to make out large numbers of people walking about or driving on the promenade. Long lines of dust along the roads showed that many of the inhabitants were hastily leaving or were sending away valuables, while on the other hand the glimmer of bayonets among the dust, told of the coming of troops who were hurrying in all directions to prevent our landing.

Odessa was, however, clearly at our mercy, and considerable controversy took place at the time as to whether the allies should not have captured it. Being defended by batteries, it ranked as a fortified town, and we should have been clearly justified in destroying these, and in putting the town under a heavy contribution, which the wealthy city could readily have paid. However, it was for some reason decided not to do so, and after lying at anchor for five days, the greater portion of which was passed in a thick fog, the great fleet steamed away towards Kinburn. The entrance to the gulf into which the Dneiper and Bug discharge themselves, is guarded by Fort Kinburn on the one side and by Fort Nikolaev on the other, the passage between them being about a mile across.

On the 17th fire was opened on Fort Kinburn, and although the Russians fought bravely, they were unable to withstand the tremendous fire poured upon them. Twenty-nine out of their seventy one guns and mortars were disabled, and the two supporting batteries also suffered heavily. The barracks were set on fire, and the whole place was soon in flames. Gradually the Russian fire ceased, and for some time only one gun was able to answer the tremendous fire poured in upon them.

At last, finding the impossibility of further resistance, the officer in command hoisted the white flag. The fort on the opposite shore was blown up by the Russians, and the fleet entered the channel. The troops were landed, and Kinburn occupied, and held until the end of the war, and the fleet, after a reconnaissance made by a few gun-boats up the Dneiper, returned to Sebastopol.

The winter was very dull. Exchanges of shots continued daily between the north and south side, but with this exception hostilities were virtually suspended; the chief incident being a tremendous explosion of a magazine in the centre of the camp, shaking the country for miles away, and causing a loss to the French of six officers killed and thirteen wounded, and sixty-five men killed and 170 wounded, while seventeen English were killed, and sixty-nine wounded. No less than 250,000 pounds of gunpowder exploded, together with mounds of shells, carcasses and small ammunition. Hundreds of rockets rushed through the air, shells burst in all directions over the camp, and boxes of small ammunition exploded in every direction. The ships in the harbors of Balaklava and Kamiesch rocked under the explosion. Mules and horses seven or eight miles away broke loose and galloped across the country wild with fright, while a shower of fragments fell over a circle six miles in diameter.

On the last day of February the news came that an armistice had been concluded. The negotiations continued for some time before peace was finally signed. But the war was at an end, and a few days after the armistice was signed the "Falcon" was ordered to England, to the great delight of all on board, who were heartily sick of the long period of inaction.

Chapter XXVI
CONCLUSION

THE "Falcon" experienced pleasant weather until passing the Straits of Gibraltar. Then a heavy gale set in, and for many days she struggled with the tempest, whose fury was so great that for several hours she was in imminent danger of foundering.

At last, however, the weather cleared, and two days later the "Falcon" cast anchor at Spithead. The next day the crew were paid off, and the vessel taken into dock for much-needed repairs.

Jack's father had already come down to Portsmouth, on the receipt of his letter announcing his arrival. The day after the ship was paid off they returned home, and Jack received a joyful greeting from his family. They found him wonderfully grown and aged during the two years of his absence. Whereas before he had promised to be short, he was now above middle height. His shoulders were broad and square, his face bronzed by sun and wind, and it was not till they heard his merry laugh that they quite recognized the Jack who had left them.

He soon went down to the town and looked up his former schoolfellows, and even called upon his old class-master, and ended a long chat by expressing his earnest hope that the boys at present in his form were better at their verses than he had been.

A month later Harry, who had quite recovered, joined the circle, having obtained leave, and the two young fellows were the heroes of a number of balls and parties given by the major and his friends to celebrate their return.

Six months later Jack was again appointed to a berth in a fine frigate, commanded by his cousin. The ship was ordered to the China seas, where she remained until, at the outbreak of the Indian Mutiny, she was sent to Calcutta. On their arrival there Jack found that Captain Peel, under whom he had served before Sebastopol, was organizing a naval brigade for service ashore. Jack at once waited upon him, and begged to be allowed to join the brigade. His request was complied with, and as he had now nearly served his time and passed his examination he received an appointment as acting lieutenant, obtaining the full rank after the fight in which the brigade were engaged on their march up to Cawnpore. He was present at the tremendous struggle when the relieving force under Lord Clyde burst its way into Lucknow and carried off the garrison, and also at the final crushing out of the rebellion at that spot.

At the conclusion of the war he rejoined his ship, and returned with her when she finally left the station for England, after an absence of five years. He was now three-and-twenty, and having been twice mentioned in despatches, was looked upon as a rising young officer.

A month or two after his return he received a letter from Count Preskoff, with whom he had, at intervals corresponded ever since his escape from captivity. The count said that he, with the countess and his youngest daughter, Olga, were at present in Paris. The two elder girls had been for some years married. The count said that he intended, after making a stay for some time in Paris, to visit England, but invited Jack to come over to pay them a visit in

Jack Archer

Paris. Jack gladly assented, and a few days later joined his Russian friends at the Hotel Meurice, in the Rue Rivoli. They received him with the greatest warmth, and he was soon upon his old terms of familiarity with them. He found, to his great pleasure, that Olga could now speak English fluently, and as he had forgotten a good deal of his Russian, and had learned no French, she often acted as interpreter between him and her parents. Jack's Russian, however, soon returned to him, and at the end of a fortnight he was able to converse fluently in it again.

He found Olga very little altered, but she, on her part, protested that she should not have known him again. He had thought very often of her during the years which had passed, but although he had steadfastly clung to the determination he had expressed to his friend Hawtry, of some day marrying her if she would have him, he was now more alive than before to the difference between her position and his. The splendid apartments occupied by the count, his unlimited expenditure, the beauty of his carriages and horses, all showed Jack the difference between a great Russian seigneur and a lieutenant on half-pay. Feeling that he was becoming more and more in love with Olga, he determined to make some excuse to leave Paris, intending upon his return to apply at once to be sent on active service.

One morning, accordingly, when alone with the count, he said to him that he feared he should have to leave for England in a few days, and it was probable he should shortly join his ship.

The count looked keenly at him.

"My young friend," he said, "have we been making a mistake? The countess and I have thought that you were attached to our daughter."

"I am so, assuredly," Jack said. "I love your daughter with all my heart, and have loved her ever since I left her in Russia. But I am older now. I recognize the difference of position between a penniless English lieutenant and a great Russian heiress, and it is because I feel this so strongly that I am thinking that it is best for my own peace of mind to leave Paris at once, and to return to England and to embark on service again as soon as possible."

"But how about Olga's happiness?" the count said, smiling.

"I dare not think, sir," Jack said, "that it is concerned in the matter."

"I fear, my young friend, that it is concerned, and seriously. When you left us in Russia, Olga announced to her mother that she intended to marry you some day, if you ever came back to ask her. Although I would, I confess, have rather that she had married a Russian, I had so great an esteem and affection for you, and owed you so much, that her mother and myself determined not to thwart her inclination, but to leave the matter to time. Olga devoted herself to the study of English. She has, since she grew up, refused many excellent offers, and when her mother has spoken to her on the subject, her only answer has been, 'Mamma, you know I chose long ago.' It was to see whether you also remained true to the affection which Olga believed you gave her, that we have travelled west, and now that I find you are both of one mind, you are talking of leaving us and going to sea."

"Oh, sir," Jack exclaimed, delighted, "do you really mean that you give me permission to ask for your daughter's hand!"

"Certainly I do, Jack," the count replied. "I am quite sure that I can trust her happiness implicitly to you. The fact that you have nothing but your pay, matters very little. Olga will have abundance for both, and I only bargain that you bring her over to Russia every year, for two or three months, to stay with us. You will, of course, my boy, give up the sea. Now," he said, "that you have got my consent, you had better ask Olga's."

Jack found that the count had not spoken too confidently as to the state of Olga's feelings towards him, and a month later a gay wedding took place at St. James' Church, the count and his wife staying at the Bristol Hotel, and Jack's father, mother, and elder brother and sisters coming up to the wedding. To Jack's great pleasure, he happened to meet in the streets of London, two or three days before his wedding, his friend Hawtry, whom he had not seen since they parted on the Polish frontier, as their ships had never happened to be on the same station. Hawtry was rejoiced to hear of his friend's good fortune, and officiated at the wedding as Jack's best man.

A handsome estate in Sussex was purchased by the count, and this, with the revenues of the estate in Poland, were settled upon her at her marriage. There does not exist, at present, a happier couple in England than Mr. and Mrs. Archer; for Olga refused to retain her title of countess. Except when, at times, the cares of a young family prevented their leaving home, they have, since their marriage, paid a visit every year to Russia.

The count and countess are still alive, although now far advanced in life. The count is still hoping for the reforms which he believed thirty years ago would do so much for Russia, but he acknowledges that the fulfilment of his hopes appears to be as far off now as it was then.

Hawtry is now an admiral, but is still a bachelor, and he generally spends Christmas with his old comrade, Jack Archer.

THE END